INSIDE SILENCE

FREYA BARKER

INSIDE SILENCE
Copyright © 2025 Freya Barker
All rights reserved.
No part of this publication may be reproduced, distributed, or transmitted in any form or by any means, including photocopying, recording, or by other electronic or mechanical methods, without the prior written permission of the author or publisher, except in the case of brief quotations embodied in used critical reviews and certain other non-commercial uses as permitted by copyright law. For permission requests, write to the author, mentioning in the subject line: "Reproduction Request" at the following address:
freyabarker.writes@gmail.com
This book is a work of fiction and any resemblance to any place, person or persons, living or dead, any event, occurrence, or incident is purely coincidental. The characters, places, and story lines are created and thought up from the author's imagination or are used fictitiously.

9781998529193

Cover Design: Freya Barker
Editing: Karen Hrdlicka
Proofing: Joanne Thompson

Savannah (Savvy) Colter is not easily overwhelmed, which is a good thing, since she is the sheriff of Edwards County. It's rare to find someone her age— a woman to boot—carrying such responsibility, but over the years, Savvy has more than proven herself worthy of the position...to most.

However, when in a matter of a few weeks an old flame resurfaces in Silence, and two particularly violent murders land on her desk, her steady and predictable life becomes a little much to handle.

New full-time single parent, Nate Gaines, reluctantly returns to his hometown, Silence, to offer his teenage daughter some much-needed stability. As a contractor he can work anywhere, and it's not like he left a particularly fulfilling life behind, but he's not too sure how much work he's going to get here.

Although, some of the changes he encounters in Silence are a surprise. The most shocking one is seeing the woman he once craved like air, now wearing the sheriff's badge he so despises.

Coming home is definitely not turning out the way he'd envisioned. Especially when a sudden crime spree has the law knocking on his door...again.

CHAPTER 1

S*avvy*

THE MOMENT my foot crosses the threshold the scent hits me; roasted coffee and warm sugar with a hint of cinnamon.

"Am I too late?"

Bess, who owns Strange Brew, looks up from her perch behind the counter and raises one perfectly arched eyebrow.

"Hello to you too."

"Hi. Sorry," I quickly correct with what I hope is an appropriate amount of contrition as I approach her. Trying to peek around her into the kitchen, I can't resist repeating my question. "So, am I? Too late? Is there any left?"

With an exaggerated roll of her eyes, Bess ducks into the kitchen and reappears a second later with a plate. With my mouth already watering, I study this week's culinary creation. It looks like a standard square but, knowing my friend, it'll be much more than that.

Every Friday, Bess tests out new recipes for her coffee shop menu, and for as long as she's done that, I've been first in line to test her efforts. I'm usually here by around eleven, when I'm about ready for a decent cup of coffee after forcing down the clichéd pot of law enforcement tar back at the station. When I took over as sheriff several years ago, I suggested perhaps investing in a new coffee machine, but that did not go over well with Brenda, who had served as my father's office manager for twenty years before I took over, although the title does not do her justice. The woman runs the office and, since things would fall apart without her, I wisely retracted my suggestion and have been chugging down the sludge she makes on a daily basis without complaint, ducking out to Strange Brew, which is just down the block from the station, for a proper cup of java.

"I had to fight off a crowd to save you the last one," Bess guilts me.

"Well, I'm sorry if I was held up. Mrs. Dixon's alarm went off; she fell again," I retaliate with my own guilt card.

Mrs. Dixon is an octogenarian insistent on living independently in her little bungalow, when she would probably be better off moving into some assisted living facility. She is still sharp as a tack, but her balance and eyesight leave much to be desired. She has a son, but he lives in Alaska, and only visits a few times a year. Last time she ended up in the hospital after a nasty fall that left her with a fractured wrist, he and I tag-teamed her in to conceding to a health alert necklace which—when deployed—not only sends an alert to the emergency dispatcher, but to my cell phone as well.

"Oh no. Is she hurt?"

"She's gonna have a lovely bruise on her hip, but EMTs checked her out and she should be okay," I fill her in, bringing the first forkful of square to my mouth.

Blueberries, and I smell a hint of something floral, recognizing it as lavender when the flavors hit my taste buds.

"Blueberry lavender coconut squares," Bess confirms when I groan my approval. "I wasn't sure about the flavor combination, worried the lavender might get buried by the coconut, but Phil said it was perfectly balanced."

"Phil dropped by?" I ask with my mouth full.

Phil is Phyllis Woods, aka Phyllis Dubois, singer of former rock band *Listen Phyllis* and also my father's new wife. She rolled into town in a rattling motorhome two years ago and rocked my father's world, blowing new life into him. It's impossible not to love Phil and the breath of fresh air she brought to our little town of Silence.

I'm the one who introduced her to Bess's Friday tastings and I don't think she's missed one since.

"Stopped in with the sheriff earlier. They were on their way to Spokane for an appointment."

After serving this town for well over thirty years, everyone still calls my father *sheriff*, despite being retired for several years now as a result of health issues. It doesn't bother me; I love seeing how my father's chest still puffs up at hearing the honorary title. He lived for that job until it just about sucked the life out of him. It had been a hard transition, but since Phil's arrival in town, he seems to be enjoying his retirement a hell of a lot more.

I bet you that's why they're heading into Spokane; to see Dad's cardiologist.

"Latte?" Bess asks, moving to the complicated espresso machine.

I nod and quickly swallow my bite before mumbling, "Please."

While she busies herself with my coffee, I hop on to one of the barstools at the counter and let my gaze drift around the coffee shop. It's after two, the lunch crowd has already come and gone, but a few tables are still occupied. I smile and nod a greeting at Dana Kerrigan, our local nurse practitioner and a good friend. Her parents own the town's British-style pub where my father hangs out for his weekly poker game. If Dana wasn't sharing a table with a man I don't recognize—a handsome one at that—I'd pull up a chair, but she seems engaged in deep conversation. Curiosity around who the guy might be is killing me, but maybe Bess knows more.

Then my eyes catch on a familiar person in a booth near the washrooms.

Carson, teenage son of Hugo Alexander, my chief deputy. Hugo mentioned a while ago his boy had been getting into some trouble since his mom died early last year after a valiant battle with cancer. I had a sneaking suspicion he might be involved in a few incidents of vandalism, most recently a dumpster fire behind the Safeway in town. I've been keeping my eye on a small group of troublemakers I've seen Carson hanging out with. My gut tells me they are the culprits, but I don't have anything tangible, so my hands are tied.

However, I know for damn sure the kid should be in school right now and not hiding out in a coffee shop, and I can definitely do something about that.

Carson sees me coming and his eyes dart around, looking for an escape. It's not until I'm almost at the table I notice the young girl sitting in the shadows across from him.

Both of them look like deer caught in the headlights, guilt written all over their young faces.

"Really, Carson?"

He winces at my firm tone and stern look, but only momentarily, before he visibly straightens his shoulders and shores up his bravado. My guess is, for the benefit of the girl across from him. She's pretty, in a wholesome kind of way; long dark hair tucked behind her ears, and a sprinkling of freckles covering her pert, upturned nose. Her big brown eyes look panicked at my approach. She is young, younger even than Carson's sixteen years.

"Skipping school?"

"We're working on an assignment," Carson bluffs.

There's nothing but two carryout cups and an empty paper bag I'm sure held some of Bess's baked goods on the table in front of them.

I fold my arms and cock a hip, staring him down. I don't have to wait long before he lowers his gaze.

"We're not doing anything wrong."

"Except skipping school," I remind him, my eyes drifting to the young girl. "Who's your friend?"

When Carson ignores my question and stubbornly keeps his eyes averted, I address the girl directly.

"I don't think we've met," I start when suddenly the door bangs open behind me and the girl's eyes dart over my shoulder, widening even more.

An angry man's voice carries, "What the hell, Tate?"

I freeze, every cell in my body recognizing the timbre long before my brain clues in.

"Oops, I meant to tell you," Bess whispers behind me. "Guess who's back in town?"

∼

Nate

Jesus Christ.

I grind my teeth. It's all I can do to keep from throwing her over my shoulder and marching her out of here.

Fourteen-freaking-years old, just started her new school last week and already skipping classes. That bodes well. My blood runs cold thinking perhaps she's a chip off the old block after all, because then her path going forward will spell nothing but trouble and pain. I don't want that for her.

After getting a call from the school office asking if Tatum was home sick today, a churning mix of worry, frustration, and anger propelled me to start driving around town to try and find my daughter. By the time I noticed the sheriff's cruiser parked in front of the coffee shop on Main Street, I'd been aimlessly driving around for damn near an hour and was fit to be tied.

I rarely ask for help, and would never voluntarily approach law enforcement of any kind, but worry and anger had started morphing into fear for my girl. Heck, one of the reasons I swallowed my pride, and packed her up to move back to a place I vowed I'd never return to, was because nothing ever fucking happens in Silence.

At least it didn't use to. A small, safe, quiet, boring town that held too many ghosts and regrets for me. But then the daughter I'd barely known most of her life landed on my doorstep three months ago. The social worker who dropped her off informed me Tate's mother had been found dead of an overdose.

Fatherhood had been something I barely dabbled in and suddenly I was a primary parent. Don't get me wrong, I love my daughter with a fierceness that still surprises me, but raising her is a whole different ball game. Although, if I'd known Charlene was back on the hard stuff, I'd have stepped up earlier. Maybe I could've done something, saved my girl from the worst kind of heartbreak.

Heartbreak I recognize, even behind the defiance she is showing me now, with her little pointed chin lifted high and her mouth set tightly. A boy in the booth across from her, who is definitely older than my daughter, looks like he just shit his pants.

"Oh, hell no," I growl, reaching into the booth to grab my daughter's hand and pull her to her feet.

"Let go of her."

I've barely noticed anyone else in the coffee shop, but turn to look at the owner of that understated but forceful voice that has the hair on my arms stand up.

It takes me a minute to see beyond the uniform to the woman who fills it out nicely. *Damn.* Savannah Colter, I shouldn't be surprised she would follow in her father's footsteps.

What shocks me though is the visceral reaction I still feel at seeing her. It's been what? Fifteen years? A long time of pretending she never existed.

Hard to do when those familiar pretty dark eyes that could melt steel are looking right at me.

"Dad, please don't make a scene."

I drop my head at my daughter's soft plea and let go of the breath I've been hanging on to with a sigh.

"This is your daughter?"

Forcing any and all emotion down, I lift my gaze to meet Savvy's impenetrable one. I don't even attempt to try and read what she's hiding behind that stony expression.

"Yes. Tatum Colter," I volunteer. "Fourteen, and skipping what I believe is Social Studies."

A barely-there flare of her nostrils is her only reaction when she turns to the boy who was sitting with my daughter.

"Carson, I suggest you stay right where you are while I walk Tatum and her father out. But you better start coming up with a very good explanation for your father, because I'll be speaking to him next."

Keeping hold of my daughter's hand, I walk her out of the coffee shop, several pairs of eyes following us. I'd hoped to lay low, have a chance at showing myself a responsible adult and parent—at least to those who might remember me differently—before any of my past could reflect on my daughter, but I guess it's already too late for that. I'm sure that little scene back there will make the rounds before dinnertime.

Tate is quiet until I pull open the truck's passenger door for her.

"We were just talking," she whispers.

"He's a teenage boy; trust me, talking is not what he's after," I grind out, closing the door on her.

A voice sounds behind me. "If that were the case, I'm sure he'd have found a better place than the local coffee shop."

Right, I'd almost forgotten Savvy indicated she'd follow us out.

I brace myself before I turn to look at her. It appears she's had a moment to get over the shock of seeing me and some warmth has returned to her expression.

"He's too old for her," I argue.

"By only a couple of years," Savvy returns with a pointed look. "They're both in high school."

Message received. I'd been a high school dropout and was apprenticing with my uncle, who was a carpenter, when

I first met Savvy. Even though we'd been older, she'd been only seventeen to my twenty-four, but I didn't care. Neither did she, at the time.

Her father sure did though.

Fuck me. I rub a hand over my stubble at the unexpected sense of kinship with her dad.

"Look," she urges, "Carson is a good kid. He's been struggling a bit since his mother died and may not always make the best decisions, but he wouldn't hurt her."

I grunt in response. There are more ways than one to put the hurt on my girl, but learning the kid lost his mom, it's clear he has at least something in common with my daughter.

"So..." Savvy drawls, her thumbs hooked in her belt and her feet spread. "Didn't think I'd ever see you back in Silence."

I shrug. "I didn't either, but you know what they say; life is what happens when you make other plans."

CHAPTER 2

Savvy

I watched him get into the black truck, *Gaines Contracting* painted on the door panels, along with a website and phone number I memorize.

I'll satisfy my curiosity later in the privacy of my home, but first I need to call my chief deputy to let him know his son is playing hooky.

"Don't be too hard on him," Bess pleads, blocking my path when I walk inside, my eyes on the teenager who was smart enough to stay put like I told him to. "He comes in here occasionally and sits in that booth by himself, staring into his drink. Today was the first time I've seen him with someone else. That boy is hurting."

It shouldn't surprise me Bess, my sweet, soft-hearted friend, has quietly adopted Carson into her protective field. She's the one who—at six years old—scooped up a baby bird that fell from a tree and rushed all the way home from school to see if her mom could help her save it. Although the memory is a little fuzzy, I'm pretty sure the poor thing perished, but it did start a trend of Bess taking in hurt creatures of all kinds and creed in an attempt to rescue them. Some successfully so, but some—mostly of the two-legged variety—would abuse her kindness.

I don't like seeing my friend hurt, but that doesn't stop me from giving her a stern look.

"Fine, but don't think you're off the hook for not giving me a heads-up about Silence's prodigal son returning."

Then I step around her and walk up to the aptly remorseful looking boy.

"Your father is on the way," I inform him.

The news appears to deflate him even further, so I slip into the booth across from him. Bess hurries over with the coffee I'd almost forgotten about and slides it in front of me.

"Is Tatum okay?" he asks, his head hanging low as he peers at me from under his eyebrows. "Her dad seemed angry."

I'm glad for the question, it reassures me his heart was and is in the right place. The mention of her father requires a little more processing, something I will save for later, when I'm home and can safely throw things. Nate Gaines is the last person I would ever have imagined in the role of a parent, or back in Silence for that matter.

"She's fine," I reassure him, quickly adding, "Other than the trouble she'll be in for skipping school. I don't think you're her father's favorite person right now though. You may want to keep your distance."

He shakes his head. "Her locker is across from mine. A couple of little bitches were razzing her. I overheard them say something about her mom being a junkie and killing herself."

I wince at the derogatory term but let it go since it apparently was deserved.

"They made her cry and she ran," he continues. "I told them off and followed her outside, but she didn't want to go back in so I brought her here."

There is definitely a good kid hiding inside the troubled teen the world sees.

"She lost her mom," I surmise.

He nods. "She said it was an overdose. Just three months ago."

Christ. Poor kid. I feel a rush of sympathy not only for the girl, but her father as well. Like Carson, I know what it's like to lose someone you love, but losing them like that is particularly harsh.

"A little close to home, right, Carson?"

"Yeah," he mumbles, wiping his nose with the back of his hand.

At sixteen, Carson isn't small; almost six feet and with a good set of shoulders, but in that moment he's just a little kid trying to deal with the loss of his own mother.

"You did a good thing stepping up for her, but can I make a suggestion?" I offer gently. I wait for his eyes to come up and meet mine. "Next time, take her to the school office, or at least let someone know where you're going. She's only fourteen and her father was really worried."

He snorts.

"I doubt there's gonna be a next time. Her dad already hates me."

"I'm sure he'll be more understanding after Tatum explains to him what happened," I assure him.

But just to be safe, I might actually run Nate down to

make sure he's aware. From my experience, fathers can be quite protective of their daughters.

Talking about fathers; from the corner of my eye, I catch a glimpse through the coffee shop's window of Hugo's cruiser pulling up to the curb. I quickly get to my feet to intercept him before he stalks in here with proverbial guns blazing.

I catch him right outside the door.

"Where is he?"

He looks like an angry bull, nostrils flaring, and I'd swear you can see steam coming from them.

"Ease up," I caution him. "And once you're done barking at him, don't forget to listen too. His heart was in the right place."

Of course, I'm one to talk, I didn't exactly stop to listen first either.

Hugo does little more than grunt before pushing past me. Instead of returning inside, I choose to head back to my office. Hugo can handle his son, and I'm not ready to get into a conversation with Bess. I'm going to need some downtime to come to terms with the fact he's back in town before I tackle the subject of Nate.

The moment I walk in to the lobby, Brenda pokes her head out of her office.

"There you are. You turned off your radio."

Shit. I did when I called Hugo, not wanting any interruptions, but I forgot to turn it back on. I immediately reach for the radio clipped to my duty belt and turn the dial to the on position.

"Sorry. What's up?"

"KC took a domestic call on Quarry Road."

"By himself?"

KC Kingma is a good deputy—one of my younger ones

—but I still would've preferred he not take a domestic call alone. We generally pair up for calls like that since they involve more than one individual and can be very unpredictable and, therefore, dangerous. Especially when there is only one deputy to try and control the often volatile situation.

"We're shorthanded, and with Hugo bolting out of here and you incommunicado, there wasn't anyone else to send after him."

I'm already on my way back out the door when she calls after me.

"Dozer called it in. It sounds like Ben is on a tear again."

Oh, great. Ben and Wanda Rogers are what we call frequent fliers, who live in a modular home just outside of town, and Dozer Combs is their neighbor. Ben is an angry drunk, which he is often, but since he lost his job as a long-haul trucker after I pulled him over for driving under the influence about six months ago, it's gotten progressively worse. This is not the first call this month.

I groan when I pull up and see KC ducked behind the driver's side door of his vehicle, sidearm drawn. On the small porch of the house, I can see Ben stalking back and forth, waving his hands. One of them is holding a nasty looking gun.

Just what I need on a Friday afternoon.

∽

NATE

I TAKE another sip of beer, walk over to the sliding back door, and step outside.

The house was in decent shape, but the backyard was sorely neglected by the previous owners. Maybe tackling that is a better outlet for my frustration than pacing around the house, waiting for my stubborn daughter to come out of her bedroom, where she barricaded herself the moment we walked in the door.

Kids, man. I don't know.

When she first came to me, I'd taken her to see a therapist recommended by the social worker. The woman suggested Tate might need some help processing her mother's death, but it was clear after a couple of sessions she wasn't engaging. She wasn't with me either. Wouldn't talk about her mother or much of anything else, for that matter. Although I'm probably as much to blame for that.

I was far from prepared to take care of a young teenage girl, living in an apartment that suited my solitary lifestyle just fine, but was not really suitable for her. That's when I started wondering if it might not be better to get a fresh start somewhere.

Here we are, a trip down memory lane for me, but a fresh start for Tatum. A safe place, where people will keep an eye out for her, should I fall down on the job. I scoff at the irony. Yet, Tate is still not communicating. Still not letting me in, and I'm scared shitless I'm already fucking up, and we haven't even been here two weeks.

Yard work proves to be therapeutic, and by the time I have weeds yanked, the soil turned in the beds, and what passes for a lawn mowed, I'm feeling a lot better. Even a little accomplished.

Working with my hands has always been an outlet for me, hence my chosen profession. I was a pissed-off teen, and physical labor was a way to stay out of trouble. Those hands have been able to build me a good living over the years. A solid reputation for quality work. But I'm a long way from Las Vegas and I don't think my reputation stretches quite this far.

I need to get my hands on some work. I'm not hurting for money, but I can't sit by idly. I'm better when I'm busy.

I glance over at the stairs when I walk into the kitchen, hoping perhaps Tate has surfaced, but I can hear the muted sounds of Taylor Swift coming from her bedroom. After a lifetime of listening to rock, my ears took a little time to adjust to the perky sounds of the pop diva. I'll never admit it, but the music may be growing on me.

I wash my hands at the sink and check the fridge in search of inspiration for dinner. That's another thing that I've had to adjust to. I don't mind cooking when I'm in the mood, but since Tate moved in with me, it has become more of a chore. Especially since she's so damn picky and if she doesn't like it, she just won't eat. It scares the crap out of me, I've read about eating disorders and I don't want my daughter to fall victim to that. It's probably not something I can control with my cooking anyway, but I'm not taking any chances.

Tate likes Asian foods and it looks like I may have the makings for a decent pad Thai. I pull out bean sprouts, peppers, carrots, green onions, chicken, and an egg. I've barely started chopping when the doorbell startles me. Wiping my hands on a towel, I head for the door.

"Savvy?"

I realize too late I probably should call her Sheriff Colter instead of her given name, which rolls off my tongue with too much familiarity.

"Sorry to disturb," she mumbles, the ball cap with her job title embroidered at the front of it pulled low, obscuring most of her face. "Rowan told me you bought the old Miskin place."

If not for Grace and Gloria Miskin—the two sisters I grew up living across the street from—my childhood would've been nothing but bad memories. They looked after me when no one else did. Unfortunately, I lost touch with them after I left town, and apparently Gloria passed away and Grace moved to a care facility, but when I saw their old house was up for sale, I couldn't resist.

On the other side of the street, where my childhood house used to be, is now a newer development of semi-detached homes, housing mostly younger families, which only added to the appeal.

Plus, whoever owned it in the interim had done some decent renovations to the place, giving it a more contemporary look but without taking away the warm, welcoming feel I remember from my younger years. It seemed like a good place—maybe a healing place—to bring my daughter to, and I'm holding out hope for that to be true.

"I did," I finally answer Savvy, returning my attention to her. "What brings you out here?"

I can hear the edge in my question. She hears it too and finally lifts her head so I can see her face.

A deep red mark, already turning blue in places, covers the right side of her face. Without warning, a hot rage bubbles to the surface.

"Who?" I bark, my hand involuntarily reaching for her face.

She winces and takes a step back, only adding to my anger.

"Who the fuck did that to you?"

"Calm down," she snaps, placing her hands on her belt.

"I got caught up in a domestic call. Bumps and bruises come with the job."

"On your fucking face?" It flies from my mouth before I can check it.

Those big brown eyes narrow to glimmering slits and her lips press together tightly.

"Not your concern," she articulates sharply.

I feel myself jerk back, as if she'd slapped my face. Put in my place, I take a deep breath and force all emotion from my face.

"Fine. What brings you out here, Sheriff Colter?" I repeat my earlier question.

I can tell she doesn't buy into my attempt at a friendly tone, but she doesn't call me on it.

"I don't know if your daughter has had a chance to tell you what happened at school."

"School?"

I instinctively dart a glance at the stairs over my shoulder, only to catch a flash of what I assume is Tate ducking out of sight. When I turn back to Savvy, a faint smile is playing on her lips.

"I remember what it was like to be a teenage girl and reluctant to share anything of a sensitive nature with my parents," she offers, confirming her accurate read on the situation before she explains. "Carson, the boy from earlier, caught a couple of girls being cruel to your daughter at school."

Instantly, my anger flares up again.

"What do you mean, cruel?"

She gives me a sympathetic look before she answers.

"It was about her mother. Carson mentioned she bolted out of the school and he took off after her to make sure she was okay. She wasn't, which is why he took her to Strange Brew."

"Her mother died a few months ago," I share. Then I decide to add, "Of a drug overdose."

"I'm so sorry for your loss. And I'm sorry to have to bring it up, but I wanted to make sure you knew what happened. In case you want to report the incident to the school."

"No!"

This time Tatum doesn't try to hide herself when I turn around. Her face is blotchy, probably from crying, and I feel instantly guilty. I should've made sure she was okay instead of assuming she was moping.

"It'll only get worse if you do," she cries, before turning on her heel and running upstairs.

Her bedroom door slams and Taylor Swift's "Cruel Summer" suddenly blasts through the house. All designed to keep me out, but this time I'm not going to let it deter me.

I already have my foot on the first step when I hear Savvy behind me.

"I'll just see myself out."

CHAPTER 3

S*avvy*

Dammit.

Frustrated, I toss the container of concealer I bought on a whim years ago, and used only once, in the trash bin. Then I wash off the pathetic attempt at trying to cover up the bruise on my face. I only made it look worse than it already does.

Damn Ben Rogers for leaving us no option but to take him down by force yesterday afternoon. Drunks are unpredictable, and despite Ben's wiry frame, he did not go down easy. Even with two of us trying to control him, he managed to put up quite a fight and my face bears the evidence of that.

I was hoping I could cover it up so I didn't have to answer the inevitable questions all day long. Looks like I'll have to keep the bill of my ball cap pulled down low to obscure as much of it as I can.

Resigned, I dismiss my reflection in the mirror and head to the kitchen for my pre-workout drink designed to boost energy, before I head out for my morning run.

Most mornings I like to get to the office early, but on the weekends I make sure I get my runs in. It's the only real organized exercise I get, and it's good for me. Running helps me think, process things, and work through problems. It wouldn't be the first time I solved a crime on one of my morning runs.

I don't have any job-related puzzles to solve this morning, but I do have some stuff to process. Namely Nate's surprise return to Silence, with his teenage daughter, and the unexpected emotions it triggers in me.

Tossing back my drink, I grab my phone, clip it to my waistband, and tuck my AirPods in my ears. In the hall I slip my running shoes on and open the door to a crisp September morning. I don't allow my thoughts to flow until I hit the trail at the end of my street.

Nathan Gaines was nothing but a distant memory until yesterday. Any feelings associated with him have been long buried under another lifetime. Another one of love and loss that ended almost four years ago when a call came in about an industrial accident at the Lizard Peak Quarry.

I was a deputy and responded to the call. I arrived at the quarry and my father, who was still sheriff of Edwards County at the time, blocked my path with a devastated look in his eyes that told me more than I ever wanted to know.

A tragic accident crushed a mining engineer working for the Lizard Peak Quarry under a collapsed, thirty-foot rock wall. His name was Matt Farkas, and he was the man I was supposed to marry only a few weeks later.

There isn't much I remember from what followed, but what is vivid in my mind is the dark ache that seemed to shadow any and all other feelings. Including the hurt Nate Gaines had once put on me.

I breathe deeply from the fresh morning air in an attempt to release the sudden tightness around my chest. Ironically, it's not the loss of the man I loved enough to want to spend the rest of my life with causing it, but the remembered pain of betrayal and abandonment when Nathan Gaines disappeared without a word.

Reaching the banks of the creek, I stop and bend forward, bracing my hands on my knees as I wait for the feeling to pass. Something my father advised me is not to fight pain or grief, but accept and move through it.

I grab for my phone when it starts buzzing against my hip. It's the station.

"Talk to me."

My hair stands up when I recognize the urgency in my chief deputy's voice.

"We've got a situation."

～

"Oh yeah, he's gone."

I step back as Buck Wilson approaches and studies the body on the ground. He's not only our local veterinarian and my father's good friend, but he's also Edwards County's elected coroner.

You don't need a medical degree to come to that conclusion. It's pretty obvious, given the man was eviscerated and most of his face is missing. I've seen a few dead bodies before but nothing quite this gruesome.

Not what I expected when Hugo told me to join him at

the bridge over Watts Lake on the south side of town for a fatality. I thought there'd been an accident, or perhaps a drowning, but nothing prepared me for the mangled corpse under the bridge on the edge of the water.

A fisherman staying at the campground, on the far side of the lake, noticed something caught on branches that were stuck on a bridge pile when he decided to cast his line over here. As soon as he realized it was a body facedown in the water, he dropped his line, waded in, and pulled the body to the shore. When he rolled the body over, he quickly realized there'd be no reviving him and dialed 911.

"You think an animal got him?" Hugo asks as Buck kneels down to closely examine the body.

The older man shrugs. "Possible. We'll have to get a better look back at the lab."

The coroner's lab is in the basement of the Silence Medical Clinic next to the morgue. I've only been in there a handful of times, the last time we were trying to identify the charred remains of the victim of a vehicle fire after a crash on the highway south of town. It's not my favorite place, and it generally takes me days to get the smells out of my nose—especially after that last time—but I will definitely attend this autopsy myself.

I watch as Buck goes through the man's pockets for anything that might reveal his identity, but he comes up empty.

I note the victim is wearing a running shoe on his left foot but he appears to have lost the other one. He has on what looks to be black track pants and what is left of a white, short-sleeved T-shirt. Part of a small logo is visible right where the material was ripped away. I can't quite make it out.

"Hugo, could you grab the camera from my trunk?" I ask my second-in-command.

The body has obviously already been moved, and the scene disturbed, but I still want to record what I can before we load the body into Buck's van. Sometimes pictures can reveal small details that might otherwise get lost.

It may well have been an animal attack, but something feels off. The man's injuries seem almost too purposely violent.

Unfortunately, since we are a relatively small county, we don't have the luxury of a crime scene tech. Some of us have had some basic forensic training so we can at least preserve as much of the evidence as possible in cases where a crime is not immediately obvious. On those occasions it's clear we're dealing with a crime scene, I would call in help from the Washington State Patrol, who have far more resources than we do here, including a designated forensic lab and several crime units they can send out to assist.

But first I need to know if a crime was committed.

"I can hear you thinking," Hugo observes when Buck goes to his van to grab a body bag and I start snapping photos. "What's wrong?"

"I don't know. It looks too clean for an animal attack." I point at the entrails spilling from the man's abdomen. "Other than the obvious injury to his stomach, the bowels look almost untouched."

"Something could've spooked it. Interrupted its lunch," he returns morbidly.

He's testing my point, which is exactly why we work so well together. We don't let the other run on a mere hunch or get stuck on an unfounded theory. We push each other to find the evidence to support any speculations.

"Have you ever heard of an animal tossing its unfinished lunch in the lake?"

He shrugs at my question.

I guess there's only one way to find out, and when Buck returns with the bag, we quickly help him wrap up the body and load it into the van.

Before I slip behind the wheel of my cruiser to follow the van to the clinic, I turn to Hugo with an afterthought.

"Where is the guy who found him?"

"I told KC to drive the guy back to his trailer and question him there. The man was pretty shaken."

"Okay, when KC returns, tell him to join me in the morgue. It's a good opportunity for him to learn a thing or two."

∼

Nate

"I'll be fine, Dad."

Tate sticks her chin out and challenges me with her eyes.

My daughter's sweet appearance is deceptive, she has a stubborn streak a mile wide.

"I just don't—" I start before she cuts me off.

"It's not like I can go anywhere without you knowing anyway. I'm living in a prison," she pouts.

She's referring to the tracker I installed on her phone last night. She'd been pissed off, and no amount of me explaining how worried I'd been when I couldn't find her and, it was for her own safety, made it any better.

Clearly, she's still mad this morning.

"I wouldn't go if it wasn't an emergency," I offer, referring to the call I received half an hour ago.

Normally, I don't take on work during the weekends, but I'm trying to rebuild my business here, I'd be a fool not to take what is offered. The call was for a partially collapsed ceiling as the result of what is suspected to be a busted pipe. Lucky for me, the local plumber is on a hunting trip this weekend and not available so they called to see if I could help. I'm not a licensed plumber, but with over twenty years' experience in construction, I've picked up a thing or two along the way, so I told the woman I would see what I could do.

Despite the scowl on her face, I bend down and kiss my daughter's cheek.

"Show me a prison with an endless supply of chocolate chip waffles in the freezer," I whisper in her ear before grabbing my cell phone and keys off the counter and heading out the door.

So much for my plans to make sure Tate eats healthy. Last night I caved at the sight of a cooler full of my daughter's favorite breakfast at the grocery store when I was picking up a few things.

Parenting 101; when all else fails, try bribery.

What can I say, I'm desperate to get my daughter to actually talk to me instead of arguing or giving me the silent treatment. It's exhausting.

The irony doesn't escape me when I pull up to the sheriff's station. Last time I was here, I was basically run out of town. Today I'm here by invitation.

I vaguely recognize the woman who is waiting for me when I walk in the door. I take the hand she offers me.

"Thanks for coming on such short notice. Good to have you back in Silence, Nathan."

The derisive snort escapes me before I can check it. She takes it with a smile.

"You probably don't remember me, it's Brenda. I've worked for the county sheriff's department for over twenty-five years. I remember you," she states, wagging a finger in my face. "And for the record, I think you got a bum deal."

Not what I expected to hear and I'm not quite sure how to respond to it, so I move on to the reason I'm here.

"Where is the damage?"

"The holding cells in the back," she indicates, suddenly all business. She motions for me to follow her as she briskly moves toward the rear of the building.

I hate to say I'm well acquainted with the holding cells. I should be, I spent enough time there as the juvenile delinquent I was. Vandalism, breaking and entering, public intoxication, a brawl or two. What can I say? I was your proverbial bad boy from the wrong side of the tracks and for a while tried to live up to that reputation. A reputation that turned out to be difficult to shed after I smartened up and stuck to the straight and narrow.

Three cells side by side against the back wall, floor-to-ceiling steel bars securing what currently appears to be a single drunk, sleeping it off on the narrow bunk at the far left. He seems oblivious to the mess in the cell on the right, when wet insulation is spilling out of a giant hole in the ceiling.

"Never mind him," Brenda suggests. "It'll be at least another four or five hours before Chance realizes where he is." She chuckles. "He didn't even wake up at the loud crash when the ceiling came down."

Then she claps me on the shoulder. "Well, I'll leave you to it. I turned off the water main in the basement through there." She points at a door on the far side. "But I managed to make a fresh pot of coffee first. It's in the kitchen, help yourself."

With that she disappears down the hall.

I subject the hole in the ceiling to closer scrutiny before heading back the way I came in to grab a ladder off my truck. In passing, I glance over at the drunk who hasn't so much as twitched.

I have a feeling it's going to be a long morning.

∽

"THE FUCK ARE YOU DOING HERE?"

I try to swing around at the booming voice but am suddenly, violently shoved up against the counter, the coffeepot slipping from my hand and shattering on the floor.

Next thing I know, a thick arm wraps around my neck, closing on me in a chokehold.

I'm so stunned, I don't have a chance to react, when that same voice hisses in my ear.

"You must be some kind of fucking idiot to show your face here, you useless piece of shit."

That emphatically slung insult triggers my memory. It used to be Deputy Sanchuk's favorite. Unbelievable that bully bastard still wears a damn badge.

Just as I grab at his hand and start to peel his thumb back, I hear Savvy's voice.

"Jeff! What the hell is the matter with you?"

Followed by Brenda's. "Let him go, you big oaf! He's here to fix the ceiling."

While the women are yelling, I manage to get a firm grip on his digit and bend it back sharply. Immediately the pressure on my neck releases as he lets out a satisfying yelp. I cough a few times as I turn around.

"Serves you right if he broke it," Brenda scolds Sanchuk, who is now cradling one hand with the other.

Savvy puts her hand on my shoulder and leans her face close to mine.

"I'm so sorry about that. Are you okay?"

I grunt, unable to form any words...and it has little to do with the condition of my throat.

CHAPTER 4

S*avvy*

"Not an animal, Daddy."

My father shoves a hand under his hat and scratches his head.

When I got here, Phil directed me to the barn, where I found my father making repairs to a hole in one of the pens. Apparently Angus, my father's Houdini goat, tried to make a break for it again. It's an ongoing battle between man and beast, with Angus holding a firm upper hoof over my dad, who seems to be a constant step behind.

I sought my father's counsel after waiting all afternoon for Buck to send me his official coroner's report.

He performed the autopsy as soon as we got the body to the morgue. I was there, which was not exactly the way I'd envisioned spending my Saturday morning, but if there was any chance of foul play, I wanted to know right away. Unfortunately, Buck wasn't talking during the autopsy and said he wasn't willing to draw any conclusions until he had a chance to study his findings.

I had no choice but to return to the station, where I walked in on Sanchuk trying to choke out Nate Gaines.

What a mess.

The sheriff's department is housed on the ground level of an old building on Main Street, which dates back to the early nineteenth century. There are offices up on the second floor but most of them are now empty, except for a lawyer's office. The place is in need of major repairs, which the county commission has informed us are not in the budget. So, we're doing patchwork every time something breaks, which is often. That's why most of the upstairs offices now sit empty. The broken pipe is just the last on a long list of problems.

The tense situation in the kitchen was quickly resolved when Brenda explained to Deputy Sanchuk, she had called Nate Gaines in to do the repairs, so he had a legitimate reason for being there. Of course, that did not solve the issue that is Jeff Sanchuk. His reaction was way over the top and it's not the first time I've had to caution him on his hair-trigger temper.

The man has been a thorn in my side since well before I was sworn in as sheriff, but it hasn't improved since. In large part because he had eyes on my job, but even more so because he's a misogynistic son of a bitch—who doesn't believe women should be in the workplace—let alone in law enforcement—and definitely not in a role of authority. On top of that, he has a narrow view of a black-and-white world that does not allow for any flexibility or compassion toward his fellow man.

The only reason he is still with the department is

because in 2003, he took a bullet for my father when someone pulled a gun during a bar brawl they were trying to break up. Sanchuk saw the gun, managed to shove Dad out of the way, and ended up getting shot in the arm. Just a flesh wound, but it was enough for my father to feel perpetually indebted to him, despite his godawful attitude on the job.

My father's asked me to let him stay 'til his retirement, but I can't wait for Sanchuk to make that decision. Not after today. If Nate wanted, he could file assault charges on the deputy and that would put the department in a difficult position.

I don't need the added stress, definitely not now that it turns out I have a murder to solve.

"Murder?"

I nod at my father. "Looks like it. I've called in the WSP for more comprehensive forensic support."

"Good. Who's the victim?"

"We think it's Franklin Wyatt, a forty-three-year-old bank manager from Coeur d'Alene on a fishing trip. He rented one of the Sterling's cabins on the north side of the lake. Apparently, he went for a hike around the lake yesterday afternoon and hasn't been seen since."

"And you're sure it wasn't an animal attack?" he asks again.

"Our county coroner is convinced it wasn't," I reiterate. "But he's called Tom Richter to have a look at the body as well."

Richter is the medical examiner for a neighboring county Buck has called before when he wanted a second opinion. Since we may be dealing with a possible crime, I had no objections when he suggested it in this case.

Dad nods his approval.

"We'll know for sure once Tom has a look at the body," I add.

"And when is that?"

"They'll try for tomorrow. The body was picked up this afternoon already."

"How are you planning to confirm identity? Dental records?"

I nod, recalling the difficult phone call I had with Franklin's partner, Jeremy, who mentioned he hadn't thought twice about not being able to get a hold of his husband last night because cell phone reception out by the lake is spotty at best. Poor guy. I could hear the fear in his voice when he told me he would drive up as soon as he got the kids he'd stayed home to look after to a babysitter. I don't think there was anything I could've done or said to stop him.

"They're being sent straight to the medical examiner's office," I share, feeling the weight of the world on me.

Dad throws an arm around my shoulders and turns me toward the house.

"You sound already defeated, Toots."

I turn my head to shoot him a tired smile. "I'm not. I actually didn't come here about the case."

Although, I hadn't been surprised news of the discovered body had already reached my father. He peppered me with questions the moment I got here.

His eyebrows pop up. "You didn't?"

"It's about Sanchuk."

He stops and turns to face me. "Jeff? What has he done now?"

"He assaulted someone. At the station," I add with emphasis.

"Assaulted? How?"

"He had him in a chokehold, Dad. In the kitchen."

"Are you sure he wasn't just trying to restrain a suspect?"

I drop my head back and stare up at the clouds in frustration. This has always been the issue; my father tries to find excuses or justifications for Sanchuk's behavior that would've been unacceptable from anyone else—out of a misplaced sense of guilt because the guy took a bullet for him decades ago.

That loyalty has held my hands tied for years, but this has gone too far. I don't need a loose cannon in my department. I don't need the distraction when I may have a vicious murder on my hands.

"Dad...the person he was assaulting was Nathan Gaines." I watch as my father's face darkens at the mention of that name, but he doesn't seem surprised. I note it but forge ahead with my point. "Nate was there to fix the ceiling that fell down in the holding cells. Brenda called him, for crying out loud. He was there to help and Jeff attacked him, unprovoked."

I recognize the stubborn set of my father's jaw and brace for his reaction.

"If he was there to fix the ceiling, what the hell was he doing in the kitchen?"

As I anticipated, he's making it seem like Nate must've done something wrong. Nothing has changed, even after all these years. But I have, and I'm not going to stand for it this time. There are many things I can blame Nate for, but this is not one of them.

"That's enough. You know Sanchuk is a problem and has been for years. The man is a liability and if Nate wanted, he could file charges. That might encourage others he's manhandled or mistreated to come forward and file complaints as well. Can you imagine the stain that could put on the department's reputation?"

Those words seem to cool my father's temper somewhat. The sheriff's department is everything to him.

"So is he? Going to file charges?"

I'd honestly been bracing for it after I'd sent Sanchuk home for the day. Nate would've had every right to and I wouldn't have blamed him. I still remember all the times he was brought in to be questioned for some crime he didn't commit. The price he had to pay for having been what my father called a juvenile delinquent. A title he had to carry and atone for well into his twenties.

He's paid enough.

"No, although it would be well within his rights. He owns his own business, is a single father, and from what I can tell hasn't broken one law since the last time you arrested him at seventeen. That was twenty-five years ago, Dad. A lifetime. It's time to let that shit go, because I won't stand by while you and the rest of the old guard left at the sheriff's department continue to judge and condemn a man for his childhood transgressions. That is over."

I wait a moment, expecting a protest, but it doesn't come. My father is staring at the dirt on his boots, his hands tucked in his jeans pockets.

"So I'm here to give you a heads-up, I will be calling Jeff Sanchuk into my office tomorrow, and I will request he take his early retirement effective immediately."

At that his head snaps up. "The man saved my life, Savannah."

Dad doesn't often use my full name, it's either Savvy or Toots, but I won't let his stern tone affect me.

"Enough with the misplaced loyalty, Daddy. He needs to go," I insist. "He's a liability. I am giving him a chance to walk away with his record and his pension intact, otherwise I will be forced to take steps that will not end well for him."

My father grabs his hat off his head, slaps it against his thigh, and gives me a dirty look as he turns on his heel and marches back toward the barn.

I figured he'd be upset, which is why I came to warn him. He'll get over it, eventually.

When I turn around, I catch sight of Phil standing on the deck of the house, softly clapping her hands.

"Good riddance," she says when I get closer. "Never could stand that man."

"Dad liked him," I offer, but she shakes her head.

"Nah, he didn't. Not really. He just felt he owed him. But you don't, so good for you. Your dad will get over his snit."

"Yeah, eventually."

"Now...I'm curious..." Phil bumps my shoulder with hers. "Who is this man you so passionately advocated for?"

∽

NATE

I OBSERVE my daughter as she puts in her order.

Apparently, she can spare a smile for the waitress, I'd almost forgotten what that looked like.

At least she was willing to come out with me to grab a bite to eat, although she may have had an ulterior motive for agreeing to dinner with her old man. I should've been suspicious when she suggested the restaurant.

I spotted them the moment we walked into Bread & Butter, the local diner; that kid, Carson, and his father. I remember Hugo Alexander, but I doubt he remembers me. He was a big deal for small-town Silence back in the day. Star quarterback for the high school team before he wrecked his shoulder his first year in college. I was still in elementary school when I would sneak out on a Friday night and hide in the bleachers to watch the games, dreaming of playing ball like him one day.

What can I say, I was young and stupid, I had stars in my eyes, much like Tate does now, glancing over at Hugo Alexander's kid. *Fuck me.*

"And for you?"

I turn to the waitress, who is all smiles.

"I'll have a bacon burger with mushrooms and Swiss, and a loaded baked potato instead of fries, with a Caesar salad on the side."

"A healthy appetite, I like it," she comments before adding, "Can I top up your drinks?"

I've barely touched my iced tea and Tate still has half of her drink in front of her, and I'm definitely not in the market for whatever else she has on offer.

"We're good."

"All right, then I'll get the kitchen going on your order right away."

"Thanks."

When she walks away, I turn to Tate, who is scrutinizing me.

"What?"

"Eww, you know she's hitting on you, right?"

I nod. "I'd noticed. Why the 'eww'? Think your old man is that hideous?" I joke, encouraged she is talking at all and hoping to keep the momentum going through dinner.

"No. She is," Tate sneers, glaring over to the counter where the woman in question is talking to a colleague.

I'm surprised at her tone. Just moments ago, when she was placing her order with the waitress, she'd been smiling and friendlier than she has been with me lately. I guess that changed when the woman showed an interest in me.

Truthfully, I'm more flattered my daughter does not find me hideous.

"That's not a very nice thing to say," I point out, fulfilling my parental duty.

Tatum rolls her eyes and leans forward across the table.

"Dad, seriously? She's hitting on you with your daughter sitting right across from you. For all she knows you're married. *That's* not nice, and pretty tacky."

Can't argue with that.

Two seconds later, Tate is making eyes at that boy again. When I look over at their table, I catch sight of his father looking this way. He lifts his chin in a silent acknowledgement and I give a nod back.

The next thing I know, he is walking over here with his mortified-looking son in tow.

"Sorry for interrupting." I take his offered hand as he identifies himself. "Hugo Alexander, and this is my son, Carson."

"Nate Gaines and my daughter, Tatum."

"I know. I believe my son has something he'd like to tell you."

You wouldn't know it by looking at the kid, who appears about as mortified as my daughter does.

"I'm...uh...sorry."

"For?" his father prompts him.

The boy shoots his father an angry look, but I'd swear it shows a hint of betrayal as well. I remember that feeling, where people expect the worst of you. Even when you're trying to do the right thing which, from what I understand, the kid was doing by looking out for my daughter.

The sudden, unexpected kinship I feel with this kid prompts me to turn to his father.

"No, actually, Carson's got nothing to apologize for. Your son took care of my daughter, helping her out of a difficult situation at school. Granted, taking her to a coffee shop instead of alerting a teacher or the principal was probably not the smartest move, but I think he had the right intentions."

Alexander looks taken aback and glances over at his son, whose face registers surprise. Guess it doesn't happen often that someone speaks up for him. I get that too.

"It's true," Tatum softly affirms. "I'm new at school and some kids were mean. Carson was just being nice."

"I see," the man mumbles, dropping his head before twisting his neck to look at his son. "Why didn't you tell me?"

"You were too busy being mad at me."

Ouch. That's got to hurt. Eating crow isn't fun and I should know, I did a bit of that myself after finding out my daughter didn't just skip school.

"Have you guys eaten yet?" I change the subject.

"We're just waiting for our dinner," Alexander answers.

"So are we. Why don't you pull up a couple of chairs?"

I'm not sure where that came from, being social is not my style, but if I'm going to make a go of it here in Silence, I could probably use a friend.

Plus, the beaming smile Tate sends me feels pretty damn good.

CHAPTER 5

S*avvy*

"Like hell I will!"

Jeff Sanchuk surges to his feet, kicking the chair back. Then he plants his fists on my desk and leans in. I ignore his attempt at intimidation and meet his furious glare.

"Like I said, up to you. But I suggest you think about it a minute, because the alternative is a straight dismissal for misconduct, and that could well impact your pension eligibility. I don't know if you've checked the particulars of our pension plan, but it is subject to some strict rules. What I'm offering is a way for you to walk away with both your pension and your reputation—for what it's worth—intact. I strongly suggest you consider your decision carefully. I'll give you twenty-four hours."

"I was doing this work when you were still in diapers," he points out, barely suppressed anger lacing his voice as it raises in volume. "That chair should've been mine, and the only reason your ass is in it is because your daddy put it there. I took a bullet for your old man and this is how I'm repaid?"

He swipes at the container of pens on my desk, sending it flying against the wall. I quickly grab my laptop before that suffers the same fate. There's no contingency fund in the department budget for a replacement.

"Everything all right in here?" my second-in-command sticks his head around the door.

Well timed, since the irate man was just making a move to come around the desk.

"It's all good. Jeff was just leaving, weren't you?"

The glare he throws me sends a chill down my back, but I don't waver and hold his eyes until he finally huffs, turns on his heel, and stalks out of the room, aggressively brushing by Hugo. It's not until he disappears out of sight I let myself relax.

"Are you okay?"

I force a smile for Hugo. "Yeah. I figured he wasn't going to go quietly. Thanks for sticking around."

"Not a problem. Carson had after-school practice anyway," he explains, sitting down across my desk.

"How are things with him?"

He smiles and shakes his head. "Surprisingly good. We had a decent talk this weekend after bumping into Gaines and his daughter at the Bread & Butter and ending up sharing dinner with them."

The mention of Nate piques my interest. He was back today to work on the repairs in the holding cells, I saw him in passing a few times, but other than saying hello, I haven't had a chance to check in with him.

I've been too busy with the investigation into what

almost certainly was the murder of Franklin Wyatt. His partner Jeremy arrived in town Saturday night and has been staying at The Carriage House, our local bed-and-breakfast, and I've been in regular contact with him, the state patrol's forensic unit, and the medical examiner's office. We're still waiting for official confirmation, but I have no doubt Wyatt will turn out to be our victim.

But that doesn't mean Nate Gaines hasn't entered my thoughts a couple of times these past days, and I've been curious to find out how things are going with him. So Hugo's mention of him has my attention.

"You had dinner with Nate?"

Hugo chuckles. "Yeah. I can't for the life of me remember the guy, but he seemed to know who I was. Are you aware he's actually a Silence native?"

I'd say so.

"I am."

There must've been something in my voice that caught Hugo's attention, and like the good investigator he is, he immediately follows it up with, "Did you know him from before?"

It's not that it's a secret, but I'd rather not have that old drama dragged up again. There's been plenty of more recent drama in my life to keep the town gossips busy.

But Hugo is not only a colleague, he's a friend. The last even more so since his wife's death last year. Dealing with the loss of a spouse was something I could identify with.

"He's an old boyfriend," I admit. "It was a long time ago. He left town and I hadn't seen him since."

"I see." He quietly studies me. "Is his return a problem for you?"

"No. Not at all," I firmly state, convincing myself as much as him. "Like I said, a lifetime ago."

It doesn't matter memories of his strong, callused hand holding mine wherever we went, or the way his kisses used to make me feel, have begun to resurface. I dismiss them the moment they pop up. It is not a place I'll ever go back to. A lifetime has passed between then and now, and I am not the same person. Nor is he, for that matter.

The ship has not only sailed, it was run to ground.

However, there is nothing saying he and I can't be civil. Friendly, even. After all, like Hugo, Nate clearly has lost a loved one as well. Between the three of us, we could form a support group.

"What's funny?" Hugo wants to know when I snicker at the concept.

"Nothing. Silly thoughts. Listen," I abruptly change the direction of this conversation. "Did you have any luck getting anything more from the tenants at the Sterling's cabins?"

I'd sent Hugo and KC out there this afternoon to follow up with a few of Wyatt's neighbors we hadn't been able to track down yet.

"The guy in cabin four was able to confirm Franklin left around three Friday afternoon. He remembers thinking it was odd the lights never seemed to come on next door that night."

His chair creaks ominously when he leans back. A reminder we need more than just the ceiling replaced. I don't think many improvements have been made to the office during my father's tenure. He never saw the need. But things have slowly been falling apart, and I had been trying to squeeze the budget to find room for a few things—like new office furniture to replace some of the pieces being held together with duct tape—when the ceiling came down. I already had a few items on my wish list, but I may as well throw that out now.

Besides, I have my hands full with more important stuff at the moment.

"Good. Now if only the medical examiner would get back with a time of death so we have a timeline to work with."

"Nothing yet?"

"No. He's still waiting for dental records, and the tox screen has to come back before he can put his report together."

I sigh deeply, frustrated things aren't moving faster. We have so little to go on, and I've already spoken with Franklin Wyatt's partner several times, working from the assumption he is the victim, just to keep the investigation going, but there hasn't been a lot I can do anything with at this point.

Jeremy was able to tell me Franklin needed a mental health break and to do some soul-searching, which is why he was in a cabin in the woods by himself. He'd been burning out, working long hours, dealing with employee conflicts, and other bank-related issues that had him questioning whether or not he should just quit. His struggles started having an impact on his personal life, which is why Jeremy suggested he take a short sabbatical to get his head together and figure out what he wanted to do.

Normally, I'd be calling around, questioning a few of his coworkers to see if there was anything there worth looking into, but I can't do that until his identity is confirmed.

It's a hurry up and wait situation, which is sadly not uncommon in law enforcement.

"It's already closing in on six," Hugo points out. "More than likely you won't get anything until tomorrow. Why don't you head home? You've been going full steam all weekend."

He's not wrong. I've only been home to shower and roll into bed for a couple of hours of sleep before returning to the office. There isn't a whole lot I can do here I can't do at home, and Lloyd McCormick and Warren Burns are on duty tonight. If anything happens, I'll get a call.

"Fine," I concede, getting to my feet.

Hugo follows suit.

"I'll walk out with you."

I call a general goodnight to whoever is left in the office as I cross the lobby. Hugo holds open the door for me, and I walk outside, turning right toward the parking lot.

An engine revs as I step off the curb to get to my vehicle, and I snap my head around to see a black F-150 approach at a fair clip from the back of the lot. When the truck slows marginally as it passes by, I notice Jeff Sanchuk behind the wheel, his eyes on me.

"He's not happy," Hugo observes behind me.

I snort. "I think that's an understatement, but he brought this on himself. I'm hoping a good night's sleep will bring him to the right decision. But either way, he's gone. I can't afford loose cannons in my department, which reminds me, I should start looking for a new deputy. I wouldn't mind a female to cut down on all this testosterone flying around."

"Do what you gotta do, but in the meantime you may wanna watch your back."

I turn and toss Hugo a tired smile.

"Yeah, I know."

～

NATE

. . .

"These two okay?"

The butcher holds up two thick cut, nicely marbled striploin steaks.

"Perfect."

I'd planned a stir fry for dinner tonight but in my rush to get out the door this morning, I forgot to get the chicken out of the freezer. Then I had to drive into Spokane this afternoon for more supplies and thanks to an accident just south of Colbert on the way back, I only now got back to town.

When I called Tate to check in with her and let her know I was going to stop in at Safeway to grab something quick for dinner, she suggested steak. I already grabbed a tub of potato salad and a bag of the sweet kale salad she seems to like. Anything to keep my girl happy.

Things have been pretty good over the weekend and I'm hoping it can stay that way.

I toss the steaks in my cart and steer toward the freezer section to pick up some ice cream. My stomach does this weird little flip when I catch sight of Savvy, halfway down the aisle, staring into the freezer. She's not moving.

She jumps at my "Hey."

"God, I'm sorry. Hi, am I in your way?" She immediately steps aside.

"Nope. I was heading for the ice cream at the end."

"Maybe that's what I should do; grab a pint of Ben & Jerry's and call it dinner."

I glance into the freezer she'd been standing in front of, filled with frozen meals.

"Couldn't be any worse than this stuff," I volunteer. "Do you know the crap they put into these?"

"Oh, come on, those meals are better than the take-out

food I've been scarfing down all weekend, and right now I'm too exhausted to cook," she shares, a tired smile on her face. "Besides, I seem to recall you could wolf down a Hungry-Man Salisbury steak like nobody's business."

I grin at the memory. She's right. I didn't cook back then and existed on pizza and TV dinners.

"What can I say? I've changed. Improved, even."

She gives me a smirk and a sideways glance. "Have you now?"

Jesus, I'm standing in the fucking freezer aisle of the Safeway in Silence, flirting with fucking Savannah Colter. You'd think I'd have learned my lesson, but apparently not.

Before I can stop myself, I blurt out, "I can prove it to you. Come over for dinner. Nothing fancy, but honest food. I'm heading straight home because Tate's waiting, but you can follow me. I've got a couple of big steaks that'll feed three easily. Hell, I'll even supply the ice cream."

I fully expect to be blown off when I see the shadow slide over Savvy's face. But she surprises me.

"Okay. If you're sure."

Fuck, no, I'm not sure at all. In fact, I have a feeling I may be making a huge mistake, but that doesn't stop me from leading the way down the aisle, grabbing a massive tub of ice cream, and heading for the checkout lane.

Tatum's eyes widen when I walk in the door with Savvy in tow.

"Sheriff Colter is having dinner with us," I announce.

"O-kay?"

"Call me Savvy, please," Savannah suggests, taking off her baseball cap and running a hand through those lush curls.

"Tate, can you grab Savvy a drink? I'm gonna fire up the grill."

I leave them both standing in the kitchen and step out on the deck. The chill hits me and I suppress a shudder. The days are still comfortably warm but are getting shorter, and as soon as the sun starts slipping behind the mountains, the evenings cool off fast.

I'm seriously questioning my knee-jerk decision as I turn on the propane and ignite the flame. Through the window I can see Tatum pulling a beer from the fridge and setting it in front of Savvy, who easily twists off the top.

I can't recall her being a beer drinker, I remember she used to like those sweet premixed cocktail drinks, but apparently her tastes have changed as well.

I deadhead the begonias in the planter the real estate agent dropped off to welcome us to the new house. I'm stalling to avoid going back in there right away. It looks like they're talking, and although I can't hear what they're saying, it looks amicable enough.

I watch as Tate pulls a bowl from the cupboard and hands it to Savvy, who throws together the kale salad while my girl sets the table. I'm surprised, we don't usually eat at the table but in front of the TV. It makes me wonder if Tate and I have genuinely turned a corner at some point during the past few days.

Maybe I don't suck at this parenting thing as badly as I thought I did.

"Dad, do you need the steaks out there?" Tate calls from the open sliding door.

"Thanks, but I'll come grab them. I need to season them first," I respond as I approach her. Deciding to capitalize on the positive vibes she gives off, I kiss the top of her head as I slip by.

As I liberally grind black pepper and sprinkle sea salt over the meat, I listen with half an ear to a discussion about hair products between my daughter and Savvy. Tate is more animated than I've heard her in months. The topic is definitely way the hell out of my scope, since the only thing I do with my hair is buzz it as short as I can every couple of weeks. I do it myself.

All through dinner Tate is carrying the conversation, peppering Savvy with questions about the best place to find cool clothes, and whether or not Silence has a library because she doesn't like the books they have at the school one.

That launches a discussion about favorite books and authors, something I also know little about because the only thing I read is the newspaper, trade magazines, or the occasional biography.

I end up being an observer at my own table, and I don't mind it one bit. The only thing I'm required to contribute is an occasional grunt when someone looks at me for an acknowledgement or confirmation.

"Sorry if we left you out of the conversation," Savvy notes when I walk her to the door after dinner.

"No need. I was glad to see Tate come out of her shell."

When Savvy stops in the open door and smiles up at me, I resist tugging at one of her curls, which is stuck to her lip.

"It's tough, losing your mother. I was older, but I lost my mother at a very vulnerable time in my life and I struggled for a while."

As far as I know, her mother had been alive when I left.

"I'm sorry to hear that."

She shakes her head and waves it off. "Long time ago. Anyway, I enjoyed talking to your daughter, she's a sweet girl and it was just what I needed after the day I've had."

"Bad?"

She glances over her shoulder at the dark street before answering.

"Let's just say, it's not one I'd care to repeat. Except," she adds quickly, turning back to me, "for that dinner. It was delicious. Thank you for that."

"Hey, I couldn't in good conscience let you eat a frozen tray of artificial food for dinner."

I take a small step closer before I continue, "And if you are serious about a repeat, I would love to cook for you again."

She lifts her hand, touching a few fingers to the center of my chest before thinking better of it. Her cheeks stain a deep blush as she looks up at me, but the next moment she turns around and walks toward the cruiser, parked along the curb.

I'm not sure whether to be relieved or disappointed.

CHAPTER 6

S*avvy*

I CLOSE my eyes and squeeze the bridge of my nose but it doesn't help.

Opening my desk drawer, I rummage around to find the bottle of Advil I was sure I had in there. I need something to kill this headache building behind my eyes. I can't afford it, there is too much to do.

I only got maybe four hours of sleep before spending the rest of the night staring at my ceiling, mulling over the case. At about five, I gave up and came into the office to find an email from Tom Richter confirming the identity of our victim.

I've talked to Tom on the phone in the meantime, going over some of the remarks in the report he attached to the message. He agreed with Buck; this had not been an animal attack, but a particularly brutal murder. He'd found some lake water in the victim's lungs, suggesting that when he went in the water, he'd likely still been breathing. It turns my stomach to think he was still alive after sustaining those horrific injuries.

Richter informed me there was blunt force trauma to the back of the skull, suggesting a blow to the back of the victim's head, disabling him. He further noted the injuries to the man's face and abdomen indicated a determined precision that didn't match the severity of the wounds. The resulting damage alluded to a violent, enraged attack, but the cuts had been clean and confident, which would be more in line with a very controlled and measured killer looking for maximum impact.

For a murder you generally investigate those close to the victim first, which is the direction I'd been looking. But Richter's conclusions have me consider the possibility the killer was unknown to the victim, making Franklin Wyatt a random target.

I suspect this perpetrator wanted the body found, or he wouldn't have bothered with the graphic mutilations. Tossing the victim in the lake is another indication he was, at the very least, not concerned with the body's discovery.

"You don't look so good."

I look up from my computer screen, displaying the digital autopsy photos I'd been studying, to find Trooper Auden Maynard standing in my doorway.

A Silence native, like myself, I've known Auden most of my life. We went to school together, hung out in the same crowd, and he was the one who introduced me to Matt when I came home from college.

"Thanks, pal." I scowl at his amused expression. "What are you doing here?"

"I'm here to assist in whatever way I can." He pushes

away from the doorpost and takes a precarious seat on the rickety visitor chair. "And before you start objecting," he quickly adds when I open my mouth to do exactly that. "The captain himself sent me here, so put me to work."

I grind my teeth. This is my father's doing, I know it is. He knows Auden's boss and put a bug in his ear, I'm sure. It's my own fault for conferring with him about the case and needing to let Sanchuk go. It's tempting to refuse the offer of assistance, but I'm even more understaffed now than I was before. I've been leaning on Hugo heavily and he already has his hands full running the department while I spend all my time on this case.

I'm going to have to suck it up.

Auden is a state trooper, he's got a good head on his shoulders, and he's not going to give me any sexist bullshit for having to answer to a woman in charge. I'd be a fool not to swallow my pride and grab all the help I can get.

"What do you know about the case?"

"Mutilated body found floating in Watts Lake by a fisherman. Victim was renting one of the Sterling's cabins. Medical Examiner concludes murder," he rattles off.

That's a good enough start. I can get Brenda to make a copy of the case file for him. He'll have to read that tonight because I have a job for him now.

"Right. The ME's report suggests the victim was surprised from behind and hit with a blunt object, leaving a substantial wound to the back of his head, likely incapacitating him. The man was taking a hike around the lake when—"

"You want me to look for the primary site," Auden jumps in, guessing correctly.

"Yes. My guys checked the immediate vicinity of the bridge and didn't turn up anything, but it turns out he was still alive when he was placed in the water. Not only that, but Richter discovered some splinters under the man's fingernails, and he was found tangled up with a large branch under the bridge."

"You think he got those trying to hang on?" He winces. "Jesus."

That detail has been burning in my gut since Tom Richter shared it. Clearly Auden gets the picture too.

"Yeah, he could've been attacked and dumped in the water anywhere along the shoreline. Other than my own two feet, I don't have anyone else I can spare right now, but I need to find the scene of the actual attack before the rain hits later this week, so I can give your forensics guys something to work with."

The forecast is for a large system moving through this area the second half of the week, as cold air from the north pushes its way south. It'll be a welcome change from the unseasonable, almost oppressive temperatures of the past few days, but it's going to wash away any possible evidence left behind.

"So let's go," Auden urges, getting to his feet with an energy I can't match.

The loop around the lake is about five-and-a-half miles over pretty rugged terrain in places. I know, I've hiked it before, but that was under much different circumstances. Today, I'm looking for the scene of a violent crime, one I'm responsible for solving. It's the hottest part of the day, and I'm already exhausted. This is not an excursion I'm looking forward to.

Still, I push myself out of my chair and grab my ball cap and my radio.

"Yeah, let's."

Nate

"The drywall is up, but I have to run out to Spokane to pick up some more tape and compound. I should probably get ceiling white while I'm at it."

I'm thinking I have a day or so of mudding, then sanding, and hopefully I'll be done by the end of Thursday. This was a small job, much smaller than I'm used to, but it was a good way to get my foot in the door here. I even have something lined up for next week. Nothing major, just a bathroom makeover for Brenda, which won't take me that long, but it's a start and one job will lead to the next. Hopefully.

Small steps.

I'm not hurting financially, but I need to keep my hands busy and I want to be able to do things for my daughter. Also, I have a reputation to fix if I'm going to make Silence our home. If not for me, for Tatum's sake.

I have something to prove here, maybe even to myself.

"Ginny at Nuts & Bolts can probably help you with that," Brenda suggests.

"What happened to Will?"

Will Collier, owner of the small local hardware store, was the reason I went into construction in the first place. One of the very few people here who meant something to me.

Hell, I'd been a little punk and he caught me stealing a fistful of Dum Dums. He kept those suckers in a mason jar by the cash register for kids who came in with their parents. My mom would never step foot in a place like Nuts & Bolts, she was too busy getting drunk or high, or both.

Instead of calling the sheriff on me, Will let me keep the suckers and told me if I came in to help him in the back of the store after school, I could have all the Dum Dums I wanted and make a little pocket money to boot. To a kid like me it felt like I'd hit the jackpot.

I loved tinkering around his shop in the rear of the store. He had a million little projects on the go; building bird feeders, bread boxes, industrial table lamps, and other small stuff he would sell as a little sideline. He taught me how to use power tools, weld metal, mix concrete, make dovetail joints, and gave me a chance to be good at something.

Yeah, I definitely owe the old man a lot, and I've been avoiding the store because I'm not sure how to face him.

That's why when Brenda tells me a moment later that Will died only two years ago, I'm hit with a feeling of regret so heavy, it momentarily robs me of air.

I left many years ago without looking back, but in my mind Silence and its people stayed the same. Frozen in time. I guess I thought there'd always be an opportunity to set the record straight, to right old wrongs. Time to atone to those I might've hurt when I took off.

Looks like I let time run on too long.

Too late to tell him I'm sorry.

"It was a massive stroke. Fast," Brenda explains. "We buried him in Potter's Field."

Potter's Field is the town's cemetery, where most of Silence's residents go after they die. Including my mother.

"The store was closed for two months while Savvy did her best to track down his only living survivor. His niece, Genevieve. She found her living in Montana. Ginny came here with plans to sell the place, but ended up sticking around. She moved into Will's apartment upstairs, and has been running the store ever since. She keeps the place pretty well stocked, so you can probably find what you need right here in Silence."

Somehow this feels like a test to see how committed I am to being back here. If I go into Spokane to hit up one of the bigger box stores, I'll have failed.

Great.

"I guess I'll give Nuts & Bolts a try then," I concede to a brightly smiling Brenda.

"Good choice." Is her verbal pat on the back, cheerfully delivered.

Not sure there was any choice, but okay.

As I walk out of the station, I immediately notice Savvy leaning with her back against her cruiser. At first, I don't recognize the big guy in a state trooper's uniform bracketing her in with one arm braced above her head against the roof of the SUV and his body leaning close. I watch as he brushes at a hank of her hair that's slipped from her ball cap and tucks it behind her ear.

My hands instantly close into fists and before I realize I'm doing it; I've taken two steps in their direction. I don't know if his attentions are welcome. He's at least six two and built like a tank to Savvy's compact, five-foot-four frame. It's not until Savvy lifts her hand and touches the guy's face, I recognize him as Auden Maynard.

I stop in my tracks.

Jesus, the scrawny kid from down the road my mother would occasionally watch has certainly grown up. The prominent hooked nose is unmistakable, as are the dimples in his cheeks. Kinda cute on a kid, but ridiculous on a grown-ass man. And he sure has grown. Only kid I knew who came from a more fucked-up household than I did. Why else would his mother leave mine in charge of her kid? She couldn't even take care of me.

Hard to believe this is the same Auden. Even harder to believe he's obviously quite comfortable with Savannah. Not sure why I assumed she was single. It shouldn't surprise me she has someone in her life. She's gorgeous and smart, and every bit as irresistible as she was years ago.

The moment Savvy catches sight of me, I change direction and head to my truck. None of my damn business what she does and who she does it with. I have no desire to live in the past anyway.

Moving forward.

∽

NUTS & Bolts is much like I remember, too much stuff crammed into too small a space. The store is relatively small and the aisles so narrow, with shelves stocked to the brim, half the time you have to shuffle sideways to get through. It was almost impossible to find what you needed, but Will knew where every little washer or screw could be found.

The first thing I notice as I work my way to the left of the store where I remember the counter to be, is how well the shelves are organized. All the small hardware is in clearly labelled bins, sorted by size. Everything is neatly arranged. Each aisle is numbered and a sign shows clearly what is there.

"Can I help you?"

The voice belongs to a well-shaped blonde, leaning forward on the counter.

"Hi, are you Ginny?"

She straightens up, and I try not to get distracted by her curves. She's got plenty of them.

"Ah, I am, but you've got me at a disadvantage. I know

most everyone who's ever as much as looked at a hammer, but I can't recall you. Trust me, I would've remembered."

The woman's suggestive scrutiny combined with those words teases a chuckle from me. She reminds me of some of the women I've dated over the years. Generally uncomplicated, easy, and fun while it lasted, which was never that long. That was just fine by me.

After burning my bridges here in Silence, I ended up getting caught on the rebound by Tate's mother, Charlene. The pregnancy had been her attempt at getting what she wanted from me when it was more than I'd been prepared to give. It backfired on her because, although I did stick around for the baby, Charlene and I were done.

I can't bitch and moan about it too much, because I got Tatum out of the deal and she is everything.

But it did make me a bit more cautious with my choices after that, and I made sure any woman I dated understood I was not in the market for anything permanent.

There's only one person who would ever fit that bill, but I burned her too. Despite the grain of hope sprouting that perhaps there might be something to salvage here in Silence, it looks like I may have been too little and too late.

So when the pretty woman with the great curves beams an even better smile at me, I lean forward with my elbows on the counter.

"I stopped in for some drywall compound and tape, but for your information, I swing a mean hammer, and I'll be happy to introduce myself properly over a cup of coffee or a drink sometime."

CHAPTER 7

N*ate*

THIS WAS A MISTAKE.

I know it as soon as we sit down in a booth at The Brew House.

The scene here is a little too hip for me and the crowd is on the young side. I suggested it, because it was new since I was here last, and I figured I couldn't go wrong with a brewery and taproom. Not to mention, the only other option would be The Kerrigan Pub, which has been around since before I was born, and was always the local hangout for the old sheriff and his cronies. I have no desire to bump into any of them, not when I'm taking a pretty girl out for a drink.

Except, that was probably a mistake as well.

It seemed like a good idea, a nice distraction for what otherwise might have turned into a night of solo drinking to nurse the sting of rejection I have no right to feel, but Ginny is not the right solution.

Don't get me wrong, she's a knockout and clearly in the market for a little diversion, but she also owns the local hardware and supply store. I'm a contractor who does not want to have to drive into Spokane, wasting a couple of hours, whenever I need a box of screws or some duct tape, only to avoid her when whatever this might be is over.

Also, she is not Savvy.

There are so many things wrong with this situation I created.

It started when I walked out of the house, followed by the look of disappointment on Tatum's face when I mentioned I was going out for a drink, and now I'm sitting here, waiting for a server to show up and take our order, realizing I suck at this parenting shit. Or maybe I just suck at life in general.

"That bad, huh?"

I lift my head and meet Ginny's eyes. The look in them is sympathetic, so instead of insulting her by pretending nothing is wrong, I opt for honesty.

"I'm sorry. It's just, I realize I'm here with you for all the wrong reasons, and it isn't fair to you."

She waves me off with her hand and shakes her head, chuckling.

"My...you are a serious one, aren't you?" Then she leans forward, patting my forearm resting on the table. "Honey, you need to lighten up a little. When you walked into the store earlier—wearing that serious look on your face—I was just flirting with you a little to see if I could get you to crack a smile. You did me one better than that and offered a drink. I'm not gonna say no to a drink with a handsome guy like you. I may be a fool on occasion, but I'm not an idiot. Besides, you looked like you could use a friend, and I'm always in the market to expand my slim circle."

I search her eyes for any sign she might be covering up hurt feelings, but all I see is open honesty. When I blow out an audible sigh of relief, she laughs, the sound as bold and attractive as the woman herself. It puts a grin on my face.

"Yessss. There it is," she claims triumphantly as she points at my face.

"Good evening, folks." The server is a young Black guy with a friendly smile. "What can I get you?" He points at two massive blackboards on the wall behind the bar listing names of what I assume are the resident brews on one of them, and the other lists choices of easy pub grub. "We have ales and IPAs at the top, followed by our selection of lagers, and if you're looking for a bolder flavor, we have a sweet German-style bock and a dark stout. Of course you're welcome to try a selection of your choice with our three or five glass tasting flight."

Ginny indicates for me to go first, perhaps waiting to see if I'll pass on drinks with her after all.

"Line me up three of your favorites," I tell the guy, adding, "and maybe bring us that fried combo platter to share." It basically offers a sampling of everything on the menu. A little belatedly, I turn to my companion. "If that's okay with you?"

"Honey, fried is the magic word with me. I came by these curves honestly."

I notice our server trying to check out said curves covertly. He fails miserably when Ginny catches him staring and points two fingers at her own eyes.

"Up here, my friend. Up here. I'll do a flight of three as well. The blond ale, your pilsner, and the bock beer."

With a mumbled, "Of course," the guy slinks off in the direction of the bar, and I'm about to return my attention to the woman across from me, when I notice the front door opening. In walks Savvy, out of uniform this time. She looks more approachable, younger even, in a simple pair of jeans and an unzipped hoody over a tank top. I'm too busy studying her, it takes me a moment before I catch sight of Auden Maynard behind her. Also no longer in uniform.

"I see..."

I turn my head and find Ginny smiling at me.

"Only one reason a man looks at a woman like that," she shares.

I shake my head. "Nah, old news. Very old."

"Maybe so, but I'm thinking there's a story here."

I scoff. "Not a pretty one."

"Well, you've got a flight of beers coming, a fried combo platter on the way, and a new friend who happens to be a good listener sitting across from you."

In the end, it turned out to be exactly that simple. I haven't really talked about my life before leaving this town with anyone. Why would I? It became a past I didn't care to remember the moment I walked away.

But being back in town, confronted with everything I thought I'd forgotten, I find I want to talk about it. Especially with someone who seems understanding and kind, and who is new enough to town, she has no preconceived ideas about who I am.

I end up giving this virtual stranger my life's story. From my rough childhood, my brushes with the law, the support of her uncle Will in finding my path, my relationship with Savannah, and the reason for my abrupt departure from Silence a decade and a half ago.

When I take the last sip of the stout—my preferred

beer of the three—and sit back, I've even shared how I ended up a single father to a beautiful teenage daughter.

It's pretty sad when you can sum up your whole life in less than forty-five minutes.

"I'm sorry, I've been yapping off your ear," I apologize to Ginny, who has been listening attentively, which makes me feel like an ass. I haven't even asked her a single damn question. "I'm not usually a big talker so I'm not sure what got into me, but let me apologize."

She ignores what I say, waving it off with a hand, before she pins me with a serious look.

"You need to tell her."

It takes me a moment to clue in she's talking about Savvy.

"Water under the bridge."

"No," she disagrees, shaking her head. "It isn't. The whole time you were talking to me, she's been glancing over here."

I continue to resist the temptation to turn around I've been battling since seeing her walk in.

"Pretty sure that ship has sailed," I insist. "Clearly, she's moved on."

"With Auden? I don't think so. For one thing, the man is a natural flirt who hits on anything with two legs and a heartbeat. She'd never put up with that. Look, I could tell you all the reasons why, but most of that is hearsay and not mine to share. Which is why I really think you should talk to her. There's obviously a lot you don't know about each other."

She leans forward and places a hand on my arm.

"You don't want to live the rest of your life wondering what if. Trust me on that."

Savvy

I can't believe I let Auden drag me out here.

I should've been back at the office, or maybe grabbing a few hours of rest in my bed after slogging through the rough terrain around the lake most of the day. Instead I'm sitting here, wishing I could stop glancing over at Nate's broad back. His date sitting across from him caught me looking a few times already.

I caught sight of them almost immediately as we walked in. I would've turned right back around if Nate hadn't already seen me. Not that Auden would've let me walk out that easily. He was pretty insistent, suggesting we could easily discuss the case over some food and a drink. I'd still been tempted to duck into bed and hide out there after I stopped at home for a quick shower and change.

The shower had been necessary. I was covered in mud, and God knows what else, and was pretty rank by the time the state police forensic team showed up to the site.

We discovered the original crime scene midafternoon when the sun was at its hottest. It was the loud buzzing of flies that allowed us to pinpoint the location, just steps from the trail. We probably would've walked right by it otherwise.

There was a fair bit of blood once we knew where to look, and we also discovered what looked like the blunt object—the thick end of a tree limb with biological material stuck to it—used to knock our victim out. Rather than inadvertently mess up the scene, I made the call to bring back the state crime scene techs. I guarded the scene while Auden hiked back to meet them and guide them in.

It was already getting dark out by the time the techs processed the scene.

"Feel better?"

I look up at Auden, who appears to be studying me.

"Maybe," I reluctantly admit.

The greasy food may not have been the healthiest choice, but it was tasty and it filled my belly. Comfort food was just what I needed.

"Good. You were starting to look a little the worse for wear. You're not doing anyone a favor by running yourself into the ground."

Ironically, these are similar words I used on my father, back when he was still sheriff and burning the candle at both ends. He didn't listen and ended up getting hit with a major heart attack that landed him in the hospital, where he underwent open heart surgery.

I'm painfully aware I carry at least half my father's genes, and already my doctor cautioned me about elevated blood pressure last time I had a physical.

Again, I have to reluctantly agree with what Auden points out. We're already short-staffed after Sanchuk smartly, but surprisingly, sent me an email this morning stating he would be taking his early retirement effective immediately. The last thing the department needs is a leader out of commission for any reason.

"Noted," I concede his point. "And to that end, I'm going to call it a night. I don't expect to hear anything from the lab until tomorrow morning at the earliest, so I'm going to try for a full night of sleep."

Auden won't let me leave a few bills for my share of the tab, but he doesn't stop me when I get up. He has, in fact, already turned his attention to a baseball game playing on the big screen behind the bar before I even get to the door.

There, I chance a quick glance in Nate's direction, only to find the booth he was occupying with Ginny Collier is empty.

I try not to read too much into that, but I have a healthy imagination.

I'm annoyed with myself as I walk out and cross the parking lot to my vehicle. Why am I still so drawn to the man? I try to force myself to look at him as just an old acquaintance who moved back to town, but it's not working. Old emotions make a resurgence, both the good and the bad.

The man left me, for crying out loud. He literally disappeared from my life from one moment to the next. It took me a long fucking time to get over that—get over him—but I did, eventually. At least I thought I did.

Up ahead, a dark shape pushes away from my cruiser as I approach. My hand automatically goes to my hip before I realize I'm not wearing my uniform, and I left my sidearm in the glove box of my SUV. My body tenses, bracing for an attack, when the headlights of a passing car reveal the man's face.

"Can we talk?" Nate asks, taking a step closer.

This is the last place I imagined him to be.

"Where is your date?" is the first thing out of my mouth, and I immediately wish I could take it back. It's far too revealing.

"Home by now, I guess. And it was only drinks with a friend."

"A friend," my treacherous mouth echoes.

He hums once before turning the tables on me. "What about you? Didn't I see you in there with Maynard?"

"Yeah, we're working a case together."

I manage to hold back the snide, "What's it to you?"

comment wanting to roll off my tongue, but I'm sure Nate can hear my defensive tone.

He drops his head and appears to shuffle his feet as an uncomfortable silence settles over us.

It's a strange situation, an awkward standoff in a dark parking lot. Still, I can't bring myself to move, the silent limbo feeling oddly safe. Safer than whatever subject he wanted to talk to me about.

It's not until an SUV turns into the parking lot and pulls into a vacant space a few spots down, I finally manage to prompt him.

"What did you want to talk to me about?"

He raises his head slightly and lifts his eyes to look at me from under his eyebrows.

"Us."

It's like ice water is poured down my spine with that single word.

"There is no us to talk about," I return coldly.

He tilts his head slightly. "Are you sure?"

The bark of laughter bursting from my chest is incredulous.

"Are you serious right now? Because I don't have the time or energy to explain to you how fucked up that is. Coming up on sixteen years ago soon, Nathan... *You. Left.* Without a word, I might add." I pull back my index finger from where it was poking into his chest. "You've been back here...what? Less than a month? Now you want to talk about us? Newsflash. There is no us! A lifetime was lived in the decade and a half since you vanished off the face of the earth."

I'm well aware I'm yelling at this point—I appear to be drawing some attention—but I can't help myself, I'm beyond pissed off. How dare he?

I curl my hands into fists and press them into my thighs to keep from punching him.

"You barely cleared out of here before you cancelled your phone, Nathan. Like a coward, you denied me an explanation. So don't you dare suggest there is an *us*. You killed that right a long time ago."

"I did," he concedes easily.

Too easily.

"But I'd like a chance to explain anyway."

I shake my head and let my eyes drift over his shoulder. Why am I even tempted to listen? Did I really believe I could forge a casually friendly connection with this man by going to his house, and having dinner with him? Or am I really that helplessly drawn to him?

"I fell in love and had a life with a wonderful man after you left," I volunteer in a last-ditch effort to create some emotional distance.

"I heard. I'm so sorry for your loss," he echoes the words I shared with him only a few days ago.

Of course he heard. Silence is a small town and nothing stays quiet for very long.

He bends down until our eyes are level before adding, "But I'm glad you found some happiness for a while."

He looks sincere enough, until his gaze slides down to my mouth.

Unnerved, I bite my lip, which causes his eyes to snap back up to mine.

"I'm exhausted. I should head home," I state, breaking whatever voodoo has me drowning in his blue-gray eyes.

Immediately he straightens up and backs away, giving me space to get to the driver's side door.

I'm about to climb in when I hear his voice close behind me.

"Give me a chance, Savvy. A chance to talk, that's all I ask."

"I'll think about it," I mutter, quickly pulling the door shut.

My hands are shaking when I start the engine.

Damn you, Nathan Gaines.

CHAPTER 8

S*avvy*

THE MAN across from me looks absolutely broken.

There are times when I hate my job with a passion, and this is one of them.

I've dealt with the death of a lover and I've been betrayed by one as well, but not at the same time or by the same person. I can't even imagine what this man must be going through right now.

Yesterday, I was going over photos sent to me by the state forensic lab once again. The crime scene Auden and I discovered yielded blood and tissue we could confirm as the victim's, but there had been little else to come out of it. No new leads, and I needed one desperately.

There was a picture showing the small bathroom trash can from the cabin Franklin Wyatt had rented. I'd seen it before, but this time the edge of a foil wrapper visible between discarded tissues jumped out at me.

It looked like a condom wrapper.

A quick check of the content list for the cabin confirmed the presence of a handful of condoms of the same brand in the drawer of the bedside table. When I called the state lab and asked the tech to check the contents of the victim's wallet, they found a receipt for condoms from Walgreens in Coeur d'Alene, dated the same day Franklin left home for his mental health break.

That made me wonder; why would a man need condoms for a soul-searching expedition?

With the help of his telephone records and his text log, I was able to come up with an unknown individual, who Franklin had communicated with several times in the days leading up to his trip. The number that stood out was connected to a pay-as-you-go phone or, as we call it in law enforcement, a burner phone. Basically, a dead end.

Except, in one of the text exchanges between our victim and this individual, Jeremy's name is brought up in a way that implies he might actually know who the unknown person is. It left me no choice but to visit the Carriage House for a word with the dead man's husband.

"I can't believe it," he sobs in the wad of tissues I grabbed him from the bathroom. "It has to be David. He's the only one who calls me Jerry."

"And who is David?" I prompt him as gently as I can, even though I am vibrating with excitement on the inside.

This could be a genuine lead. Something for me to put my teeth into when I feel I've done little more than spin my wheels these past days.

"He's been my best friend since high school. At least I thought he was." Jeremy covers his face with his hands and rocks back and forth. "Oh my God...he was the best man at our wedding," he wails.

People suck. They really do.

My heart goes out to this poor man whose reality has so dramatically and painfully changed. He's lost his husband, his trust, and now his best friend all in one cruel sweep. I feel like an absolute bitch for pushing him, but I still have a vicious killer to find.

"I'm so sorry, Jeremy. More than I can express. Can you tell me David's last name?"

"Trotter. David Trotter."

"Have you been in touch with him at all these past days?"

Jeremy shakes his head. "I left a message for him. He travels all the time; he does the buying for several online fashion outlets. I didn't think much of it when he didn't get back to me right away, he's supposed to be traveling through parts of Asia until the end of the month. It's not unusual for him to be out of reach for days when he's on the road."

He lifts his head and pins me with red-rimmed eyes.

"Except he's not in Taiwan or Korea, is he?"

I can't answer that question. Not with any degree of certainty anyway, not until I track him down. But my gut says we'll find David Trotter much closer to home.

∽

"Silver Lexus RX, Idaho license plate K32682."

"Nice ride," KC observes.

It is.

It's also a vehicle you don't see very many of out here. It wouldn't necessarily be out of place in Coeur d'Alene or

Spokane, but here in Edwards County we don't see too many luxury vehicles.

The good news is that will make it easier for us to find it. Provided David Trotter is indeed somewhere close by, and he didn't rent a car or something. I put a call in to the Coeur d'Alene police department for an assist on trying to locate the man. I'm hoping I don't have to wait too long, but the detective I spoke to in their investigations department mentioned they had their hands full with a double murder that just landed on their desks.

It may be a while.

They never show you that on those TV cop shows; the amount of waiting involved. Most investigations take longer than the forty-eight-hour sweet spot they always tell you about. Hell, lab results alone can take weeks, and sometimes months to get back.

But, we try to do what we can while we wait, which is why I want Deputy KC Kingma out there looking for Trotter's Lexus.

"Motels, B&B's, rental properties. I want you to check anywhere someone might be staying temporarily."

"Do we know for a fact he's here somewhere?" he asks.

"No. We don't," I admit. "But it's the only real lead we have at the moment and we're going to work it until we hear otherwise."

He shrugs, fits his cap on his newly shaved head, and gets to his feet. By the door he stops and turns around. "Want me to bring him in if I find him?"

"I want you to call me immediately and then sit on him but at a distance until I can get there. No more one-man heroics, you hear me?"

It's clear he's not happy with those instructions, and

with a light tug on the bill of his cap and an exaggeratedly polite, "Yes, ma'am," he disappears down the hall.

The soft ping on my phone signals an incoming message. It's from Nate.

> Hope you like salmon. I caught it myself.

IT'S FOLLOWED with a picture of a sizable Chinook on a large rock at the edge of the water. I smile with the memory of an early morning, many years ago, when an excited Nate dragged me out to the creek because the salmon started running. Usually sometime mid-to-late-September, when the weather starts getting colder, the salmon run upstream to spawn. It's a sight to behold, all these large fish, struggling against the current, turning the creek into a living, breathing thing in their desperation to get to their spawning grounds.

Growing up in a small town like Silence, you get your entertainment where you can get it.

I guess it's that time of year again. Usually, I would be over at my father's place, tossing a line in beside his, but I've been so overwhelmed with this murder case and distracted by Nate's return, I hadn't even noticed they were running.

Yes, I called Nate after I had a chance to think about his offer to talk. I slept on it, or rather, lost sleep over it. I didn't want to hear what he might have to say at first, comfortable with pretending the past is behind me. That might've been possible before Nate came back, but is obviously not working when I bump into him all over town. I don't think those old feelings, hurts, and grievances, will ever go away unless I deal with them head-on. Part of that is listening to what he has to say.

So I agreed to dinner, tonight, at his place.

He mentioned his daughter would be at a friend's and he was available tonight. I'm the one who opted to go to his house. Eating out would've meant other people around, and I don't want witnesses to my discomfort. His place would give me the option of bailing if things get to be too much, and besides, he offered to cook.

I don't bother changing out of my uniform before I go. It's not like this is a date, and the uniform might serve as an imagined shield. At least I hope so.

I have a feeling I may need it.

∼

NATE

I'M NERVOUS.

I can't remember the last time I felt this jittery. It feels like a lot depends on tonight going well.

Funny, a few weeks ago my daughter was all I could think about, yet I just dropped her off at the Alexander house for a barbecue and almost forgot to say goodbye. I was too preoccupied trying to figure out what I'm going to say to Savannah when she gets to my place.

For some reason, setting the record straight has become my priority. I can't control what Savvy will do with that information—hell, it may all blow up in my face—but at least she'll know the truth. She'll be mad, I have no doubt about that, but I'm braced for that.

At least when she unleashes on me it'll be for the right reasons.

I toss together the Asian coleslaw, quarter the fingerling potatoes to pop in the air fryer, and have the large salmon steaks marinating in soy sauce, lime juice, and sesame seeds. The fish won't take more than fifteen minutes on the grill, so dinner can be on the table quickly once she gets here.

I'm out on the deck, drinking a beer and staring off at the mountains when I hear the doorbell. As soon as I open the door, the words I so painstakingly gathered these past hours evaporate from my mind.

Despite her raised, almost defiant, chin, the armor of her uniform, and her crisp "Hello," she looks utterly vulnerable standing on my doorstep. It's her eyes, they're swimming with questions and uncertainty, and I hate what I'm about to tell her may be hurtful to hear.

I'd convinced myself the truth would be the best way forward, for her and for me, but suddenly I'm wondering if I'm not being selfish. Maybe the truth is overrated.

Regardless, Savvy makes it clear there is no turning back now when she says, "I'm here, so talk," before stepping past me into the house.

"Care for a beer? Wine? Or are you still on duty?"

She stops by the kitchen island and turns to face me.

"I'm always on duty," she bites off sharply. Then she lifts a hand and presses her fingers to a spot at the base of her nose as she closes her eyes, following it up with a much more subdued, "Sorry. Been a tough day. A tough couple of days. Maybe I'll have that beer."

"The murder case?" I ask as casually as I can, while grabbing a beer from the fridge before taking out the beer glass I popped in the freezer earlier.

"Bottle is fine," she indicates, ignoring my question.

I twist the top off and hand it over, watching as she brings the bottle to her lips and tilts her head back. I study her slender throat moving as she takes a long drink, and remember how she used to love me kissing and nibbling the softs skin at the base of her neck.

The sudden rush of blood to my crotch has me whip around and head for the back door.

"Just gonna heat up the grill," I mumble, looking for a bit of distance to get my head in the game and my mind out of the gutter.

But Savvy follows me out, walking up to the railing of my deck where I was standing just minutes ago.

"This is pretty," she observes. "I didn't really notice the unobstructed view you have of the mountains last time."

"Yeah, on clear nights like this the view is pretty."

"Can we sit outside?" she asks, turning her head to look at me.

I'm sure it's not only the view that makes her want to stay out here, but I get it.

"Sure, and let me know if you get cold. I can light the firepit."

She nods before returning her attention to the mountains.

"Guess murder cases are pretty rare around here," I prompt her, returning to her tough day comments from earlier.

"We've had a few. Not many," she admits. "And nothing ever like this." She looks over her shoulder at me. "But I didn't come here to talk about my day."

I shrug. "Fair enough. Give me a minute to grab the salmon and my beer. Food first, and then we'll talk."

I also bring out a bowl of pistachio nuts, which has

become a bit of an addiction for me since I quit smoking when Tate came to live with me. I guess it's a healthier habit, but it sure puts the pounds on my gut. My damn jeans are getting tight. But it gives my hands something to do, which helps settle my nerves.

Conversation is sparse, mostly focused on neutral topics like the weather, but as soon as I finish the last bite of my salmon, I sit back in my chair and look at Savannah.

"I need to set a few things straight first," I start when her eyes meet mine. "Apparently, we all jump to quick conclusions—myself included—instead of asking the right questions or waiting for explanations."

Her eyes narrow slightly at that, but I push on.

"I assumed you and Auden were a thing after seeing you in the parking lot at the station, and reacted by asking Ginny out for a drink. Not the most mature reaction and not the first time I made a mistake like that, but at least I recognized it for what it was before it got me into trouble. That's what happened when I left Silence; I was feeling vulnerable and picked up the first pretty girl who paid attention to me. Charlene was a mistake, she tried to trap me with a pregnancy. Don't get me wrong," I add quickly when I notice Savvy wince. "Tatum is everything to me, but I would've wished her a better set of parents because, in the end, it wasn't just Charlene who fucked up. I did as well, by not doing much of anything."

I shrug off the discomfort at laying it all out on the table.

"But at least I have an opportunity to try and do better, which is why I brought her here."

She remains quiet as I take a quick swig of my beer for reinforcement. I have to give it to Savvy for letting me talk, but I have no doubt she'll have a thing or two to say before long.

"This may sound ridiculous, but I wasn't expecting the reaction I had to seeing you again. I hadn't really thought coming back here through at all, which seems to be par for the course for me."

I chuckle self-deprecatingly.

"I still don't know why you left in the first place," she interrupts for the first time.

There it is, the million-dollar question. The one I've been agonizing over how to respond to. The truth comes with consequences, and I'm afraid the answer will only create pain of a different kind for Savannah. But she deserves to know the reason I so abruptly turned my back on her.

"Remember my uncle Cam? I was working for him." At her affirmative nod I continue, "At the time we did quite a bit of custom cabinetry in that newer subdivision up on Forest Hill Drive. Apparently, some jewelry and money had gone missing from a few of the homes we worked on. Long story short, my uncle was in the hole with his bookie and couldn't bring in the money he needed to pay the man and his goons off fast enough."

Her eyebrows have drawn together in a deep frown, as she leans forward, listening intently.

"Despite his confession and his promise to return and repay everything he took; eyes were on me as his accomplice. I'd had no idea, and Cam vehemently denied my involvement. Still, I was given an ultimatum; leave town immediately, cut all ties, and Cam would be able to keep his business. The alternative was I'd be going down for the thefts along with my uncle, dragging everyone I cared about down with me."

Her narrow face has paled, making the odd freckle stand out on her skin.

"Who?" she asks, her voice croaking. "Who told you that?"

Fuck.

This is the part I wanted to avoid.

But before I have a chance to answer her question, she is on her feet and moving for the door.

"Never mind. I can guess."

CHAPTER 9

S*avvy*

ANOTHER SLEEPLESS NIGHT.

For once I'm grateful for the black sludge Brenda brews daily, the brand-new machine sadly hasn't improved the quality of the coffee. It packs exactly the punch I need this morning because my head is all over the place.

What I found out last night was a shock to the system. It rattled me, changed my perspective on so many things I'd held on to as fact. It had been painful but simple; Nate was an asshole who abandoned me and I was the victim. After some time, I even convinced myself it was for the better, that I'd dodged a bullet. But as it turned out, it wasn't that simple, was it?

Oddly enough, I don't doubt the truth of what Nathan shared. In hindsight, it makes way more sense than what I chose to believe for so many years. It also explains Jeff Sanchuk's violent response to seeing Nate.

I bolted last night, determined to confront him, but he wasn't home. The rundown bungalow in an older section of town stayed dark, even after I spent a good amount of time ringing the bell and banging on the door. An elderly neighbor stepped out on her porch and informed me he'd left a few hours earlier on his motorcycle. I had no idea he rode a bike, but it explained why his truck was still parked in the driveway.

All that unresolved anger turned into frustration and between that and this damn case, I couldn't get my head to stop spinning all night.

"Hey, Brenda," I call out when she passes by my open door. "KC in yet?"

She stops and peers in.

"He's come and gone. Off to check out the lodge and the two campgrounds up near Thunder Peak."

I guess that means still no sign of the silver Lexus.

"Let him know I want to see him when he comes in, please?"

She gives me a thumbs-up before continuing on her way.

It would really be helpful if the Coeur d'Alene PD could spare an officer to follow up on David Trotter for me, because I'm afraid even if the man was here at some point, why would he be hanging around and risk being found? No, I would head home, get into my regular routine as quickly as possible. That is, if I had just violently murdered someone.

Still, the unanswered messages Jeremy left for this David bother me in that scenario. If he were home, wouldn't he respond to those? Act like he's devastated by the loss of a friend?

The longer I sit with this, the more I wonder if Trotter makes sense as the killer. Even if he turns out to be Franklin Wyatt's secret lover, he doesn't necessarily fit the picture of our killer. Like the medical examiner indicated, the attack appears to have been too controlled, too precise, to suggest the kind of passionate rage you'd expect from a lover.

But we have to run down the lead before we can turn our attention elsewhere.

I really need the cooperation of the CdAPD, and not just to look into Trotter. I'm going to need their help if I want to check into Wyatt's workplace, talk to his colleagues. It's less than a two-hour drive to Coeur d'Alene, but I can't take the risk of sending someone out there to be met with closed doors.

Determined, I pick up the phone and dial the number for Detective Althof, who I'd spoken to before.

"Althof," he barks, which doesn't bode well.

"Detective, this is Edwards County Sheriff Colter. We spoke a few days ago."

"Yes. I remember. Look, Sheriff Colter, I'm sorry, but—"

"Our victim is a resident of your city, your state, and he's lying on a cold slab in the morgue, his head bashed in, his face obliterated, and his guts eviscerated," I interrupt before he has a chance to blow me off again. "I appreciate your workload, believe me, but this isn't just another murder, this is darker. The violence done to this man was not in a blind rage, as you might expect, but according to the ME, it appears to have been cold and calculated. I have a very uneasy feeling. We need to get a bead on this killer. Soon," I add with urgency.

That is what kept me up in the darkest of the night, the fear we'll find another victim at some point.

It's silent on the other end, and for a moment I fear he's hung up on me, but then I hear him clear his throat.

"Look, I apologize for unloading on you, Detective Althof—"

"Rick. Call me Rick."

"Rick, I'm Savannah, but everyone calls me Savvy."

"I'd say that nickname is well earned. You have my attention, Savvy."

I chuckle, a little surprised my rant worked.

"I appreciate it, Rick."

"So, that's not the type of killing you usually see in isolation," he deduces matter-of-factly.

"Exactly."

"Have you run a check on any similar cases?"

It's actually what Auden is doing as we speak. He was here when I got to the station this morning, and I told him about my middle-of-the-night concerns.

"I've got State Patrol helping me with that."

"Good. Now, tell me what you need from me."

For the next twenty minutes I share the details of my case, and explain what I'm hoping he can help with. When I end the call, I have his promise to look into Trotter's whereabouts immediately. He's also offered to make initial contact with Franklin Wyatt's coworkers to see if there is anything interesting to shake loose there. We agreed to keep the other in the loop of any developments.

I feel a lot better after talking to him, but I still have the other issue that kept me up last night left to deal with. This time I use my own cell phone to make the call.

"I owe you an apology," I tell Nate when he answers.

"For?" he prompts me.

"Storming out without thanking you for dinner for starters. Then, I guess, for believing the worst of you all this time. I'm still trying to wrap my head around it."

"Hmm. I get that, but there's no need to apologize. You didn't do anything wrong."

"But I feel I should. If not for myself, then for the office I represent."

"This was long before you joined the sheriff's department, Savvy."

He sounds almost amused. It's not difficult to imagine that crooked half-smile I remember well, but have only seen once or twice in recent days. It's both cocky and disarming, and had me fall harder for him than anything else.

"Be that as it may, but I still feel responsible."

"For what it's worth, I'm sorry too. For what I put you through then, and laid on you last night. But, this is all water under the bridge at this point," he insists. "I suggest we move on."

I'm silenced by that comment. Unsure of the meaning behind it, I'm suddenly unsure how to react.

KC comes to my rescue when he stops in my doorway.

"I'm sorry to cut this short, but I have to go. Duty calls," I add lamely.

"Sure thing. Talk to you later."

"Sorry, Sheriff. Brenda said you were looking for me?"

"Yes, I was looking for an update. What have you got for me?"

He scoffs, "Not a whole hell of a lot. No sign of a David Trotter or his shiny luxury car. Mind you, for all we know he used a fake name and rented a car."

He's right. If this was a premeditated murder, he may have done exactly that.

"But he would've had to use his driver's license and credit card to rent that car," I point out. "Call all—"

"Car rental places in Coeur d'Alene," KC finishes for me. "I'm on it."

As I watch him walk out of my office, I'm starting to feel a little better about my day. Don't get me wrong, I'm still spitting angry with Sanchuk and have a big bone to pick with him, but it'll have to wait.

I have a killer to catch and that has to have priority because, God forbid, my uneasy feeling turns out to be accurate.

∼

NATE

"CAN WE MAKE PIZZA?"

I barely have my foot in the door when Tatum comes barreling down the stairs with an enthusiasm I haven't seen in a long time.

"How about hi, Dad?"

"Hi, Dad," she echoes, rolling her eyes like any self-respecting fourteen-year-old would, before she repeats the question. "Can we make pizza? Because I saw this TikTok where they stuffed the crust with cheese and bacon bits, and they used salsa, taco meat, and more cheese for the topping. It looked so good!"

"It sounds like a heart attack," I return in defiance of my mouth watering at her description. It does sound good, but I'm trying to be a good parent. "Where are the vegetables?" I want to know.

"Da-ad, come on. We can make that cucumber salad you

did the other day. The one with the cherry tomatoes and the sliced radish? That wasn't too gross."

I bite off a smile. I suppose that was as much of a compliment as I'm going to get. Like a lot of kids, Tate is not too hot on vegetables, but maybe this pizza idea is a negotiating opportunity.

"I'll tell you what; we'll do the cucumber salad on the side, and we can make the pizza, but...you need to pick one vegetable to go on the pizza."

"Cucumber," she says immediately.

"We're already having the salad, and besides, cucumber is like ninety-five percent water. You can't bake that; it'll make the pizza soggy."

"Is not. How can it be crunchy if it's mostly water?" she challenges me.

I shrug and walk over to the fridge to grab a beer. Today was demolition day and I'm dusty and dirty, but I can have a quick shower when the pizza is in the oven.

The work on Brenda's bathroom is more of a renovation than the makeover she first suggested. She wants the tub out and a walk-in shower installed. She also wants to replace the old tile flooring and install a new toilet. The vanity is still in good condition, but I'm putting in a new counter and sink, and replacing the hardware. It'll keep me busy for a bit.

"Google it," I instruct Tate.

It earns me another eye roll, but she does grab her iPad and pulls up the browser. A moment later she narrows her eyes at me.

"Fine. Pineapple."

"That's a fruit, not a vegetable," I point out, enjoying the exchange.

Sure, it's more contentious than a nice chat, but it's interactive communication and I will take it in a heartbeat over the moody, often loaded, silences the past few months seemed filled with.

"Fruit is good for you," she fires back, her mouth twisting in a little smirk.

My girl is enjoying the banter too. Fuck if that doesn't make my heart swell in my chest.

"The deal was a vegetable," I persist, sending her a full smile before I walk over to the fridge and pull open the produce drawer. "Your choices are: red pepper, broccoli, cabbage, tomatoes, or spinach."

She follows me into the kitchen and as I list the options, her face goes through several grades of horrified expressions. I can't hold back a burst of laughter. She grins back, clearly hamming it up for effect.

"Drama queen."

"Dictator," she returns, her eyes twinkling.

I hook my arm around her neck and playfully pull her against my chest, rubbing the knuckles of my other hand on the top of her head. As she tries to pull away, I quickly press a kiss to her crown.

"What'll it be, kiddo?"

"Spinach," she finally concedes. "But can you cut it up really small?"

I pull out the bag of spinach and fish a knife out of the drawer.

"You cut it up small. Weren't we supposed to make this pizza together?"

The stuffed crust she wanted is a little more involved than anticipated, so it takes us a good hour before the pizza is ready for the oven, but neither of us minds. It's an hour of us working side by side, listening to music—mostly Taylor Swift, but I'm not complaining—and casually talking about her classes, the town's upcoming Harvest Fest she really wants to go to, and the local track and field club she wants to join.

All those things have one thing in common—Carson Alexander. Even though my daughter probably has a little crush on the kid, he's also the only friend she seems to have. His dad is a good guy and Carson has been nothing but polite with me, which is why I've let her hang out with him. That boy probably understands better than anyone what my girl is going through, both of them losing their mothers so young.

I can't deny it seems to have done her good, having someone her own age—or close enough—to talk to. She appears more approachable, hasn't been hiding out in her room quite that often in recent days, and seems more engaged.

When I come back down after a quick shower, I'm surprised to see Tate has set the table. When we eat together it's usually at the kitchen island, or in front of the TV. The only time we've used the table was that time I bumped into Savvy at the grocery store and invited her over for steak.

"Looks nice."

She sneaks a glance at me and shrugs her shoulders, looking a tad embarrassed.

"Yeah, well, I figure we'd put so much effort into making this epic pizza, we should have a proper sit-down meal."

"Agreed."

The pizza is pretty tasty and I'm about to grab my third slice when the doorbell rings.

"Were you expecting someone?" I ask Tate as I get to my feet.

She shakes her head. "No."

When I open the door it's a bit of a shock to find Auden Maynard on my front step. He's in uniform and, judging from the expression on his face, not here for a neighborly visit. I don't even know if he still lives in this neighborhood.

"Hey."

"Thought I recognized you the other day," he says by way of introduction. "Nathan Gaines, back in Silence."

I don't like the vibe I'm getting from him. His feet are slightly apart and both thumbs are hooked into his belt as he looks me dead in the eye. I can't figure out what would've brought him to my door, so I'm playing it cool. Let him be the one to tell me.

"That's right."

"How long have you been back in town?"

"Since mid-August."

"And what brought you back?"

Definitely not a social visit. He's got an agenda and it's making me uneasy I don't know what it is.

"Dad? Everything okay?"

I glance over my shoulder to find Tatum behind me, concern on her face. Poor kid, daughter of a father with a juvenile record and a drug addicted mother, I guess she comes by her mistrust of law enforcement naturally.

"It's fine, honey. Finish your dinner, I'll be right there."

When I catch Auden looking at her, I step outside, crowding him back, and pull the door shut behind me.

"Who's that?"

"My daughter."

"Is that a fact? Does she live with you?"

"She does. Look..." I've had enough of this game and hold up my hand. "You're obviously not here to welcome me back to town, so why don't you tell me what brought you to my doorstep tonight?"

It figures I'm still an outsider in Silence, I always was, even though I was born and raised here. I could say I have my mother to thank for that—she was a drunk who slept with anyone who'd pay her rent or buy her the next bottle—but I guess I did a good job alienating everyone in town myself during my teenage years. I tried for a long time to earn my place here, but any gains I might have made were negated when I left town the way I did.

I'm really starting to wonder if I made a big mistake coming back.

"I'm just asking a few questions as part of an investigation, that's all."

"An investigation of what, exactly?"

He doesn't immediately respond but stares at me sternly, as if that might elicit some kind of confession out of me.

Jesus, I thought we'd passed the days I was getting tagged for shit because of my transgressions as a kid.

"Where were you last weekend? Friday late afternoon and evening specifically?"

My blood runs cold when I realize he's not talking about some traffic violation, but that body they found in Watts Lake on Saturday morning. The case that has Savvy looking tired and drawn.

"You have got to be kidding me."

CHAPTER 10

S *avvy*

"Are you out of your fucking mind? What the hell were you thinking?"

From the stubborn set of his chin, I can tell he either does not feel any remorse, or is hiding it well.

"I was thinking the guy is the only new arrival in town."

I try to get a handle on my outrage. Screaming like a banshee—even though it feels really fucking good to let my anger fly—is not an appropriate representation of the office I hold.

I was surprised when Brenda patched through an urgent call and I heard Tatum Gaines's timid voice on the other end. She said there was a cop in a blue uniform at the door, and he and her dad were yelling.

The description of the State Patrol's blue uniform was a

dead giveaway. I immediately got on the radio and told Auden to get his ass into my office ASAP.

"Seriously, Auden? New in town? We have tons of campers and vacationers filing through the county every week, what about all them? You singled out Nathan?"

"They don't all have a rap sheet, Savvy," he persists.

This is so ridiculous; I bark out a harsh laugh.

"That's not a rap sheet, that's a juvie record for relatively minor stuff that should've been sealed years ago, and you know it."

He avoids looking at me, and I see a crack in his stubborn armor.

"You *know* I'm right," I hammer home.

A brief silence falls over my office as I watch his demeanor change. The squared shoulders relax and the stubborn set to his chin softens. Then he flashes me a dimple.

"I'm just looking out for you."

"What?"

I'm not sure what he's getting at.

"I saw you talking to him in the Brew House parking lot the other night, Savvy. The man did a number on you when he left, or have you forgotten? You walked around like a shadow of yourself until I introduced you to Matt." He takes a step closer and spreads his hands apologetically. "I'm your friend, I'm just worried this guy is gonna hurt you again."

"So you thought you'd go to his house, and put the heat on him for something he's not even remotely on the radar for, and in front of his daughter?"

All efforts to contain my anger have officially flown out the window as my voice rises to a shrill level. Even for Auden, who has a bit of a protective streak—even more so since Matt's death—this is beyond the pale.

"You say he's not on the radar, but did you know the Vegas PD currently has an open case very similar to this one? A badly mutilated body found floating in Lake Mead early this year. And did you know Gaines lived in Vegas before he moved here?"

I laugh mockingly.

"Oh my God, Auden. Do you know how often bodies are pulled from Lake Mead? Just a few years ago when the waters were low, they found six skeletons and who knows how many are still lurking under the surface. Aside from being a suspected mob dumping ground, you're talking about a recreational area with some of the country's highest deadly incidents. You want to attribute all of that to Nathan as well? Because he has a juvie record?"

He throws up his hands.

"Fine. It was a stretch. But it can't hurt to have him on notice."

"Except it does hurt," I correct him sharply. "His daughter, who was scared enough by your confrontation with her dad she felt the need to call me. She's scared and traumatized. And don't even get me started on Nate, who already has plenty of reason to distrust law enforcement—believe me on that—and all you've done is justify his misgivings.

"It's a slippery slope when you use professional leverage for personal interests. Especially when you're law enforcement. I just had to let a man go who routinely crossed those lines. Don't go down that road, Auden."

His head is hanging by the time I finish my speech. I'm sure he'd convinced himself he was doing the right thing when he decided to knock on Nate's door, but I hope he sees the error of his ways now.

"Shit," he mutters.

"Yeah," I confirm.

"Should I go apologize?"

I roll my eyes. Normally, I'd say absolutely, but in this case I think I should probably do a little damage control myself.

"I'll handle it. Go home, Auden. I need you to get your head clear before I see you back here tomorrow."

"Sure you still want my help?"

"I have a killer to catch and I am desperately short-handed. Beggars can't be choosers."

He winces. "Ouch." Then he throws me a wry smile. "Guess I'll see you in the morning."

When he's gone, I shut down my computer, shove my phone in my pocket, and fit my ball cap on my head.

"Everything okay?" Brenda asks when I pass her office on my way out. "It got pretty loud."

"I know."

"Anything I can do?"

I flash her a tired smile. "Yeah, find me a couple of new deputies. We're in desperate need of new blood in here."

"We only have budget for one," she reminds me.

"Well, I need at least two. I'll put in a request with the county commission."

Maybe I can get my dad's help with that. He still has a bit of clout.

I'll stop by there first.

∼

"Two?"

"At least, Dad. Even if it is one additional full time and one part-time deputy. The mayor called this afternoon, getting on my case to solve this murder because he's afraid it's going to hurt the fall tourist industry with a killer on the loose."

The man had been overly dramatic, which tends to be his MO, but he's not entirely wrong. This will have an impact on some of our small businesses that rely on the additional income tourism brings in.

Edwards County is known for its phenomenal fall colors and it brings out the tourists in droves. Anything from outdoor enthusiasts to day-trippers from the bigger cities start flocking in once the colors change. This is why the campgrounds and rentals are generally booked up for the end of September, early October.

The mayor's point only enforces why I need the extra hands on deck.

"Do you want some coffee and dessert?" Phil pokes her head out the kitchen door.

"Not tonight, I still have got something I need to take care of, but thanks."

"Okay, but it's been a while since you stopped in for dinner, and you need to eat anyway. It would be good to see you."

"As soon as I get a breather, I'll call. I promise."

I return my stepmother's smile and thumbs-up, and watch her disappear back inside.

"So, what's happening with the investigation?" Dad asks, returning to the subject of my visit.

"The one promising lead we had has not panned out so far. I heard from the detective in Coeur d'Alene last night. The guy we thought was our victim's secret lover turned out to be a bust. He's been in Taiwan the past couple of weeks on business, and that has been confirmed."

It was a blow when Althof dropped that bit of news, because it meant we're back to square one.

"Not a total bust," Dad offers. "It's likely he used that condom with someone. That's still a lead to pursue, even if there isn't an obvious love interest for you to focus on. Since the wrapper was in the victim's cabin, it's safe to presume his lover came to visit him there. Talk to the neighbors again. Talk to Milt Sterling and get a look at any renters whose time at the cabins overlapped with your victim's time there. Follow up. Boots on the ground, sweetheart."

I shake my head and smile at my dad's pep talk.

"Right, but I need more boots to do that," I point out.

He chuckles and claps me on the shoulder.

"I hear you. Guess I have my work cut out with the county commission."

∾

Nate

To say I'm angry is an understatement.

I'm fuming and it's not healthy for me.

I remember spending a lot of my youth angry and that got me in trouble in the first place.

The cold beer I grabbed from the fridge and took back out on the deck helps a little, as does the calming view of the mountains. But my blood still boils remembering the sight of my tearful daughter when I came back inside after blasting Maynard out on the front step. I guess my outburst could've gotten me in some hot water, but he got a radio call and ended up taking off without another word.

Tate went up to her room after I managed to reassure her I wasn't in trouble, and I've been out here stewing ever since.

I'd been too mad to answer his question about my whereabouts Friday night a week ago, but I thought of it after. Friday was when I'd spent the longest hour of my life looking for my daughter who was missing from school, and my first encounter with Savannah Colter since returning to Silence. Not a day I'd forget lightly, in part because later in the afternoon she stopped at my house with a bruise on her face to explain why Tate had taken off.

I'm not sure what brought Auden Maynard out here tonight, but I'm pretty sure Savvy didn't know about it. There's not a question in my mind she would've remembered my whereabouts last Friday as well.

I'm surprised when I hear the doorbell, and my first thought is the bastard came back. Stepping inside, I see Tate already at the door. My "Wait," falls on deaf ears as she opens it.

"Hey, Tatum. Thanks for calling," Savvy, who is standing on my doorstep, tells my daughter.

Wait. Tate called her? When?

I reach the door and the confusion must show on my face, because my daughter scrambles to explain.

"You were yelling outside and I couldn't see what was happening and got worried, so I called the sheriff's office. I didn't know what else to do."

Before I have a chance to react, Savvy steps inside and puts a hand on Tate's shoulder. "You did the right thing calling, honey. I'm afraid Trooper Maynard knocked on your door by mistake. It was a misunderstanding." Then she flashes a quick apologetic smile at me before turning back to Tate. "Do you think I could chat with your dad for a bit?"

I slide my hand around the back of Tate's neck and press a kiss to the top of her head.

"We'll be out on the deck, all right, kiddo?"

Savvy follows me to the kitchen where I grab a couple of cold ones from the fridge on the way out the door. I don't drink every day and rarely more than one or two, but today is definitely a three-beer day.

"I'm so sorry," she starts when I slide the door shut, cutting Tate off from hearing us. "I had no idea Auden was coming here."

"I came to that conclusion already," I volunteer, catching the relief on her face. "Although, I'm not sure how I got on his radar in the first place."

Unless it has something to do with her. Maybe the first impression I had when I saw him crowding her in the parking lot of the sheriff's station wasn't too far off the truth after all.

Her eyes slide beyond me to the mountains.

"It's complicated."

"Try me. Is he more than a colleague?"

Because that might explain why he ended up here. It's possible he saw us talking outside the Brew House, saw me as competition, and decided to flex his muscle.

"No," Savvy responds immediately before correcting it to, "Yes."

"Helpful," I grumble, taking a swig of my beer.

"What I mean is, he's a friend. I went to school with him. He was Matt's best friend and, after Matt died, was there when things were tough. He's like a big brother. Protective like one too," she explains.

"I see. So, this was a warning for me? To stay away from you?"

She shrugs. "I'm not sure what exactly he was thinking, and I'm not saying this to excuse him, but he remembers what a mess I was when you left."

Immediately the old guilt rises its head and I react defensively.

"So we're right back there again."

She takes a step closer and puts her hand on my arm.

"No, you and I aren't, but he doesn't know what really happened yet, because I didn't tell him. I've barely had a chance to process that information myself."

She drops her hand and turns her back to me, bracing herself against the railing of the deck as she looks out at the view.

"I'm overwhelmed, Nathan. I have had the biggest case in my career land on my doorstep, I've got pressure from the mayor's office to get it solved but I'm shorthanded on deputies, I haven't had much sleep in a week, and, to top it off, your return to Silence has stirred up a lot of confusing feelings I'm not quite sure what to do with."

She turns and leans back against the railing, a hint of vulnerability in those pretty brown eyes when she fixes them on me.

"I had no idea he was coming here or I would've stopped him. I'm sorry you have to defend yourself against a reputation you didn't deserve in the first place. I want to set the record straight, not just with Auden, but the whole town. Let them know we failed—"

I don't let her finish and cut off her words when pure instinct has me lean in and cover her mouth with mine.

There was no thought involved in the kiss, just an overwhelming need to taste her lips, feel her body against me, to see if we still fit as smoothly as we did a decade and a half ago.

Her arms slip around my neck as she presses her front against mine, and my hands automatically settle in the small of her back, one hand up, and one sliding down to the curve of her round ass.

Yes.

This is what I remembered in unguarded moments when my resistance to dwell in the past was at its lowest. This is what I have been imagining for the past few weeks since I first looked her in the eye again.

This is what I sacrificed years ago, because I was made to believe leaving was my only choice.

I was wrong. As I taste her and feel her breath brush my skin, I know it down to my soul; I should've stayed and fought for her.

For myself.

CHAPTER 11

S*avvy*

"Take a breath, Wanda."

The poor woman is hysterical, and I can't blame her.

Dispatch called me twenty minutes ago that an incident call had come in from the Rogers's place. Since our last encounter there, I'd instructed dispatch to call me first for any future disturbances at that address.

Another sleepless night and another interrupted weekend.

At least I got my run in this morning. I needed it to try and clear my mind. Last night's unexpected kiss had been dominating my thoughts, when I should've been focused on my case. Only one kiss that stopped as abruptly as it started when Nate's daughter came looking for her father, but it had packed a punch. One that made me question everything I thought to be true, and left me feeling guilty.

The crisp morning air on my run went a long way to gaining some perspective, and by the time I received the call, I was buried in the case file I brought home.

I quickly changed into my uniform and contacted Hugo to meet me at the Rogers's place. I figured I should have some backup—I'm not an idiot—and we showed up here in tandem, prepared to tackle Ben Rogers.

Except, he wasn't here.

When the judge allowed Ben to be released on bail on the Monday after we booked him for assault, Wanda wisely decided to head out of town to visit her sister and let things cool down a bit. But when she wasn't able to get a hold of Ben for the past day and a half, she drove back home, only to find her husband gone.

She was sitting on the porch steps when we arrived, rocking back and forth. I left Hugo to check her out while I went ahead inside, sidearm drawn just in case. Despite his truck in the driveway where it's usually parked, there is no sign of Ben anywhere in the house.

However, when I entered the garage through the mudroom, it was clear something had happened here. A sizable brownish-red coagulated pool of what likely was blood, marked the concrete floor. Laying right beside it was a ball peen hammer, the blunt side coated in the same sticky red substance. I immediately contacted Auden and asked him to call in the crime scene techs.

I may be jumping the gun, since I don't know what happened here yet, but my gut tells me my worst fears may have come true.

I hope I'm wrong, and there is a simple explanation for this. Perhaps he injured himself, became disoriented, and wandered off somewhere, but either way, I'm making sure all bases are covered.

"Try again, deep breath."

While Hugo continues to try and calm the woman, I put in a few more calls. I have an ambulance on the way for Wanda, and I have Brenda dispatching a couple of deputies to assist us. First priority is looking for Ben, and I am silently praying we'll find him alive somewhere.

My eye is drawn to Dozer Combs's place next door, but his vehicle is not parked out front and I don't see any movement.

"Wanda," I draw her attention. "Have you seen Dozer?"

She blinks a few times and glances over at Dozer's single wide. Then she looks at me, shaking her head.

"Okay, you stay here with Hugo, I'm just going to check if he's home."

As I walk over, I'm silently praying whatever fate found Ben Rogers hasn't befallen Dozer as well. There's no answer when I knock on the door, and nothing looks out of order when I peek into the mobile home's windows. It's entirely possible he simply isn't home—which I hope is the case—but I do want to speak with him as soon as possible. He may have seen or heard something.

There are a few other houses to canvass in the neighborhood, but those places are farther up the road. Still, it's possible one of the neighbors noticed something, and as soon as I get some backup here, I'll send someone to start knocking on doors.

Auden pulls up just as I return from Dozer's place, an ambulance turns onto the driveway right behind him. I leave Hugo to handle Wanda and the EMTs, and motion for Auden to follow me.

"Fuck," he curses when I show him the garage.

We stay in the door opening, making sure not to disrupt the scene.

"No drag marks or blood trail I can see," I fill him in. "Just that pool of blood and the hammer."

"It's too clean, it almost looks staged," Auden observes.

He's right. I noticed that too, and it's part of the reason I don't really believe this could've been an accident. If some kind of mishap caused him to bleed this profusely, he would've left a trail for sure.

"I don't think he left this garage under his own steam," I share. "The only way out would've been through the house, or out the garage doors."

"Could've been under the cover of night," Auden suggests, pointing at a stack of folded tarps on a shelf of the storage unit along the wall. "Maybe wrapped in one of those tarps."

"Even though Ben wasn't a particularly big man, you'd have to be pretty damn strong to be able to carry that kind of dead weight very far," I contemplate out loud. "If Ben is actually our victim," I add. "We don't technically know who the victim is yet."

And unless we find a body, the only way to get an identification would be through blood testing in the lab.

"Very true. So, whoever the victim is, they've likely been moved to a vehicle," he suggests. "Someone was attacked, maybe surprised from behind, or it could have been someone the victim knew. Hit them with that hammer to disable them and took them to a different location."

"That would be my guess, and we need to send out a patrol car to check for security cameras in the neighborhood that may have picked up anything. But first we still should search the immediate surrounding area. In case our theory is way off base."

"One thing though, Savvy; I think we're looking for a body."

I was already resigned to that very possible outcome. Whatever happened took place many hours ago, judging by the mostly dried blood stain on the concrete floor. There is also a lot of it, so even if the victim survived the initial attack, I don't think they would've lasted long with that amount of blood loss.

By the time we get back outside, Wanda is being loaded into the back of the ambulance.

"What's happening?"

Hugo turns at my approach.

"She's shocky and tachycardic. They want to take her in for observation."

"Okay."

It's probably better for her not to be around when the crime techs arrive and we start searching the neighborhood.

"Want me to go with her?" Hugo wants to know.

"No. I need you here. Call Dana, tell her Wanda is on her way and fill her in on what's going on. She can probably find someone to sit with Wanda, but make it clear she should not be left alone at any time."

Soon after the ambulance leaves, two of my deputies arrive and I quickly get them up to speed. Then I split the men up into two groups to get this ground search underway, I pair Hugo up with KC and Auden with Warren Burns, who is a former detective for the Seattle PD.

I stay behind to do another walk-through of the house—in case I missed something the first time—while I wait for the crime scene unit. I'm about to head inside when I spot Dozer's old pickup truck coming down the road.

"What's going on?" he asks as soon as he gets out of his truck. His expression is one of concern as he takes in the vehicles parked in front of his neighbor's house. "Is Wanda okay?"

I guess it's not so surprising that would be the first thought in his mind, that something might have happened to her.

"She'll be okay, Dozer."

"I don't understand, what happened? Why are you guys here? Did that bastard harm her?"

"You mean Ben? Have you seen him?" I question him.

He switches his attention from the house next door to me.

"Ben? I saw him when I was loading the truck to head up to the cabin. That would've been Wednesday. He was on the porch, drinking."

"You haven't seen him since?" I prompt.

Dozer shakes his head. "Been up at the cabin 'til now, fixing the roof. Tree fell on it in that big storm last month. Why? Where is Wanda? Is she inside?"

His eyes are fixed on his neighbor's house as he starts moving toward it.

"Hold up, Dozer. You can't go in there. Wanda isn't there."

That stops him and when he swings around on me, I'm startled by the intense expression on his face.

"Where is she?" he snaps.

"The hospital, but, Dozer..." I start, but he's not listening anymore. "Hey...wait!"

Before I can stop him, he rushes past me and despite his advancing age and rickety frame, hops behind the wheel. He narrowly misses hitting the crime unit's van coming up the road as he speeds off.

He seems very concerned about Wanda.

Interesting.

∽

Nate

Jesus, this is so not my thing.

I probably shouldn't be using that name, considering where I find myself this morning. It's just that I've never felt more out of place.

It's for Tatum, that's what I need to remind myself of. Trust me, I would not be spending a perfectly good Sunday morning sitting in my truck, at the edge of the parking lot outside the New Horizons Church, if anyone but Tate had asked me to.

She didn't actually ask me to sit outside, she asked me to come, because she wanted to attend a Christian youth music group. I suspect maybe she hoped I'd attend the service taking place at the same time in the church part of the building, but the parking lot is as far as I'm getting. Already I feel like I'm committing sacrilege simply by being on church property.

Still, I wasn't going to tell my daughter no when she's making efforts to connect with the new-to-her community. Of course, it was at Carson's suggestion, but I figured there are worse things the kid could have gotten Tate into.

Busy place, the parking lot was pretty much full when I got here forty minutes ago. I've been killing time playing Sudoku on my phone. Something to engage my brain and my hands, otherwise I might've run out for a pack of smokes from the convenience store across the street.

The temptation to light up has been strong these past few days. I blame that kiss. I guess that was a little bit like falling off the wagon as well. It's basically what the kiss was; indulging in something that may not be healthy for you, but is satisfying in a way nothing else can touch.

I mean, I've had entire wild sexual encounters that did not leave me feeling like an almost modest brush of Savvy's lips did.

Even back then, I knew we had a number of odds stacked against us. A seven-year age difference—which doesn't seem to matter that much now, but fifteen years ago it felt like a big gap—a not-so-stellar background on my part, and the fact her father was the sheriff and already not my biggest fan.

Never mind she lit up my world in a way I knew was a once-in-a-lifetime deal, or that she made me feel wanted when rejection was what I was used to. In the end, I knew in my gut it couldn't last; she gave me so much when I had little to offer in return.

Maybe that's why I didn't put up much of a fight when I was being run out of town.

But I'm back now, and the years away have given me a chance to grow out of a reputation that crippled me, and gain a better sense of self-worth. Not only do I have something to prove, but I feel I have something to offer. To Silence, but mostly to Savannah.

I'm pulled from my thoughts when I notice the church doors opening and the congregation spilling into the parking lot.

I recognize several church-goers, including an old school buddy of mine, Roy Battaglia, with what I assume is his family. It sure looks like he's done well for himself. I hear he has his own business, installing home security systems, which is pretty ironic, seeing as he and I did more than a few break and enters in our youth. Guess we both landed on our feet, but he went a step farther and appears to have established himself as one of Silence's upstanding citizens in the past fifteen or so years.

I watch as he helps his wife and daughter into a nice Cadillac Escalade parked about twenty feet from my truck. Might be nice to say hello, but before I have a chance to get out of the truck, the rain that has been looming all morning starts coming down, and not just a little. Roy scrambles to get in his vehicle and is already pulling out when I catch sight of Tate, standing in a crowd of people seeking shelter under the portico over the front entrance.

I start the truck and make my way around the parking lot, pulling up right in front of the group. I can feel every eye fixed on me and do my best to ignore them as I focus on my daughter.

Leaning over, I open the passenger side door for Tate, who is trying to stay dry by covering her head with a stack of papers she's holding.

"What's all that?"

"Some permission forms you need to fill out, and a schedule for upcoming events for the rest of the year."

"Okay...I'm guessing you had a good time?"

She flashes a bright smile at me.

"It's really cool, Dad. It's like a choir and dance group with a band, and they make these reels for TikTok or Instagram to help them raise money to build a school in Burundi. Get this, last year they raised over three thousand dollars!"

I don't have the heart to tell her three thousand is only a drop in the bucket of what would be needed to erect a building—even in Burundi, I imagine—instead, I grin at her enthusiasm.

"Sounds like a worthy cause. Tell me more."

She does, all the way home. About the young guy running the program, who apparently is a sheriff's deputy, and about other kids in the group. She rattles off names I don't recognize, except maybe one; Naomi Battaglia. I'm thinking that might be the pretty blond girl I saw getting in the back seat of my old friend's Escalade. His daughter.

I'd forgotten how small the world can be in Silence, Washington.

Tatum's normally timid voice sounds excited and much more confident than I'm used to. I know she loves music, and she has a pretty voice—I've occasionally heard her sing along to her favorite tunes in her room—but I wasn't aware she's this passionate about it.

It's a good thing. She's settling in, and as a result I'm beginning to feel some solid ground under my own feet again.

It feels good.

Now, if only Savannah didn't have this murder case taking up all her time, perhaps I could convince her to spend some of it with me.

Fuck, I hope she'll give me this second chance.

CHAPTER 12

Savvy

I DROP my head in my hands, frustrated and overwhelmed.

It's been nine days since Franklin Wyatt's body was found floating in Watts Lake, and I have made little headway in tracking down his killer.

Then yesterday afternoon, Ben Rogers's remains were found in a dried-up creek bed in the woods behind the mobile home community where he lived. Aside from a traumatic head injury to the back of his skull, which probably would've been lethal on its own, the man looked like he had been severely kicked and beaten. There was damage all over his body, including several obvious broken bones.

Other than the fact we haven't seen many violent deaths in Edwards County, and now we suddenly have two in short succession, there really isn't anything obvious connecting them. That doesn't mean there isn't—it could be we simply haven't found it yet—but I have to work these murders as separate cases.

I don't have enough manpower and there aren't enough hours in the day for me to do either of these victims justice. It sucks, because it means I'm going to have to call in help from the CID, the State Patrol's Criminal Investigation Division.

"I heard about Ben."

I look up to find my father standing in the doorway of my office.

"Dad. What are you doing here?"

I'm equal parts annoyed and relieved he's here. I've been doing this job for several years now, and I do a damn good job, if I say so myself. But this is a lot to shoulder.

"Thought you might want to use me as a sounding board. Talk through things, bounce ideas off me. Whatever you need."

He takes a seat in the chair across from my desk and looks at me with concern.

I hate this. I really do. Asking for help or accepting it is hard for me. But I have to recognize the limitations of this department as well as my own, and something has to give.

"Do you have any reason to think these two cases are connected?" he asks.

I shake my head. "Nope. And until I learn differently, these are two separate investigations."

He grunts.

"I've decided I'm calling in the CID," I add.

Dad nods, studying his folded hands. "Don't think you have a choice, Savvy," he agrees.

"I know."

"But—if you don't mind me making a suggestion—run the investigation into Ben's death yourself. You've dealt with him before, you know his background, all the people he regularly associates with. You're better equipped to investigate that case, and let the CID handle the Watts Lake murder. Divide and conquer, and if it turns out the cases overlap you can join forces. More eyes on the ball."

"That's what I'm aiming for."

Dad's lopsided grin makes an appearance.

"Phil told me not to come. Actually, she told me to quit meddling in business that wasn't mine anymore. She said you'd have a handle on things and don't need me looking over your shoulder." He pushes up out of the chair and leans forward on the desk. "Phil is a wise woman, and I should've listened. However, me showing up here is not because I doubt your professional capacity in any way, but you'll always be my daughter, and I'll always want to look out for you."

I flash him a smile of my own as I get up from my chair and round the desk.

"I know, Daddy, and I love you for that."

A brief shadow passes over his expression before he straightens up and turns to face me. I lift up on my toes and kiss his stubbled cheek.

"I'll leave you to it." He moves toward the door where he stops and glances back over his shoulder. "But you know where to find me."

As soon as he's gone, I bite the bullet and make the call.

Next, I summon KC to my office.

"I need you to make copies of everything we have on the Watts Lake case and get a file ready for the CID."

He looks puzzled. "CID?"

"Yes. They'll have a team here in the morning."

"They're taking over?"

"I called them in for support, and they'll be taking lead on the Watts Lake case, yes."

My young deputy does not look happy, and I can't really blame him. He's put a lot of hours in on that case, even attended Franklin Wyatt's initial autopsy. He's eager, and a bit cocky at times in his youthful enthusiasm, so I can see how stepping aside would not sit well with him.

Truthfully, my pride is a little dinged as well, but I can't let it get in the way of doing what is best for the case and the victim. I guess that's why they pay me the big bucks. *Ha.*

"It's bullshit," KC reacts, shocking me a little since I've rarely heard a curse word from his mouth. "We could've done it. Worked double shifts or whatever. We never get cases like this and now you're giving it away. That's bullshit," he repeats vehemently.

"Deputy Kingma, may I remind you who you're talking to?" I sternly call him to task.

I'm all about keeping a relaxed atmosphere here in the office, but that doesn't mean we shouldn't behave professionally. I will not tolerate insubordination.

"For your information, our department will continue to focus on the murder of Ben Rogers. And, not that I owe you any kind of explanation, but I have a responsibility to both the victims as well as the residents of Edwards County, and trying to juggle everything ourselves would be a disservice to them all."

His cheeks stain a ruddy color and his lips press thin, whether from anger or embarrassment I'm not sure, but his apology sounds sincere.

"I'm sorry, Sheriff. I was disappointed, I didn't mean to be disrespectful."

I wave him off. "I get it. Now, if you wouldn't mind

getting that file together, I need you to follow up with some of the Rogers's neighbors we haven't spoken to yet after you're done."

"Yes, ma'am."

"Call me if anything pops up. I'm heading over to The Kerrigan to see when the last time was they saw Ben."

The Kerrigan is his favorite hangout and I know the owners well. Jacob and his wife Stella are good friends of my father's, and Dad still plays poker Thursday nights in the smaller back room of the bar.

"Anything pressing before I head out?" I ask Brenda on my way out the door.

"Nothing Hugo or I can't handle," she returns. "About time you took an early night. Not to push my luck, but you might want to consider a proper meal too. Judging by the food wrappers in the trash bin, you've been eating like crap."

She's not wrong. I'm feeling perpetually bloated with all the unhealthy takeout I've consumed over the past week or so.

"Yes, mother," I mock her. "I have to stop into The Kerrigan anyway. I'll see what special Stella has cooked up for today."

I could do with one of her hearty stews or scrumptious lasagnas.

My stomach is already growling when I walk in the pub ten minutes later.

∽

NATE

"DAD?"

"Yes, Tate."

I'm balancing my phone between my shoulder and my ear while I load my tools in the back of my truck.

"Naomi's mom invited me to stay for dinner. Can I?"

She'd mentioned yesterday Naomi Battaglia had offered to teach her some of the youth group's dance routines before they meet again next Sunday. She'd called me once again already during her lunch time, asking if she could go home with Naomi. That resulted in me asking for a number to get hold of one of the girl's parents to make sure they're okay with my daughter showing up, and I ended up talking to Roy's wife, Maggie. She told me she'd be fetching the girls from school, and I told her I'd swing by after work to pick Tate up again.

"Yeah, if she's sure."

"Wait, she wants to talk to you."

I hear rustling as her phone changes hands, and Maggie's bubbly voice comes on.

"Hey, Nathan. Listen, on Monday nights Naomi and I are usually on our own, because it's Roy's dart night, so we'd love for Tate to hang out for pizza with us. The girls can do their homework together. Oh, by the way, you didn't tell me you and Roy used to be friends. I mentioned your name when I had him on the phone earlier, and he told me you were once thick as thieves."

A snort escapes me at his description of us. I hope to God she has no clue how accurate it actually is.

"I wasn't sure if he'd remember me."

Or if he'd care to, for that matter.

"Of course he does. You should totally drop in for a beer. The guys usually congregate at the bar after work and grab something to eat before they play. Roy would love it."

Sweet of her to think so, but time will tell. I didn't exactly make an effort to stay in touch or leave a forwarding address when I left Silence. I bailed on him too.

Of course, if our daughters are becoming friends, chances are I'll bump into him at some point, and I'd rather get any potential confrontation out of the way on my terms before that happens.

"I may do that. Where are they at?"

"The Kerrigan."

Figures.

With my luck, Roy won't be the only pissed-off blast from the past I'll be bumping into.

Oh well, may as well get it all over with at once.

"Sounds good. I'll swing by for Tate around eight thirty?"

I might as well grab a bite at The Kerrigan if I'm heading there anyway. From what I recall, they had pretty decent wings.

We'll see if I'm welcome.

∽

NOT SURE WHAT I was expecting walking into The Kerrigan, but no one really paid any attention to me.

That is, until Roy noticed me, stood up from the table, and abandoned his buddies to come and greet me.

"Well, fuck me sideways. Nate Gaines. I didn't believe Mags at first, but I'll be damned, it *is* you!"

His loud, booming voice is accompanied by a wide grin, a big bear hug, and several bone-jarring slaps on my shoulders and back.

I'm actually stunned into silence. I definitely hadn't anticipated a greeting like this and it's taking me a moment to process.

"Back in Silence," Roy continues undeterred. "I didn't

think we'd ever see you again, man. You left nothing but dust clouds and hurt feelings, but I tell you, I'm sure glad to see you back and in one piece. Mags says your daughter is a sweet kid. How'd you manage that?"

He laughs heartily at his own joke and claps me on the shoulder again for good measure, while I swallow the unexpected lump in my throat.

Luckily, Roy's boisterous personality makes up for my silence as he starts dragging me toward his table of friends. Before I know it, I'm being introduced to Larry, Omar, and Tim, pushed down in a chair beside Roy, and served a beer from the large pitcher in the center of the table.

Conversation around me resumes as if I'd been sitting here all along. The subject is rather predictably sports, although they also briefly discuss the suspicious death of an old drunk who was a regular here, and some ongoing issues Omar is apparently having at his place of work. I don't really know a whole lot about records and stats, the dead guy's name doesn't ring a bell, and I don't have a clue where Omar even works, so I simply resign myself to an occasional grunt.

But I listen, learn, and sip my beer, and when at some point several baskets of wings and a boatload of fries are set down on the table, I dig in right along with them.

Even though I've always been a bit of a loner, it feels kind of nice being one of the guys.

"Play darts, Nate?" Larry asks at some point.

"Not with any kind of accuracy," I admit.

I mean, I could probably hit the board, but that's the extent of my abilities.

"He couldn't throw a ball to save his life either," Roy jokes.

He's referring to the one time I had the misguided idea to try out for the school football team, because the players got all the hot girls. What little appeal I might've held to the opposite sex at the time evaporated during the two hours of those tryouts. My athletic ambitions did as well.

"Yeah, well...all it takes is a little practice," Larry suggests, following it up with, "You're welcome to join us any time. Monday nights, come early like today for drinks and some food, and the games start at seven and run to ten, ten thirty."

"You should," Tim, who seems to be the quiet one in the group, contributes. "It'd be nice to have an extra player."

Roy gets to his feet and also pipes up, a teasing grin on his face as he shakes his head. "Y'all, this guy will need a *ton* of practice. Don't say I didn't warn you lot."

I ignore him, but turn to the other three. "I'll think about it. I'm still settling in."

Sort of.

Mostly, I'm not sure if I want to commit to something that requires me to show up at The Kerrigan on a weekly basis. It would only be a matter of time before I'd be forced into a confrontation with some of the town's old guard. I'd rather that not be in front of this group of likable guys who—other than Roy, of course—didn't know me back then.

"You gonna stick around?" Roy asks.

I glance at my watch and shake my head. "I told your wife I'd swing by to pick up Tate. Another time."

He claps me on the shoulder and starts heading toward a dart board at the rear of the bar. Omar and Tim follow him, but Larry hangs back.

"Nice meeting you," he says, holding out his hand.

"You too," I return.

"Whenever you're ready, you know where to find us."

"Appreciate it."

When he heads after the others, I pull my wallet and toss a few bills on the table, before turning toward the exit.

That's when I notice Savvy sitting at the bar by herself, picking at the fries on a plate in front of her. Her back is turned to me, but her head swivels around when I walk up to her.

"Hey."

She sounds surprised. I guess she hadn't noticed me either.

"We've gotta stop bumping into each other in bars," I observe.

She flashes a tiny smile. I can read the strain and fatigue on her face.

"I know. Did you just come in?"

I shake my head. "No, I was sitting over there with Roy and his buddies. I'm actually on my way out. I need to go pick up Tate from a friend's house. What brought you here?"

"Work. My latest victim was a frequent visitor here."

"I see. Guess when it rains, it pours."

She chuckles. "You can say that again. It's disturbing."

Without thinking I brush a strand of hair that slipped from her stubby ponytail behind her ear. When she turns her eyes on me, I try to read the message in those deep, dark pools.

"You should get some rest," I suggest gently.

"I should," she agrees. "And you should go and pick up your daughter."

Shit. Tate, that's right.

"Yeah. Hey, call me when you have a chance or need an ear or something. Okay?"

"Sure."

She turns back to her half-empty plate.

It may be my imagination, but I'm almost positive that's

disappointment I hear in her voice. I brace my hands on the bar on either side of her and lean in, my mouth brushing the shell of her small ear.

"Day or night, Savvy."

Then I kiss the sensitive spot behind her ear, my lips lingering against her skin to feel the slight tremble, before I tear myself away and walk out the door.

CHAPTER 13

S*avvy*

SURPRISE REGISTERS on his face when he sees me standing on his doorstep.

To be honest, I'm not entirely sure what I'm doing here either.

I left the pub not long after him and went straight home. I took a quick shower to wash the day's grunge off before putting on my pj's and slipping into bed. But it was clear to me twenty minutes later that sleep wouldn't come. Not with my mind refusing to quiet down.

So I pulled on a pair of yoga pants and a hoodie, fully intending to try and get some work done, but once my feet were moving, I walked right past my laptop and the case files I'd dumped on the coffee table and out the door.

And now here I am, without a clue what to say to Nate when he looks at me questioningly.

Then his expression softens and he steps aside, motioning me in. As I pass by, he gently grabs hold of my wrist as he closes the front door. Then he pulls me toward him, sliding his other hand under the loose curls at the back of my neck where his long fingers cup the back of my head. When his lips hit mine, I'm ready, already experiencing the inevitable charge surging through me from his touch.

It's surreal how well the body remembers what the mind worked so hard to forget.

I willingly give up control, letting myself float on the wave of sensations.

His kiss so achingly familiar but also provocatively new. The taste richer and his tongue bolder as he claims my mouth.

I'm floating, held in place by an arm pinned behind my back and a hand cradling my head, while his mouth devours me, leaving no room for any coherent thought in my mind.

This. This is what I was looking for.

I manage to slide one of my hands between us, and rub the heel firmly along the hard ridge of his cock. I can feel his responding moan in my mouth all the way down to my core. I'm instantly wet, or maybe I was already when I knocked on his door.

Not that it matters. The only thing that matters right now is the slide of his callused palm into my waistband and down the curve of my ass. My fingers curl around his length, as his brush my crease, slipping into the wet of my arousal.

All I can think of is having this man inside me. Clearing my mind and filling that void I've been living with for too long.

I'm so focused on reaching that goal, it startles me when Nate abruptly stops kissing me. Next, he pulls his hand from my pants.

"Wait," he whispers.

The first word spoken between us.

We're both breathing heavy as he leans his forehead against mine. I'm starting to feel a little self-conscious with my hand still wrapped around the outline of his dick through his sweats, so I drop it to my side.

"I'm sorry," I start apologizing automatically. After all, I'm the one who showed up on his doorstep unannounced with need in my eyes. "I shouldn't have—"

"Stop." He grabs hold of my chin and tilts my face up. "I'm not sorry about anything. But...I have a teenage daughter who is right up those stairs, and as much as I'd love to strip those yoga pants off you and fuck you up against the front door, it doesn't seem like a good idea with her in the house."

His crass words do little to settle the wobble in my knees and, in fact, make my heart race a little faster.

I'd forgotten how direct he could be, or how much I liked that about him. But the point he makes gives me pause. The mention of his daughter is a good reminder life isn't as simple as it used to be when it was just him and me.

I'm not quite sure what—probably need— drove me to his door at almost eleven at night, but I'm positive Tatum was not part of the equation. It's a bit embarrassing, and a lot sobering, making me realize perhaps getting involved with Nate in any way deserves a bit more thorough consideration.

"Maybe I should go," I offer, trying to slip from his arms I'm wrapped in.

"No." He buries his face in my neck and holds on tight. "Stay a bit. Come out on the back deck with me. It's a beautiful night."

"It's a little chilly, don't you think?"

I know I was cold coming here just in a hoodie.

"I'll grab us a blanket."

His lips brush mine before he releases me, takes my hand, and leads the way through the living room, grabbing a throw off the back of the couch in passing.

There's a dining set on the deck—a table and four chairs—and one lounger, which is where he leads me.

"Here, sit and I'll grab us some drinks. Beer?"

"Sure."

I lean back and let him arrange the blanket over me before he disappears back inside. I lift my eyes to a clear sky, dotted with countless stars. It's one of the many perks of living in a small community in the mountains; there is little to no light pollution like you'd see in the more populated areas and bigger cities.

I hear the sliding door and turn my head to see Nate approach.

"Scoot over."

I sit up and shift forward, making room for him to slip in the chair behind me.

"Lean back, Sav."

It feels a little like coming home, leaning back and feeling his solid body behind me. He reaches around and hands me one of the bottles he was carrying.

"Now, relax," he whispers by my ear. The light brush of his breath is like a caress.

Then his free hand slips underneath the blanket, stroking down my chest and curving around my breast. He finds my pert nipple through the thick fabric of my sweater and tugs lightly, sending a signal straight down between my legs, and I shift my hips restlessly.

"Patience..." I can feel the rumble of his voice against my

back. "Take a sip of your beer, baby, I will get to your pussy when I'm done playing here."

I can feel the cold liquid slide down my throat as Nate builds the heat in my body. His hand is now on my bare skin, working its way down to fulfilling his promise. My beer bottle hits the deck boards when I try to set it down next to the lounger, but I need my hands free. With one hand I grab hold of Nate's neck, pulling him down as I twist my head to reach his mouth. My other hand moves down, covering his as he easily slides one, then two digits inside me.

I come embarrassingly fast. Already well-primed, it doesn't take much.

I'm grateful when he doesn't retrieve his hand right away, but leaves it where it is, gently cupping me. It feels nice, unhurried, and safe, which allows me to let all tension drain as his body cradles mine.

I close my eyes, only for a minute.

∼

NATE

"You've been awfully chipper this week."

I immediately wipe the grin I've been wearing off my face.

Brenda isn't the only one who's commented on it, Tate has too. The difference is my daughter was simply curious, but that's not the vibe I'm getting from Brenda, who is flashing me a knowing smile. I almost get the sense the woman has a decent idea where my good mood comes from, although I doubt she'd have found out from Savvy.

I still can't believe how responsive she was, and how easily she fell asleep in my arms after.

I sat there with her in my arms for a good hour and a half, enjoying the feel of her and allowing myself to fantasize a little about what a future might look like for us, before I woke her up. It was tempting to carry her inside and let her stay the night in my bed but—aside from the fact I'd need to prepare my daughter for any kind of sleepover—I didn't think Savvy would want to wake up in my bed.

Not yet, anyway.

I walked her out to her SUV and kissed her goodnight before she got behind the wheel. I haven't seen her since, but I know she has her hands full with these murders. We did exchange a few brief texts, just checking in, but I'm hoping I can catch up with her sometime this weekend.

"Always nice to make a new customer happy," I deflect Brenda's comment. "Do you mind if I take a few pictures for my new website?"

"Go right ahead. I didn't even know you had a website." She steps out in the hallway to give me room to take a few shots with my phone.

"I don't yet. My daughter is setting one up for me as part of a project for one of her elective courses. I wouldn't even know where to start, but apparently my fourteen-year-old's technical skills far outweigh mine."

Brenda chuckles as she hands me the check she's been writing. "Trust me, I know what you mean. My guys are a little older than your daughter, but I've been turning to them for years for any issues I have with my phone, or my computer or even TV. And it's not that I'm clueless, but technology changes at a pace I can't seem to keep up with. It seems so effortless for them."

"I hear you. Anyway, thanks for this." I hold up the

check. "I appreciate you picking a virtual stranger to do the job."

She waves me off. "I should be thanking you. My husband, Jim, kept saying he was gonna do it, but he's been on the road almost nonstop this past year, and I got tired of waiting. It helped your price was reasonable."

She follows me as I head for the front door.

"Glad I was able to help." I turn and grin at her. "And feel free to recommend me if you hear anyone is looking to get some work done."

She studies me, her head slightly tilted to one side. "Actually, I may have someone in mind. They bought an older house a few years ago they were going to do some work on themselves, but I guess life got busy. I'll put a bug in their ear."

"Appreciate it."

Half an hour later I'm at home, putting the tools away in my garage when I hear movement behind me, but before I have a chance to turn around, something hits me in the back of the head, knocking me to the ground.

My face hits the concrete floor hard and the pain is intense. I hear footsteps approaching and try to push up, but my body won't cooperate. Then a growling voice sounds right above me, cutting through the black fog that's closing in on me.

"You should've stayed away."

∽

THE NEXT VOICE I hear is Tatum's.

"Daddy. Oh my God, are you okay? Dad?"

It fucking hurts when I try to open my eyes, and all I see

is a blurred shape leaning in. After a few blinks Tate's face comes into focus, tears running down her cheeks.

My poor girl. After what happened with her mother, this must scare her.

"I'm okay," I reassure her in a raspy voice.

To be honest, I'm not sure I'm okay. My ears are ringing, my eyeballs are throbbing, and my head feels like it's caught in a vise and someone is turning the wheel. When I try to push up off the floor, the pain is intense and a wave of nausea hits me suddenly, forcing me to drop back to the ground. Pressing my cheek against the cold concrete, I suck in air through my nose.

"I called 911," I hear a man's voice I don't recognize. "Don't move, an ambulance is on the way."

Not moving won't be a problem.

CHAPTER 14

Nate

"What the hell, Nate?"

My head automatically swings around at Savvy's voice, and I realize immediately that isn't a good idea when I have to resist the urge to puke. Still, I manage to notice her pretty face is pale and her hand is trembling when she reaches out to grab mine.

"Brenda tracked me down and told me. What happened?"

At this point everything is a bit of a blur. I've had questions of my own no one seems able to answer, like where my daughter went. I know I'm in the hospital, but she didn't come with me in the ambulance and I haven't seen her since I got here. Of course, I was poked and prodded before getting sent for X-rays and a scan, and I've been in this small cubby hole of a room, hooked up to machines, waiting for someone to come so I could find out where she's gone.

"Have you seen Tatum?" I ask instead of answering her question.

"Yeah, she is in the waiting room with KC. He drove her here."

"Who the fuck is KC?"

I pull my hand from hers and try to sit up, but she unceremoniously shoves me back down in bed.

"Don't you dare move. Dana said I could see you but she's gonna kick me out if I upset you."

She leans down and places her palm against the side of my face. My entire body feels like it's on fire, so her cool hand on my skin is nice. Soothing.

"KC Kingma is one of my deputies and was the first to arrive at your house. Apparently, he knows your daughter from the church youth group he runs."

He must be the young guy she mentioned once or twice.

"Is she okay?"

"Upset and a little scared, but that's to be expected. She says she came home from school and saw you lying on the floor of the garage. You were bleeding and unconscious. When she screamed, a neighbor heard her and called dispatch."

That was probably the voice I didn't recognize.

I feel bereft when Savvy takes her hand back. But then she pulls a stool closer to the bed and sits down beside me, her face now level with mine.

"Now, can you remember what happened to you?"

I close my eyes, both to try and minimize the throbbing in my head, and to concentrate so I don't miss any details.

"I came home and was putting away my tools—I

finished Brenda's bathroom today—when someone walked up behind me and hit me over the head."

"Wait," Savvy interrupts. "Did they walk in or were they already in your garage waiting for you?"

I assumed whoever hit me walked in from the street, but I guess it's possible he'd already been there. I take a moment to think about that.

The garage door was closed when I got home, I'm positive. It works on either the opener I have clipped to the sun visor in my truck, or you can access from the keypad if you have the code. However, other than the overhead door and the one leading into the house, there's another access door on the side. One that leads into the yard.

I mowed the lawn on Wednesday and thought I'd locked that door after I put the lawn mower back in the garage. But maybe I didn't.

"I never saw him so I can't be sure. It's possible he came in through the side door and was waiting for me."

He certainly seemed to know me.

"You say 'he,' are you sure it was a man?"

"It was a man's voice."

"He talked to you?"

I start nodding but think better of it when a stab of pain pierces my skull.

"He told me I should've stayed away."

Savvy suddenly sits straighter and I can almost see her ears perking up.

"What did he say...exactly."

"You should've stayed away," I repeat the man's words verbatim.

"Did you recognize his voice?"

"It was more of a growl so it's hard to know for certain."

I take in a breath and give my response one last consideration. I don't have a good track record with law enforcement—I generally don't have a lot of faith in them—but I have to believe Savvy is not part of the old boys' club.

Decision made, I add, "But if I had to venture a guess, based on the message he imparted, I'd place my bet on your former deputy."

Her lips thin and her jaw tightens as she gets to her feet slowly but deliberately, and starts pacing the small room.

"I see," she finally shares. "Just for clarity's sake, other than his message, was there anything else, anything tangible that suggested to you it was him? Were you able to see anything at all?"

I hate her questions make me doubt what I felt so confident about just moments ago.

"No. His voice was the last I heard before I blacked out."

The door opens behind Savvy and the same elderly doctor who was here earlier walks into the room.

"Mr. Gaines...you are a lucky man." Then he turns to Savvy. "Sheriff, sorry to interrupt."

"Hey, Doc. No worries, we were pretty much done here."

"Good." He focuses back on me. "Like I said, you're a lucky man with an extraordinarily hard skull. The scan shows no fractures, bleeds, or obvious damage, but you lost a bit of blood and suffered a serious concussion. You'll also probably have an extra bump on your nose from hitting the ground face-first, I hope you're not too vain. I'm going to send Dana in to stitch up that gash on the back of your head. And then we're gonna keep you here for observation for at least forty-eight hours. Head injuries can be sneaky and we want to make sure we haven't missed anything. I'll be by to check on you later."

Forty-eight hours? It's the weekend, what am I going to do about Tatum?

The doctor is already gone by the time I process the information.

"I can't be in here for two days."

Savvy grins wryly. "You don't have much of a choice."

"I can't. I've got Tate."

She walks up to the bed.

"You need to rest. I'll make sure your daughter is taken care of."

Then she surprises me when she leans down and presses a kiss against my chapped lips.

"You scared me," she whispers, before turning on her heel and walking out.

I must've dozed off because the next thing I know, my daughter's voice wakes me.

"Daddy? Are you okay? They said I could only see you for a few minutes."

I notice Dana Kerrigan hovering in the doorway behind her.

"Hey, honey." I try to smile at her but it hurts my face. "I promise, I'll be fine. They want to stitch me up and keep an eye on me for a couple of days. That's all."

"I know, Savvy told me. She called Naomi's mom and I can stay there for the weekend. She asked KC to stick around so he can drive me over."

"Why? Where is Savvy?" I can't help but ask.

"Oh, she said something about an urgent matter she had to take care of. She promised to check in with me later."

"Tatum..." Dana pipes up. "Maybe let me get your dad stitched up so he can get some rest. Savvy said she'd bring you back tomorrow for a visit, and in the meantime, I wrote down your number so I can update you or get in touch with you if I need to, okay?"

Tate nods, but her eyes are welling with tears when she looks at me.

"Aww shit, honey, come here."

I spread my arms as best I can and wrap them around my daughter, who cries on my chest.

"Sweetheart, I swear to God, I'll be just fine."

Forty-five minutes later my head is stitched up, and Dana left me with instructions to get some rest. But unfortunately, rest will not come, because I can't stop worrying about the urgent matter Savvy left to take care of.

∽

Savvy

This is on me.

I should've handled this as soon as I found out Sanchuk had been responsible for chasing Nathan out of town. Worse, he used the threat of falsifying evidence to implicate an innocent man in something he didn't do.

It's just been so crazy. Even with the CID now in charge of the Franklin Wyatt case and our department only responsible for Ben Rogers's murder investigation, this has been such a busy week. It doesn't help the town's Harvest Fest is only a little over a week away and I'm getting pulled into the planning at this point. With all that going on, tracking down Jeff Sanchuk has slid way down my list of priorities.

That was a mistake.

My mistake.

The moment I leave the hospital, finding Sanchuk becomes priority one on my list. I head straight for his address. For a moment I think about calling in backup, but first I want to make sure he's home.

The bungalow is as dark as it was when I came looking for him last time and his vehicle is still parked in the driveway. I also notice some flyers and a couple of papers on his doormat that weren't there last time, and I'm starting to wonder if he's been here at all since then.

A small niggle of doubt worms its way in, as I consider the possibility he took off after leaving the department. Maybe he took a vacation somewhere. Of course, if that's the case, he couldn't have been the one to attack Nate.

I'm startled by a knock on my window and I find Mrs. Dixon on the sidewalk, holding on to her walker with one hand while trying to peer into my cruiser.

"Mrs. Dixon," I start as I get out from behind the wheel. "What are you doing here?"

Never mind that she lives right down the street, she shouldn't be wandering around the neighborhood when it's already almost dark out. The sidewalks are uneven and the streetlights are sparse. She could easily fall.

"Stretching my legs. It's a nice night, not too cold, and I'm trying to get my steps in."

"Your steps?"

She pulls back the sleeve on her right arm, revealing a Fitbit on her wrist.

"I'm short about eight hundred on my daily quota," she explains. "That's about as much as a round trip to the community mailbox at the end of the street."

"Quota?"

I'm only five four, but with her shoulders and back so stooped, the woman has to turn her head sideways to be able to look up at me.

"Yes, I'm going for five thousand steps a day. Gertrude

Vanderzand told me she does seven thousand and she's seen a huge improvement in her health. She's even lost some weight. She came to visit me after I fell and showed me a website where I could join this virtual walking group. It came with this handy watch that keeps track of everything for me, so I signed up."

Oh dear.

Gertrude Vanderzand is late fifties, maybe sixties, but definitely far from her eighties, and in good physical shape. The last I heard she was making money doing chair yoga videos for her YouTube channel. Before that, it had been selling nutritional supplements, and I believe she even tried her hand at teaching Zumba classes in the church basement at some point.

She's one of Silence's more colorful individuals and always seems to find ways to capitalize on the latest fitness craze.

"I guess there's nothing wrong with a little extra exercise," I start cautiously. "But maybe five thousand steps is a little excessive to start with? Have you talked to Doc Wilson about this?"

She shrugs her hunched shoulders. "No need, they have medical professionals virtually monitoring. Isn't technology amazing? Besides, since Doc Wilson took his partial retirement it's almost impossible to get in for an appointment."

Unfortunately, that's true. I know my friend Dana, the clinic's nurse practitioner, is constantly swamped. We have a dire shortage of primary care physicians here. That's why Doc's retirement is only partial until we can find someone to take his place, but it hasn't been easy to draw fresh blood to Silence.

"Anyway, enough about me," she declares. "How come you're sitting here at the curb?"

"I'm actually looking for Jeff Sanchuk," I explain casually. "But I guess he's not home."

"Coho are spawning. He's got a fishing shack up river. I'm guessing that's where he went."

I should've thought of that, I knew he was an avid fisherman.

"Any idea where up river?"

Up river is north of town, generally speaking, but that in itself is an obscure description, since there are about seventy miles of mostly unpopulated wilderness between us and the Canadian border. He could be anywhere.

"I wouldn't know. Can't be that far, he's never gone for longer than one or two days at a time."

I know someone who might have an idea.

"Gotcha." I smile at the woman. "Now, can I give you a ride back home?"

She checks her Fitbit. "Thanks, but I'll walk. I've got a few more steps to go."

I put a hand on her shoulder.

"Okay, but I'm going to follow you home. It's dark and I don't want you out here by yourself," I persist when she starts shaking her head. "I can't stop you from doing what you want, but it's my responsibility to make sure you, along with everyone else in Edwards County is safe."

And I've been doing a piss-poor job of it lately.

As I'm slowly rolling along, following Mrs. Dixon home, I dial my father's number.

"Savvy, we were just talking about you," Phil announces when she answers the phone.

"My ears must've been burning."

"Ha. No, here's the thing; your dad and I thought—" She's cut off when I hear my father's rumbling protest in the background. "Your father is being a stick in the mud," she shares. "Fine. *I* thought it might be fun to throw an end-of-summer cookout with a bonfire next Friday night to kick off the Harvest Fest for a few friends and family. You can make it, right?"

I pinch the bridge of my nose. *Great.* Something else to add to my already full dance card.

"And feel free to invite a friend," she adds, not at all subtly.

I stifle a groan and distractedly wave back at Mrs. Dixon, who is turning onto the path to her front door.

"All I can promise is that I'll try to be there," I tell my stepmother, watching to make sure Mrs. Dixon makes it safely inside her little house.

"Of course. That's all I can ask. I know you have your hands full, but I thought it might make for a nice distraction."

"Absolutely," I agree with her because it's the fastest way to get to my reason for calling. "And I promise I'll let you know, but before I go, could I talk to Dad for a second?"

"Yeah, he's right here. Talk to you later."

I hear some rustling as the phone changes hands, and then my father's voice is on the other side.

"Don't feel pressured, Toots."

I chuckle. "It's okay. It sounds like fun."

He grunts, clearly of a different mind.

I don't enjoy bringing up the man who has caused some tension between my father and me lately, but I've wasted enough time already.

"Reason I'm calling, though, is Sanchuk. I need to find him and I was told he's probably up river at his fishing shack. You wouldn't happen to know where that is, would you?"

"What do you want with Sanchuk now? Just leave him be, Savvy."

My dad is a gruff guy, he wasn't born with a lot of tact, or the ability to read the room. Normally, I can handle that, but today—after seeing Nate helpless in a hospital bed, with his head and face bloodied—Dad's knee-jerk comment goes down the wrong way.

"You're kidding me, right? Leave him be? For your information, Nate Gaines is in the hospital in serious condition, hooked up to monitors, and you want me to leave Sanchuk be?"

For a moment it's quiet on the other side, and when he speaks, my father's voice is cautious.

"You think it was Sanchuk?"

"Dad, did you know he's the one who chased Nathan out of town years ago? Threatened to frame him for something he didn't do. That's why Nate disappeared. Do you know what he said when he was assaulting Nate in the kitchen at the station? He called him a fucking idiot for showing his face back in Silence."

"I see. Gaines told you that?"

"No, I heard him say it myself as I walked into the kitchen. But Nate told me later what that was all about. He told me everything."

"He told you Sanchuk threatened him?"

I take a deep breath to calm my flaring temper. I should know by now people are rarely inclined to listen to someone yelling.

"Yes. And after he attacked him in his garage, he told Nate he should've stayed away. Now, do you know where Sanchuk's fishing shack is? I need to have a word with the man."

There's a brief pause before I get an answer.

"It's about ten miles north. Take Pinegrove up, past the turnoff to the Mountain View Lodge, and continue a couple more miles until you see a red-painted rock marking a small dirt road on the left side. Follow that to the end. You may have to walk in the last bit."

It's clear my father has been there before, and I'm not sure how I feel about that.

"Okay. Thanks."

I'm about to hang up when he adds.

"Savvy, wait. I don't think you should go there alone."

CHAPTER 15

S *avvy*

"What is your father doing here?"

I glance back at my dad sitting behind the wheel of his ancient Bronco. He's staying put in his truck like I told him to. At least for now.

What can I say? The stubborn old goat insisted on following me in his old beater after I told him he could absolutely not ride along with me. I was just passing Mountain View Lodge when he caught up with me. Unfortunately, his rust bucket is louder than a thunder car at the stock races, and I'm sure any living creature out in these woods could hear us coming.

"I'm not sure. I called him to get directions to this place and told him no when he wanted to ride shotgun. He didn't want me to go alone and, as you may remember, my father has a stubborn streak a mile wide, so he decided to follow me anyway."

Thank God my deputy, Warren Burns, was already waiting by the red rock when we drove up. Warren is former Seattle PD, and he was the last person my father hired. He's an excellent deputy and likes working the night shifts, which works out fine for me. His excuse for trading in a detective position in a big city like Seattle, for a post as a deputy in the smallest county of the state, is he needed a change of scenery. I always suspected there was more to the story, but his file shows he left the police department on good terms, with an excellent record and a high recommendation from his captain. I'm pretty sure it must be something in his personal life, but he's not really much of a social guy, and I rarely see him outside of work.

But I'm glad it's him at my back tonight as we start walking the trail toward the river side.

"I hope he stays put," Warren mumbles beside me as we trudge along the overgrown path, his flashlight lighting the way.

"You and me both."

From the corner of my eye, I catch Warren looking at me. "What?"

"Care to tell me why we're out here in the boonies looking for Sanchuk at eleven at night, instead of tomorrow when we can see where we're going?"

"Because I've put it off long enough and now a man is in the hospital. I can't wait until tomorrow. Not anymore."

"Are you talking about that guy who was attacked in his garage? Hugo filled me in on that case."

"Not just any guy. Nate Gaines, he's the guy who fixed the ceiling by the holding cells. You probably missed him because you work the night shift. He also happens to be the guy Sanchuk assaulted in the office kitchen."

That stops Warren in his tracks.

"He did what? How come I haven't heard about that?"

Because I made Brenda swear to hold her wagging tongue, and the only other person who knows at the station is Hugo, who happened to be there when I was giving Jeff Sanchuk his options in my office, and Hugo wouldn't share employee related stuff with others.

"Wait, is that why he retired so abruptly? I did hear about that."

"Yes, that would be why."

"I'm surprised," he states. "Don't get me wrong, from what I've seen of him, Sanchuk is a Grade A prick, a bully, and a piss-poor cop. Never liked the guy. But he's usually smarter than to shit where he eats. What made him lose his cool this time?"

I snort. He gives an accurate assessment of the man.

For both Nate's sake and my own, I wasn't going to broadcast any details, but I probably owe it to Warren since I dragged him out here and he should know what he's in for.

"In a nutshell; Nate and I were an item fifteen or so years ago when Sanchuk decided to run him out of town under the threat of bogus burglary charges that wouldn't just impact Nate, but his family as well."

"And he left? Just like that?"

I guess it's a fair reaction, but Warren doesn't know Nate's background. He didn't grow up here and doesn't understand, no matter how hard Nate worked on building a decent life, he was always struggling to overcome his bad rap with law enforcement. He had no reason to trust them. Not back then and—given what happened to him since he returned—I'm pretty sure that hasn't changed much.

"Trust me, Nathan had his reasons," I assure him. "Look, I can't be a hundred-percent sure as to what prompted Sanchuk to assault him the first time, but I'm willing to bet he was hoping to intimidate Nate. Probably worried about his own hide if it ever came out what he did all those years ago."

I have to duck for a low hanging branch and end up stumbling over the protruding root on the ground. Warren grabs my elbow to keep me from landing on my face.

"Thanks."

"No problem. So I'm guessing you think Sanchuk is responsible for this latest attack as well?"

"I do. Nate remembers his attacker saying he should've stayed away. Sanchuk is the only one who makes sense."

I catch Warren nodding.

"And you trust this Nate?" he asks, shooting me a sideways glance.

If he'd have asked me this question a few weeks ago, I'd have given him a resolute no, but after the attacks and getting the full background story from Nate, I have no doubts.

I'm about to answer him when he shushes me and stops, pointing up ahead. The flickering orange glow of a fire is visible through the trees slightly to our right.

"What's the plan?" Warren whispers.

I'd hoped that if we found him here, he'd be inside, maybe asleep already. Having him sitting out by a campfire makes it tougher to approach without alerting him. At this point, I don't trust him not to go for a gun and shoot blindly.

"We approach him from opposite sides and announce ourselves when we get close enough, or if he hears us. Make sure your body cam is on, and let me do the talking. Keep your weapon holstered unless he leaves us no choice."

"I'll take the woods," Warren volunteers.

I give him a bit of a head start to work his way around before I continue making my way up the narrowing trail, watching where I put my feet to minimize noise.

I'm just easing around a slight bend in the path when I hear a rustle and then the distinct slice and click of a rifle cocking. Immediately my hand goes to the gun on my hip.

"Sheriff's Department!" I call out as I draw my gun. "It's Savvy, Jeff. I'm just here to talk."

When there isn't a warning shot, I walk out into the open and see Sanchuk standing next to a folding chair by a small campfire. He is holding the rifle I heard loosely by his side, and he's glaring at me.

It's not until I take a few steps closer I see Warren in the shadows behind him. He has his service weapon aimed at Sanchuk.

"Drop the gun, Jeff," he tells him. "We just have a few questions."

With an angry grunt, he drops his rifle, and when Warren quickly confiscates it, I clip my weapon back in its holster.

"Thought you were a damn bear," Sanchuk slurs as he takes his seat. "What the hell are you doing here? Can't a man drink in peace?"

It's then I notice the half-empty bottle of booze next to the chair. *Wonderful.*

Warren stays closely behind him, his hand on the butt of his weapon, ready to intervene if necessary. I hope it won't be.

"Listen, I need you to come back to the station so I can ask you a few questions about an incident today."

He barks out a harsh laugh, which turns into a phlegmy cough that makes me wince.

"Ask me here," he finally manages.

"I don't think that's a good idea, Jeff. You've been drinking and I'd prefer it if you were sober."

Mostly because anything he volunteers or admits to while intoxicated makes for bad evidence. It would be reason for any defense lawyer worth his wages to challenge the validity of the testimony and argue for it to be thrown out of court.

"Then come back tomorrow."

"You know that's not the way it works."

In response, he folds his arms and stares stubbornly into the fire.

There is no doubt he'd be long gone by the time we got here, and there is no way in hell I'm going to risk losing him at this point. I have my plate full with what is going on in town right now, and it would be nice to be able to scratch one investigation off my list.

Since he is clear about not coming voluntarily, we ultimately have no choice but to put Sanchuk in handcuffs and march him back to where we left our vehicles. He doesn't resist, but appears to dig his heels in when he catches sight of my dad's Bronco.

"Had to call in your daddy, didn't you?" he taunts me. "Scared to face me alone, little girl?"

It requires a tremendous amount of restraint for me not to take the bait. It's so damn tempting to exert my power over him, but that would only make his day and turn me into another bully.

"Come on, let's go, Jeff," Warren urges him toward the vehicles. "You're only digging yourself a deeper hole."

"Put him in the back of mine," I instruct him. "Mr. Sanchuk can hitch a ride with me."

Warren places him in the back of my cruiser and shuts the door. Then he turns to me.

"Are you sure this is a good idea?" he asks in a low voice.

"Yep."

"He'll probably be mouthing off at you the entire ride," he warns.

"I know."

It's what I'm counting on, and once he realizes he's not getting the reaction he's hoping for from me, he's going to get annoyed and hopefully won't be as careful with the things he spews. I'll be listening and will have the camera attached to my rearview mirror running the entire fifteen minutes it'll take to get back to the station. Any information I'm able to glean may not be enough for the DA, but it may give me the leverage I need when I officially question him in the morning. After he sobers up.

"That's what I'm going for," I confess with a grin.

Before I get into my vehicle though, I walk over to my father's Bronco. Credit to him, it doesn't look like he's moved from his spot behind the wheel. He rolls down his window when he sees me approach.

"What's going on?"

"He's blotto. Had his rifle on us so we had to pull our weapons, but it all ended a little anticlimactically, since he's drunk. So, I'm taking him in, letting him sleep it off in a holding cell, and questioning him in the morning."

He nods, his eyes on the back of my cruiser where you can just see the outline of Sanchuk's head through the back window.

"I appreciate your concern, but as you can see, we have it well in hand. Go home, Dad."

He nods, but when I drive away moments later I notice his Bronco falling in line behind my cruiser and Warren's.

Stubborn old coot.

For the first couple of minutes, I assume Jeff must've dozed off; there is not a peep from the back seat. So when he suddenly starts talking, it startles me for a moment.

"Not sure what you think you can pin on me, missy, but I've been up here fishing since you kicked my ass to the curb."

"I'm not looking to pin anything on anyone, Jeff, unlike some people I know," I return with a taunt of my own.

"Are you accusing me of something?" he immediately fires back, already getting riled up.

Perfect. I like him hissing and snarling. His own mouth will run him into trouble.

"Not at all," I respond calmly, which probably only pisses him off more.

"Miss High and Mighty. You think your shit don't stink, but it didn't take you long to hook back up with that delinquent boyfriend of yours, did it?"

My blood runs cold at his words and I have to struggle not to show any reaction, because that's what he's after.

He's been watching. He has to have been or he wouldn't know that about Nate and me.

So much for him being up at the river all this time; it would appear he's been doing a lot more than fishing.

I force a derisive laugh. "My Lord, Jeff; you must be really hammered, you're starting to hallucinate."

"Like hell I am," he snarls back. "You're welcoming that piece of trash back with open arms and, just like that, the town is going to hell in a handbasket. I knew you weren't fit for the job. Two murders in one week since that criminal rolled back into town, and what do you do? You throw yourself at that filthy bastard instead of locking his sorry ass up."

I feel his spittle hit the back of my neck, but I don't

move, because every word out of his mouth is a nail in his own coffin.

"This town was locked down tight before you took over. There was no room for criminals like Gaines, and we made sure they didn't stick around for long. Sent his ass packing too, and boy, were we glad to see the back of him."

We?

I swallow the question hovering on my lips. I'd just be playing into his hands.

"Nathan told me how you ran him out of town," I say instead. "Threatening to frame him for a crime you knew he had nothing to do with." I glance in the rearview mirror and see his narrowed eyes shimmer from the shadows of the back seat. "It must've scared the crap out of you when you saw him back in town. Afraid he'd rat you out?"

He snorts. "I'm not scared of that piece of shit. But I bet you he realizes now he made a bad choice the day he decided to move back to Silence."

Not quite a confession, but a clear admission he at least knows about the attack on Nate. I decide to push just a little more.

"And why is that?"

I catch him watching me in the rearview mirror and his face slowly cracks with a smile that sends a shiver down my spine.

"Because I'm not the only one upset to see Gaines back in town."

"Oh?"

I try to stay casual as I raise an eyebrow. Sanchuk appears to be enjoying this exchange a little too much, and it makes me uneasy.

"Yeah…" he drawls. "But you're gonna have to look a whole lot closer to home for that."

My eyes immediately snap to my side mirror where I can see the Bronco still at the back of our little convoy.

I can just catch part of my father's outline behind the wheel.

Swallowing hard, I force down the bile crawling up my throat.

CHAPTER 16

S*avvy*

"Tell me he's talking out of his ass."

With all my heart I was hoping Jeff Sanchuk was yanking my chain, but one look at the expression on my father's face is enough.

"Oh my God, Dad. Seriously?"

I waited for Warren to escort Sanchuk inside the station so he can be booked for the night, and as soon as the door closed behind them, I turned to my father, who'd already been exiting his truck.

I can't believe we're having this showdown in the department parking lot, but Dad is the one who chose to ignore my suggestion he go home and followed me back instead.

"Let me explain, Toots," he pleads, lifting his hands in an effort to settle me down, but I'm afraid it's already too late for that.

"Don't *Toots* me. Not fucking now." I press my eyes closed and inhale through my nose in an effort to regain some control. "Let me see if I can get this straight. You didn't like who I was hanging out with, and you got your lackey to put the thumbscrews on Nate and chase him out of town."

"It wasn't like that."

I laugh bitterly at his response.

"Wasn't it, Dad? For someone who spent his entire adult life proudly representing this badge and upholding the law, I find it rather ironic to discover you were so willing to defy that badge and break your precious law to get rid of an innocent man, whose only crime was loving your daughter."

He looks genuinely shocked at my diatribe as he shakes his head.

"What? That's not...I never—"

"Oh, come on," I yell in his face, feeling out of control. "You threatened to throw him in jail over something he didn't do. How can you even justify that to yourself?"

"Savvy," Dad starts in a placating tone. "As far as I knew, Nathan stole a total of seventeen thousand dollars in jewelry and cash. He already had a juvenile record and would've gone to jail for a substantial amount of time."

"Except you were wrong; Nate didn't steal anything."

He shakes his head and stares at the building behind me. He looks old, sad, and tired, but I'm having a hard time right now conjuring up much sympathy. I'm too angry, it's boiling my blood and making me sick at the same time.

I love my dad—worship him—he's been my rock and my mainstay for so long, this sense of betrayal is almost too painful to bear. The disappointment I feel cuts deep on so many levels.

"I believed he did, Savvy," Dad explains softly. "I was trying to keep him from landing in jail and you throwing your life away, pining for him. Sanchuk said he had him dead to rights. I should've asked to see the evidence, but I had no reason to doubt Jeff at the time."

"And pegging Nate as the bad guy fit your narrative better," I add bitterly.

"Look, I'm sorry. I screwed up."

"Yeah, you did. Big time. What was done to Nate is beyond unfair, and for what? Why the hell does Sanchuk have such a hard-on for him? It doesn't make sense."

"Have you asked Gaines?"

My temper sparks and I fix angry eyes on my father.

"His name is Nathan, and no, not specifically. I haven't spoken to him since finding out Sanchuk wasn't acting alone."

However, I will be speaking with him as soon as he's sufficiently recovered, and I've had a chance to question Jeff Sanchuk. Sober.

But first I need a break: a meal, and hopefully some sleep.

I turn to head back to my vehicle when a thought strikes me, and I turn to look at my father over my shoulder.

"You know what's funny though, Dad? Nate never once mentioned your name."

∼

NATE

I'VE NEVER BEEN this fucking bored in my entire life.

There's only so much walking the halls I can do in this small regional hospital, and if I'm gonna spend forty-eight hours mostly in bed, I can think of a lot more fun ways to do that than by myself in this drab room.

Had a lot of time to think though, which isn't always a good thing. Doubts creep in, self-recriminations, rehashing shit I can't possibly change at this point in time. There's no one to talk to, other than whatever nurse pops in to check my vitals. Tate stopped in for a visit yesterday with Roy, but after half an hour I started dozing off, and they hurried to get out of this depressing room.

The whole weekend, Savvy has been a big no-show.

All in all, I'm not in the finest of moods when Doc Wilson finally shows his face, this afternoon's nurse following him into the room.

"Mr. Gaines. I hear you're doing well."

He doesn't get more than a grunt from me, which he seems to take in stride.

"Excellent. This morning's blood work looks good," he continues. "No more dizziness? Blurry vision?"

"No."

"What about the headaches?"

"Mostly gone."

"Fabulous. Let me have a quick peek at the bump on your head."

I turn the back of my head toward him and he lightly palpates the swelling that formed there. It's a little sore, but I'll bite off my tongue before I mention that to him. I want out of this bed.

"Still a bit swollen, it looks like a bit of fluid buildup under the skin from aggravated soft tissue. I expect it to disappear over time. There were no markers to indicate a possible infection in your blood work, and I don't see any excessive redness around the wound either."

He moves to the foot end of the bed and flips through

my chart, marking something with a pen before handing it to the nurse.

"If you could get Mr. Gaines discharge papers ready? Include a flyer on wound care and a list of things for him to look out for relating to his concussion."

I almost do a fist pump when he turns back to me.

"You're good to go, my friend. Be smart and don't rush back to work. I want you to take it easy for at least this coming week. Come and see me Friday for a quick checkup, and I'll take those staples out as well."

He shakes my hand and leaves the room, but when the nurse catches me swinging my legs out of bed, she stops me.

"Not so fast. It's gonna take me a while to get the paperwork done, so sit tight. I still have to finish rounds with Doc Wilson before I can get to it, and you need to find someone to take you home."

Shit.

Who the hell am I going to call? I go over the limited number of people I've interacted with since I've been back, but there really is only one person I'd feel relatively comfortable asking. I don't want her to feel put on the spot though—I know she's busy—so I send a text instead.

> Hate to bother you, but any chance you could give me a ride home from the hospital?

I HOPE that gives her enough room to say no. I hate asking.

Of course, I start overthinking when I don't hear from her immediately. Something I tend to do when I have too much time on my hands, like the entirety of the past two days. My mind shuts up when my hands are busy. I've been called a workaholic before, told I need to take a break, but in truth I can't handle sitting still for very long, and this weekend has been taxing on me.

I'm recounting the holes in the ceiling tiles when, finally, my phone pings with an incoming message.

> When?

Wow. That's rather...curt.

> Half an hour.

AT LEAST I hope the paperwork will be ready by then. The urge to add something is too great and I quickly add a message.

> Totally fine if you don't have time.

THIS TIME her message is instantaneous.

> I'll be there.

. . .

Yeah, definitely curt. I'm trying to think back whether I did or said something to piss her off, or if she is just preoccupied with work. Of course, I'm sure that's what it is.

See? There goes my mind again. *Jesus Christ*, I make myself sick.

I'm dressed in borrowed scrubs, the clothes I'd been wearing Friday cut and bloodied in a plastic bag, with my discharge papers in hand when Savvy walks into the room. My concern is instantly spiked; she does not look good.

"Why didn't you tell me?" are her first words to me.

When I don't immediately clue in to what she's talking about she adds, "That my father was part of it, why didn't you tell me?"

Oh, I know what she is referring to now, talk about coming out of left field. I'm not sure how to respond to that. I don't even know how she found out, because I wouldn't have brought it up. For what? It would only hurt her, probably even more now than back then.

But however she found out, she's looking for answers.

"When, then or now?"

"Does it matter?" She sounds aggravated.

"I think it does. I didn't feel like I had much of a choice back then. Plus, what would've been the purpose? It's not like it would've changed the outcome, and I didn't want to hurt you more than you would be already, which I knew you would be had you known. I guess I did have a choice this time, but the question would remain the same; to what purpose? It wouldn't change anything about the fifteen years behind us. All it could do was hurt the future of your relationship with your father."

The stubborn set of her chin is in stark contrast with the tears she is furiously trying to blink from her eyes.

"I'm not about hurting anyone, Savvy," I add.

"I see that," she shares. "But both you and my dad are so hung up on doing what you think is best for me, protecting me, but neither of you bothers to stop and ask *me*. You see it as something noble, when in reality it makes me feel incompetent, insignificant, and small."

Her words are a rude awakening; a bucket of ice water to my ego.

Hers is a perspective I would never have considered, which only goes to show how much my protective instincts are about me, and much less about her.

"Are you ready?"

The nurse interrupts when she pushes a wheelchair into the room.

"Is that really necessary?" is my knee-jerk reaction, which earns me a raised eyebrow from Savvy. "Never mind," I quickly follow it up with, taking a seat in the damn thing.

Nobody speaks until I'm settled in the passenger seat and Savvy slides behind the wheel of her cruiser.

"My father claims he was told you were responsible for those thefts."

Her eyes are focused on the road, but I can tell she is eager for my reaction.

"I didn't know that, but I guess it wouldn't surprise me," I tell her honestly. "Your father stayed behind the wheel of his cruiser when Sanchuk confronted me, so he was out of earshot. Besides, Sanchuk had it in for me for years."

"Why? What did you ever do to him?"

I scoff. "Other than exist? Nothing. But my mother did and I guess he took it out on me. She was a flake and a drunk who slept with anyone and everyone she thought could make her life easier. I'm pretty sure Sanchuk was one of her conquests, he'd be over at our house from time to time when I was young. I remember coming home from school one day and walking in on a screaming match between them. He yelled at me to get out and she didn't like that much so she sent him packing instead. That didn't seem to sit well with him, and I guess he thought he was getting back at her by targeting me." I bark out a harsh laugh as a wave of bitterness washes over me. "Little did he know, mother dearest didn't give even the tiniest fuck about me."

Wonderful. Here I thought I was long over all of that childhood shit, and now I've gone and dumped it all over Savvy's lap.

"I'm sorry," she whispers, her lip trembling. "For your mother, for Sanchuk, for the way even my father treated you. You didn't deserve it then and you definitely don't deserve it now."

"You don't own this, Savannah, so don't apologize. Not for any of them." I reach out and put a hand on her arm. "I have plenty to apologize for myself, but if you ask me, it's a waste of energy that might be better spent moving forward."

"It's not that easy," she laments, allowing me to pluck her right hand from the steering wheel and sliding my palm against hers. "I can't get over the fact my father was even a part of that."

I bring her hand to my mouth and brush a kiss to her knuckles.

"I don't know...now being a father myself, and given what your dad believed to be true at the time, I can't say I don't understand his motivation."

The rest of the drive is quiet again, but her hand stays in mine the entire way home.

"Hey, I'd love for you to come in. Tate won't be home

until tomorrow in the afternoon, Maggie and Roy are keeping Tate tonight and seeing her off to school in the morning."

"I'll come in and get you settled, but I don't know if I'll stay," she says with a tired little smile.

"It's up to you," I assure her, remembering her earlier point and trying not to be too overbearing. "But unless you've got somewhere to be, I thought you might be able to use a little break. We don't even have to talk much."

She snickers at that.

"Thank God there's nowhere I need to be, but I've spent too many hours this weekend in a much-too-small room, filled with disdain and anger, and smelling of hangover sweat and bad breath. I need a drink and a long, hot shower."

"Well, I'm feeling pretty benevolent myself, I haven't touched a drink in days, brushed my teeth before you came, and have a nice walk-in shower and a good bottle of scotch I've been savoring."

She turns her body to me and leans in, pressing a soft kiss on my lips.

"Seems like a no-brainer to me."

CHAPTER 17

S*avvy*

I'M a little disoriented at first, but the soft groan in my neck and warm body snuggling in behind are good reminders I'm in Nathan's bed.

It's barely dawn and I'm suddenly wide awake.

We didn't last long last night. After making sure Nate was settled in the living room with a drink and the remote, I took a ridiculously long shower in his bathroom. When I came out with my hair up in a towel, wearing one of Nate's T-shirts I dug out of a drawer, he had dozed off on the couch.

I ended up making us a couple of quick and easy peanut butter and jelly sandwiches, and opted to make a pot of tea instead of grabbing for alcohol.

We ate and drank, sitting on the couch, with a news station on in the background. His free hand was stroking circles on my bare leg as we took a little time to catch up on our lives. Nothing heavy, no talk about my work, or even my father, but we did broach the subject of his daughter, and the business he built for himself.

That then led me to bring up my house, which I bought for a steal a year and a half ago with the idea of doing the necessary renovations in my spare time. I thought it would be fun to tackle by myself and turn the house into my vision.

The reality is, I haven't even started pulling the screws and nails the previous owners left in the walls. Every day, the laundry list of work that needs to be done becomes more overwhelming, which is why, when Nate offered to take a look and help me come up with a plan, I was all over the idea.

Fatigue soon took over and when I couldn't stop yawning, Nate suggested I stay the night. Maybe against better judgment I stayed, but I knew the moment I was by myself, the full weight of my responsibilities would come down on me like a ton of bricks, making sleep impossible like it has been most of the weekend.

If you don't count the goodnight kiss and the large hand cupping my breast all night, it was all very innocent. I also slept like a log, which hasn't happened in a while.

So, despite the early morning hour, I am wide awake and very aware of Nate's morning erection pressing against my ass cheeks.

"Good morning to you too," I whisper.

I can feel his responding groan against the back of my neck as he snuggles in even deeper. When I press my ass against his groin, his hold on me tightens.

"You know I'm gonna need to fuck you now," he mumbles in my hair, rocking his hips against me suggestively.

"Didn't you say Doc told you to take it easy for a week?" I question him playfully.

"That was about work. This wouldn't be work, it would be pure pleasure, baby."

"But it may be too strenuous for you. It's been a long time; we can wait another week or so."

His displeased growl almost makes me laugh out loud.

"Or..." I tease him, drawing out the word as I turn around in his arms. "You could just let me do all the work."

His heavy-lidded eyes sparkle with a combination of humor and heat. Lifting his head, he covers my mouth with his, waking up every last one of my senses. Then he rolls on his back and scoots up so his back is against the headboard.

"Fucking great idea."

His move puts me at eye level with his belly button, which is why—since I'm already halfway there—I move down first.

He hisses when I shimmy his boxers down his hips, the elastic band brushing the sensitive head of his engorged cock. I watch his expression through my lashes as I slowly lick the bead of precum from the tip before sliding him between my lips.

I work him with my mouth and hand until I see the tendons in his neck stand out prominently with the strain of trying to stave off an orgasm. I'm as ready as he is as I quickly slip off my panties and swing a leg over his hips, leaning forward to kiss his eager mouth.

One of his hands grabs hold of my hip while the other slips between my legs, testing my slick center.

"My God, how beautiful you are," he mutters, looking up at me with an almost surprised expression on his face. "I'd almost forgotten."

"Hold yourself steady," I suggest, waiting for him to wrap his hand around the base of his cock.

I shift until I feel his crown brush my core and with a deep groan, sink down to the root. I need a moment to allow my tissues to accommodate him, but I revel in the way he stretches me. This man fills me like he was made to fit my body.

"You have to move, baby," he urges me.

It takes me a moment to find my rhythm, but soon I settle into a steady bounce and grind motion that stimulates all the right spots. When I drop my head back and give in to my body, Nate sits up, and with a hand in the center of my back he keeps me close as he latches on to one of my breasts.

He doesn't need to touch me anywhere else, with his cock buried inside me and the heat of his mouth around my nipple, I can feel this man in every cell of my body.

When I come, it's with a force that overwhelms all my senses and robs me of air. I'm nothing more than a rag doll draped over him, as I feel his powerful release pump inside me.

It takes at least a full five minutes before I can even manage a breathless, "Wow."

He does little more than grunt, his heart still racing under my cheek.

When we finally untangle, I grab another quick shower, get dressed—thank goodness for a uniform that makes it a little less obvious I didn't spend the night at home—and follow the smell of coffee downstairs and into the kitchen.

"Good morning," he rumbles, pulling me close for a hard kiss on my lips.

"Yes, it is," I agree, returning his smile.

I gratefully accept the mug of coffee he hands me and

almost burn my mouth in my eagerness for a hit of good caffeine.

"Want some eggs for breakfast?" he offers.

"Thanks, but I'll grab a yogurt at the station. I have a lot of work to do."

I need to put together my case against Sanchuk this morning so I can get him officially arrested and charged, or else he'll walk tonight when his seventy-two-hour hold is up.

"Understood."

"Not to be a wet rag, but one of the things we need to do, at some point today, is go over the statement you gave me on Friday and see if there's anything you want to add before you sign it. If I can't make it myself, I'll send one of my deputies."

"Or I can come to the station if that's easier for you. Doc Wilson didn't say anything about not driving."

"That's up to you."

I toss back the last of my coffee and walk around the island to rinse my cup at the sink. Nate steps up behind me, caging me in as he braces an arm on either side on the counter, resting his chin on my shoulder.

"At the risk of putting a damper on what was a truly mind-blowing morning," he mumbles by my ear. "We didn't use a condom. Not only don't I have any in the house, but I was so wrapped up in what was going on, I didn't even stop to think of it. I'm sorry, that never happens. Not smart."

I'd come to that realization myself when I was in the shower reliving every single moment of our early morning's activities. Luckily, I'm religious about taking my contraceptive.

I turn around so we're face-to-face and loop my arms around his neck.

"I'm on the pill. Also, I haven't had time for intimacy since Matt died."

He leans his forehead against mine.

"It hasn't been quite that long for me, but it has been a while, and I always use a condom. Still, I'll make sure to get tested sometime this week to be safe."

"I can do the same," I offer. "But now I really have to get going."

I lift up on my toes to kiss him before grabbing my belt off the kitchen island where I left it, and fitting it on my hips.

Nate follows me to the front of the house and as I open the door, I turn to look back at him.

"I'll call you later, okay?"

I lean in for another quick brush of lips before stepping outside...just as my father's Bronco comes to a stop at the curb. His keen eyes fixed on me.

Well, shit.

～

Nate

My back goes up when I see her father march up to the front step.

"Dad, what are you doing here?" Savvy asks.

She puts herself between me and her approaching father like some fierce pint-sized sentry. It's cute, but I have no intention of hiding behind her. I gently take her by the shoulders and move her to my side.

"Morning, Savvy, Nathan," he greets us stiffly, but his eyes remain on me.

The man's expression is inscrutable and I'm having a

hard time reading him, so I simply nod and wait for him to explain why he's here.

"Why are you here?" his daughter asks again.

"Didn't know you'd be here, honey. I was hoping to have a word with Nate."

"Now you want a word?" she returns.

I squeeze her shoulder in warning. I know it's her dad, but she doesn't have to fight my battles for me. Besides, I don't get the impression the man is here to try and chase me off again, and I'd like a chance to hear what he has to say. He's an integral part of Savvy's life, even of this town, and if I really want us to move forward—as I expressed to his daughter—I should put my money where my mouth is.

I didn't expect it to be easy to produce a polite smile for the man I've spent so many years despising, but it actually feels surprisingly good.

"Why don't you come inside, sir. I've got fresh coffee in the kitchen," I tell him, stepping out of the way and keeping Savvy to my side. "I'll be right with you."

"Hey," she objects when I prevent her from following her father into my house.

"I've got this, and you've got work waiting," I remind her, lowering my head to look her in the eye. "I can handle your father. I'll be in touch later, okay?"

She seems to struggle for a moment, but then concedes.

"Fine, but don't let him—"

I cut her off with a short, hard kiss.

"Go. It'll be fine."

Colter is standing by the fireplace when I walk in, looking at the few photos we put up on the mantel. Most of them are of Tatum.

"Your daughter?" he asks.

"Tatum. She's fourteen," I inform him. "She's the reason

I came back to Silence. Her mom overdosed earlier this year and Tate found her. I needed to get her away from those memories."

The look he sends me is one of unexpected compassion.

"I'm sorry for your loss."

"It wasn't really my loss," I clarify. "Her mom and I were never together for any length of time, and we didn't see eye to eye on much of anything, but we did produce an amazing daughter and she feels the loss."

"I see."

"You take your coffee black?" I guess, pushing through the awkward moment.

"Please."

I move to the kitchen and busy myself pouring him a cup and topping up mine. When I turn around, I see he's taken a seat at the island, staring at his hands in front of him. I slide his cup toward him across the counter and lean my hip against the kitchen sink, taking a sip of coffee, waiting for him to speak.

"She was heartbroken...Savvy," he clarifies. "For a long time. Her mother was furious with me when she found out I'd had a hand in driving you away. She never believed you had anything to do with those thefts."

I'm stunned. I remember Savvy's mom as a sweet lady who, unlike her husband, had made me feel welcome in their house. Imagining her furious over anything is a stretch for my imagination, let alone being angry on my behalf. It feels oddly validating, even after all these years, to hear I had someone other than Savvy in my corner.

"I was sorry to hear she passed away," I mumble, not sure what else to say.

"Thank you. She was sick for a while before she died and that was tough on my girl as well. Then she met Matt, and things were good for her for a while. She was excited about her future and then he died as well, and she was grieving again."

When he lifts his eyes to me, they're swimming with emotion.

"I'm not telling you all this as an excuse, but as an explanation. I did you wrong, and I'm ashamed to admit I've known it for a while. There is no defense for that. But the only reason I never set the record straight was because I knew how much it would hurt Savannah, and she's lived through enough pain to last her a lifetime."

His emotions get the better of him and I turn my back to give him a chance to collect himself.

I'm a little overwhelmed myself, feelings of anger, hurt, and empathy all warring for dominance. That last one is the kicker, because I do understand.

Behind me the older man clears his throat, and I turn around as he gets to his feet.

"I'm sorry. I'm sorry for a lot of things when it comes to you. I'm sorry I allowed assumptions and preconceptions skew my view of you. But I want you to know I see you now, I see everything you've accomplished in spite of people like me, and I gotta tell you, it humbles the hell out of me. You inviting me inside your house, when by all rights you could've kicked me off your property, it shows you're the bigger man."

I don't have an opportunity to react, since he is already walking out my front door, leaving me...speechless.

I never thought anything Brant Colter said could matter, but it does...a lot.

CHAPTER 18

S*avvy*

IT'S NOT until Brenda walks into my office and dumps a brown paper bag bearing the Strange Brew logo on my desk, I realize I am starving.

I was going to pick up something to eat on my way into the office, but I never got the chance. First, Detective Tessa Androtti called to let me know she wanted to meet to discuss Franklin Wyatt's case. No sooner had I hung up with her when Warren called me from the station to let me know Sanchuk was hooting and hollering from his holding cell that he wanted to see me.

Everyone wanted a piece of me this morning, and I've barely had a chance to breathe. Needing a break from what has been a frustrating two hours trying to get somewhere with Sanchuk, I just stepped out of the interview room and sat down in my office to follow up on calls and emails for a few minutes before Androtti gets here.

When I smell the sweet scent of sugar and cinnamon, my stomach rumbles loudly and I reach into the bag and pull out one of the biggest cinnamon rolls I've ever seen.

"I asked for a tomato and egg salad sandwich, but Bess packed this instead," Brenda huffs.

God bless her, she tries so hard to make sure I look after myself, and that includes eating properly, but Bess knows me best. She knows I would've probably left a sandwich sitting on my desk to eventually be forgotten about, but I wouldn't be able to resist one of her delectable cinnamon rolls and would wolf that down in a heartbeat.

"You need to eat properly, take care of yourself or you're going to wear out before you're old," she chastises me. "You probably barely slept again."

"I did okay," I mumble around a mouthful of the delicious pastry.

She huffs again and leaves my office, and I can't help the grin pulling at my lips. I may have woken up early but that was after sleeping like a baby in Nate's arms, and then proceeded to engage, in what I would call, a healthy morning exercise routine. I was feeling pretty damn skippy until my dad showed up on Nate's doorstep.

It's probably a good thing I haven't had the time to worry and stew about his early morning visit. I haven't even begun to process how mad I am at my father, and how hurt I am by what feels like a betrayal. I don't get how Nate could be so calm and collected when he's the one who was hurt the most.

I put down my cinnamon roll, lick my fingers clean, and grab my phone to shoot Nate a text.

> Hey, just checking in. How are you feeling?

When there's no immediate response—he could be napping, or in the shower or something—I take another bite of my pastry, lean back, and close my eyes briefly, focusing on a moment of enjoyment in an otherwise less than stellar workday.

"Sorry to interrupt..."

My eyes fly open to find a salt-and-pepper-haired woman in a pin-striped suit standing in my doorway with a briefcase in her hand. The suit and case suggest professionalism but her hair, haphazardly piled on top of her head in a messy knot, seems a little contradictory, as are the chunky, horn-rimmed glasses barely hanging on to the tip of her nose. Despite the gray in her hair, she looks to be maybe in her early forties at the most.

CID agent, Tessa Androtti, is nothing like I'd envisioned.

"Not interrupting at all," I assure her, jumping to my feet as I wipe my sticky fingers on my pants in a less than classy move. "I was just enjoying a belated breakfast, or is it lunchtime already? Detective Androtti?"

I round my desk to greet her.

She flashes a friendly smile as she steps into my office, her hand outstretched.

"In the flesh. Sheriff Colter, it's good to put a face to the voice."

"So it is. And let's drop the titles. I'm Savvy. Please have a seat. Would you like some coffee? Although, it should come with a hazard warning," I whisper conspiratorially.

She chuckles as she sits in one of the visitor chairs, setting the briefcase she was holding beside her.

"Your assistant is fixing me one right now. And thanks for the warning, but caffeine currently sustains me and I'm desperate enough for my next fix to chug down engine oil if I must."

Good, she has a sense of humor, and is not some stiff in a suit. Which the funky hair and glasses already kind of gave away.

"And please don't let me stop you from enjoying the rest of that scrumptious-looking thing on your desk." She points at the cinnamon bun.

"Can I at least offer you half?"

She shakes her head. "God no. Just looking at it is gonna put back the seventy-five pounds I've managed to shed since last year." Then she quickly adds, "But please, don't let that stop you. I have two sons who unapologetically stuff their faces like starved animals in front of me, so I've been desensitized."

Just then Brenda walks in and hands the agent her coffee.

"I'll hold your calls," she informs me before she steps outside and closes the door behind her.

I watch as Tessa takes a gulp of hot coffee, makes a disgusted face, and still takes another one before she resolutely places the cup on my desk and pulls a thick file from the briefcase at her feet.

"I was able to track down Stanley Greer and his wife Olivia back at home in Clinton, Missouri. They were the guests in cabin five," she clarifies when she catches my confused expression.

Right. We'd been in the process of trying to locate any and all guests whose stay would've overlapped with Franklin Wyatt's time there. A few of them were hard to chase down.

"Five is the one right across from the victim's cabin, correct?"

"It is," she confirms. "The Greers were kind enough to speak with me on the phone. Between them they had pretty detailed recollection of their time at the cabin and were able to send me their signed statements."

She pulls two sheets of paper from the file folder and places them on my desk, facing me.

"I'd like you to read them and tell me what you think."

I grab them and start reading. Pretty standard observations, the comings and goings of our victim they remembered seeing during their time at the cabins, a brief conversation they had with him when they bumped into him on an evening walk, anything unusual they might have seen, including a visitor they observed going into cabin four on two separate occasions.

What stands out immediately is that both occurrences were at night, they saw them go in, but not come out, and both times the individual seemed to appear out of the surrounding woods. It was dark so—other than the fact this was a man, and his general height and build—his face was not visible so they couldn't give us many more details on his possible identity.

What they were able to describe, however, is what he was wearing.

My breath catches in my throat as I read their description of light reflecting off shiny buttons, the appearance of a duty belt on the hips, complete with a weapon's holster, and the ball cap the visitor appeared to be wearing. The final detail is a pair of handcuffs Mrs. Greer spotted hanging from his hand.

"A uniform," I mumble under my breath, but Tessa hears it.

"That would be my guess."

"Could be a security guard," I suggest feebly.

"The ball cap doesn't really fit," she counters, pointing out what I'd already figured out.

"Role-play? A costume?"

She shrugs. "Could be, but we can't ignore the possibility this was someone in law enforcement."

I pinch the bridge of my nose. Just what I need, with everything else going on, now I have to look at the dwindling members of my sheriff's deputies with suspicion?

Unless...

∼

NATE

WEIRD MORNING.

Well, not all of it was weird. The earlier part of it couldn't exactly be described as weird, that was actually pretty mind-blowing, but after that it got weird. A bit surreal.

First there was Sheriff Colter's visit—Savvy's father, that is—which kind of shifted everything I thought I knew off its axis. After he left, I took my coffee out on the deck and spent a good hour just sitting there, staring out at the mountains, trying to process it all.

Then the neighbor, the Good Samaritan who came to my aid, pushed his own lawnmower all the way across the street and started mowing my lawn with nothing more than a wave of his hand, like it was the most normal thing in the world.

And finally, Hugo Alexander showed up at my door,

with a coffee and a breakfast sandwich from Strange Brew, courtesy of Bess, he said. He also had a box of groceries Brenda at the station asked him to drop off.

This is so unlike anything I remember from before. People caring enough to volunteer to help out, law enforcement showing up at my door for anything other than to hound me, and more than anything else, Brant Colter apologizing to me after finding his daughter basically rolling out of my bed.

It's like I woke up in an alternate reality from the one I knew, and I'm having a bit of a hard time finding my equilibrium.

The world sure has changed in this town.

Or maybe I'm the one who has changed. I'm definitely not the same since coming back here. A lot of the anger and resentment I've worn as a cloak almost my entire life seems to be sliding off me. All those negative experiences I have carried with me kept me an outsider my entire life, but now I wonder if I wasn't the one cultivating that divide.

This morning it felt like Silence may be welcoming me inside.

I tuck a pillow under my head, and briefly close my eyes, lying on the couch. As much as I feel generally okay, I also feel perpetually tired. I tried watching a bit of TV earlier, but that brought about a bit of a headache, so a nap seemed a better option, but doesn't seem to come easily.

Although, when there is a knock on my door an hour and twenty-five minutes later, I realize I must've dozed off after all. I gingerly get to my feet and head to the door, wondering who it could be.

"Hi," I say to the woman on my doorstep. "Can I help you?"

"Are you Nathan?"

I'm a little cautious in my response. "Who wants to know?"

She smiles disarmingly. A very attractive older woman who reminds me a little of the actress Andie MacDowell. A bit of a hippy, judging by the beads, flip-flops, and flowy fabrics. She doesn't look like someone who'd try to sell me insurance or some service I don't want.

"I'm sorry. Of course, you don't know me from Adam. My name is Phil—short for Phyllis, in case you wondered—and I'm Brant Colter's wife, and I guess Savvy's stepmother."

I almost laugh, the idea of this colorful woman with stuffy Sheriff Colter strikes me as funny, but I manage to hold it back and instead nod politely.

"Nice to meet you." Curiosity drives me to add, "Would you like to come inside?"

She beams a smile at me and steps into the hallway.

"I don't intend to take much of your time."

I gesture for her to precede me into the living room, where she confidently perches herself on the couch's armrest. This woman probably feels comfortable anywhere.

"What...um...can I do for you?" I prompt her, choosing to remain standing.

"First of all, I want to apologize for my husband. I'll have you know he's effectively in the doghouse until further notice. *Overprotective buffoon*," she mumbles under her breath, before flashing me another smile. "And for the fact he so rudely interrupted what clearly was a cozy morning with Savvy."

The woman obviously has no filter either, and I have to say, I like her more and more.

"It was," I feel compelled to confirm.

She gives her fist a little pump. "Yess! I knew it, and I'm

absolutely thrilled. I was afraid Savvy would start to prune up before her time."

That has me laughing out loud. What little I know of this woman; I have a feeling Phil probably has told Savvy herself as much on occasion. She doesn't seem the type to hold back much.

I'm not sure how pleased Savvy will be when she finds out her stepmother was cheering on our early morning tryst.

"But...the actual reason I'm here is to invite you. Friday night we're throwing a little end of summer cookout, to kick off the Harvest Fest on the weekend, and would love for you and your daughter to come. I'm afraid I'm not very organized and it's turning into a bit of a haphazard potluck event, but it should be good fun. Just bring chairs and if you're into fishing, a rod, or we can probably rustle one up. Oh, and tell your daughter to wear jeans in case she likes riding. We have horses," she rattles on. "There will probably be other kids her age."

Who would've thought I'd ever be invited back to the Colter household. I shake my head. Maybe it's a little too soon, and I hadn't really planned to be part of any community events, but it would be good for Tatum, and I'd have a hard time refusing this woman. She's a card.

"I make a pretty mean Bombay noodle salad and I'm sure I can get Tatum to help me bake some brownies for dessert."

She claps her hands and jumps to her feet.

"Fantastic! I am thrilled. You know where to find us?"

"Still up at the farm?"

She nods. "You've got it." Then starts moving toward the front door where she stops to add, "Nothing much changes here."

Well, I don't know about that.

Halfway to an SUV parked on the street she turns around.

"Five o'clock," she yells.

I give her thumbs-up and get a wave in return.

Somehow, I'm not surprised when a few seconds later the vehicle is burning rubber down my street. I'm laughing as I head back inside.

How's that for a *welcome to the family*?

CHAPTER 19

S*avvy*

I haven't had a chance to even look at my messages until just now, when I got behind the wheel to go home.

My eyes immediately go to Nate's response to my much earlier question.

> Good. Great, actually. Call me when you have a chance? I was just invited to an event at your father's house.

What? What the hell does that mean?

> Bit of a surprise, right? Same here. We'll talk when you can.

. . .

I'M ALREADY LOOKING for his number when I spot the time. *Shit*, it's almost eleven, a little late to be calling. He's probably already in bed and I don't want to risk waking him up, so I shoot off a message instead.

> Surprise would be an understatement. Sorry I didn't get back to you sooner. Crazy day. You're probably sleeping. Call you in the morning.

CALLING today a crazy day is a bit of an understatement as well.

After reading those witness statements from the couple in cabin five, I floated Sanchuk's name to Tessa Androtti and briefed her on him. As expected, she wanted to have a chat with him, but that chat turned into a full interview that had us both tied up for the best part of four hours this afternoon.

Androtti turned out to be a skilled interviewer, and I learned a ton just from sitting in and observing. She never lost her cool, was very friendly and exceedingly patient in how she handled Sanchuk, who flung around his usual bluster. Nothing flustered Tessa, and the fact she could not be shaken seemed to frustrate and ultimately enrage my former deputy. He's the one who lost his cool and went into defensive mode when her gentle suggestions and innuendos around his possible involvement with the victim got under his skin.

Under the constant gentle pressure, he finally started

cracking, denying vehemently he had anything to do with the slaughter of Franklin Wyatt but admitting to more minor offenses. These included shaking down visitors to our town for trumped-up traffic offenses he forced them to pay for on the spot, using his badge to gain favors, neither of which I had any clue of. He even fessed up to the attack on Nate in his garage.

According to Sanchuk, he did all those things but was definitely not responsible for any murder. It didn't sway Androtti, and it definitely didn't convince me.

I arrested him on the spot for the attack on Nathan and stuffed him back in the holding cell, where he'll now sit until his arraignment on Thursday at the earliest.

Discovering what he'd been pulling off under my nose for years made me sick to my stomach. So, when I got back to my office, I locked the door and pulled up all of Sanchuk's reports, his schedules, who he was partnered up with, and started working my way back from the day I gave him the ultimatum.

Corruption in law enforcement is something you might expect to see in larger departments, but in one the size of ours, it's rare. I'm not sure what or who to trust anymore. Was Sanchuk on his own or is this a more widespread problem I've simply been blind to?

I spent the evening making a list of steps for me to take investigating my own damn department, because one thing I know; the only way to stop the rot from spreading is to cut every little spot out.

So now I have two murders, one former deputy in custody, and a department that is falling apart around me.

I could cry, but someone is going to have to clean up this mess.

I'm stopped at the traffic light on the corner of Maine

and Pinedale Drive when my phone rings. A quick look at the screen on my dashboard shows Nate's number.

"You're still up."

His chuckle warms me. "I'm in bed, trying to read a bit, but my thoughts kept drifting to you, and then your message popped up. Must be karma."

"Must be."

"Long day?"

I blow out a shaky sigh, trying not to fall apart at the genuine concern in his voice.

"Yeah..."

"Are you home?"

"On my way there now."

The light turns green just as Nate says, "Come here instead. Let me take care of you."

It's probably not wise, I was going to go home and work a little more on the file I'm compiling on my department before hitting the sack. But I'm tempted.

A car horn behind me forces a split-second decision and I find myself turning left instead of right. I need sleep more than anything, and I know I can find that in Nate's arms.

The hall light is on when I park along the curb. For a moment I hesitate, aware Tatum is probably home, sleeping in her own bed, but then the door opens, and Nate steps into view, waiting for me.

"What about Tatum?" I ask after he pulls me inside the house with a kiss.

"She's down, and she's a deep sleeper. I usually have to kick her out of bed in the morning to get ready in time for school, she doesn't get up before seven thirty."

"I'll be gone before that," I let him know.

"I figured. Now come to bed, I warmed it up for you."

When I finally join him there—after a quick shower in

his awesome bathroom to wash off the day's grunge—he curls his body around me, and I fall asleep in no time flat.

∽

"I'M SO sorry I'm running off again. We haven't even had a chance to talk."

I woke up with Nate tapping my shoulder at ten past seven. The man is apparently my own personal sleep aid. There is no time for anything other than getting dressed and following Nate downstairs, where he shoves a travel mug of coffee and a toasted bagel with cream cheese in my hands.

"I didn't even ask you about this event at Dad's place. What's that all about?"

He grins. "Well, your father's visit yesterday morning was a bit of a revelation that requires more time to explain, and I met your stepmother when she showed up at my door later yesterday."

I groan and slap a hand over my face. Seriously, my family is too much.

"I'm so sorry."

"No. It was actually good. Phil certainly is an interesting character," Nate continues. "And not really the match I would've picked for your father."

I smile back, because he's not wrong. I love Phil, but I was a little shocked to see her and my dad hit it off.

"I hear you, but they're really good together. She forces him out of his shell and he seems to calm her crazy. It's unexpected, but it works."

"Well, she showed up yesterday and invited Tate and me to a cookout on Friday night. I said yes, but I'm not really sure if I should've checked with you first."

"With me? Why?"

He shrugs. "It's a bit odd, maybe? Your dad hated my guts and I've never met his new wife before yesterday. I feel like I'm the subject of some elaborate prank."

I can't believe I'm giggling in my current situation. Not only do I have what likely will be another day from hell waiting for me, but an impressionable teenager could walk in at any moment, making for an awkward discovery.

"No prank," I quickly tell him. "With everything going on, I'd forgotten about the cookout. I plan to be there too, although I can't make any guarantees. There are a lot of things unraveling at work I can't really get into now, but I'm bound to be tied up for a while."

He hooks me with a hand behind the neck and pulls me in for a hard kiss on my lips.

"Do what you need to do, but you're going to have to eat at some point. Why don't I show up with lunch, and you take fifteen minutes to feed yourself and decompress or talk or make out, or whatever you're in the mood for. I'll take whatever you can spare."

My eyes well up. I remember this caring side of him no one but me seemed to see.

"Okay, but don't be too nice to me or the wheels may come off."

He kisses the tip of my nose.

"So noted. Now get out of here, I need to get my kid up and ready for school."

Despite knowing the pile of shit I was heading into at the office, I'm wearing a smile when I get behind the wheel.

∽

Nate

. . .

"Do I have to go?"

I glance over at Tate beside me.

"I'd like you to. We don't have to stay long, but I think it would be a good idea to make an appearance. We can face the townsfolk together."

She hums, not sounding too sure, but the more I thought about this last night, the more I think going to this cookout on Friday is a good thing. I have never been particularly social or outgoing, which was fine when I was on my own, but I have Tate in my life now. I don't want her to grow up like I did; an automatic outcast because of who my mom was.

I'm sure those who want to think badly of me will do so anyway, but maybe showing myself to be just a regular guy, who also happens to be a single father to a fantastic daughter, will change the preconceived opinions of one or two of them.

I pat Tate on her knee as I pull up in front of her school.

"I'm sure we'll have a good time."

Her huff as she gets out of the truck makes it clear she's not convinced. I have no doubt she'll make other attempts to get out of it—the week is still long—but I'm not going to budge.

After dropping Tate off, I spend the morning doing some laundry and cutting vegetables for the quick Thai curry I'm whipping up to bring Savvy for lunch.

This is only my second day home and already I'm itching to get productive. I don't like sitting still, but maybe I could have a look at Savvy's place, see what needs to be done. It sounded like it would be quite the project, so I could start working it out on paper to get a bit of an idea of the scope. If she'll let me grab a key off her at lunch, I could get started this afternoon.

Brenda is behind the reception desk, engaged in an animated conversation with a guy in a suit when I walk into the station. She catches sight of me and lifts her finger to the guy, asking him to hold on.

"You can walk right in, Nate. She's expecting you."

Apparently, that doesn't go over well with the man she was talking to, who loudly proclaims his displeasure. I gather he's here to see Savvy as well.

Leaving Brenda to handle him—I'm sure she's got that covered—I duck down the hall and make my way to Savvy's office. The door is closed so I knock.

"Yeah," she calls out, sounding distracted.

When I poke my head in the door, I'm greeted by a tired smile.

"Oh good, it's you. Come in, and please, close the door."

Her desk is covered in file folders and paperwork, a yellow-lined notepad is filled with scribbles and sports a few coffee rings from where she set her mug. I notice she did stop in at home to change this morning, because she's wearing a pair of jeans and a black golf shirt with the sheriff's department logo.

"You look swamped," I tell her as I look for a place to set lunch.

She solves it by unceremoniously shoving all her paperwork to one side.

"You have no idea."

I have no idea how she feels about public displays of affection, but I set down the insulated bag holding the containers and round her desk to give her a soft kiss on the lips. She looked like she could use it.

When there is no protest, I kiss her again, with a little more heat this time. Her arms snake around my neck as I brace myself on the chair so I don't land in her lap. Not like that would be a bad thing—I can see some interesting scenarios playing out in her office—but this is definitely not the time.

"Let's eat," I suggest, gently peeling her arms from my neck.

The first few minutes we eat quietly, only a few appreciative moans from Savvy breaking the silence.

"This is good," she voices, with a little smile sent in my direction. "All of it, the food, the break, and the kiss. It's a little oasis in the middle of a hectic day."

She shoves in another bite before covering her mouth, asking me, "Did you see the guy giving Brenda a hard time?"

"Yeah. Who is he?"

"Jeff Sanchuk's lawyer. He's demanding to see me, but I don't want to see him. He can have all the access he wants to his client, but I'm not about to let him try to badger me into releasing his client, because it's not going to happen. Sanchuk is lucky to be arraigned on Thursday, they can plead their case to the judge."

"Do I need to be present for that?" I ask her.

"No. The judge will read Sanchuk his charges and ask what plea he wants to enter. Then they'll discuss bail, which we'll have to wait to see if the judge will grant, and set pre-trial dates. The district attorney's office will likely be in touch with you to discuss all that."

"Okay." I point at the papers on her desk. "What have you got going on this afternoon?"

"I have a few meetings here in the office and then I have to head out to Quarry Road to follow up with Wanda Rogers about her husband's case. What about you?"

"Actually, I wanted to talk to you about that. I was hoping you'd let me poke around your house a bit to see the scope of the work, maybe take some measurements."

She wags a finger at me. "Didn't the doctor tell you to take it easy?"

I shrug. "I wouldn't actually be doing any work, nothing physical anyway, and it'll keep me busy. Added bonus is I'll be able to give you a cost projection so you know what you're up against before any work starts."

"That would be very helpful," she admits. "I have money set aside, but I don't really know if that'll be enough."

"I'll be happy to help you figure that out, but I'm gonna need a key to get in."

"All you need is the code. Zero nine zero six."

I open my mouth to thank her when the significance of those numbers hits me.

"June ninth, that's my birthday," I share.

She looks at me, a little smile playing on her lips.

"I remember."

CHAPTER 20

Savvy

"I NEED at least four volunteer deputies on this. We're short bodies."

Hugo and I are trying to work out a schedule for Saturday morning's harvest parade and the weekend's festivities.

"I'll call around," my right-hand man offers.

We're not getting very far trying to fill the vacant spots in the department. I have to follow up with Dad to see if he's been in touch with the county commission, but I'm still pissed at him. Besides, I doubt much can be done in time for the Harvest Fest anyway.

I don't like calling on the volunteers for jobs like this, when they'd probably rather be participating, but I am spread so thin right now, I can't afford not to.

Earlier I had both Warren and KC come into my office to

ask them some specific questions about their experience with Sanchuk. Warren had already suggested to me he knew something was up with Sanchuk, but it took me assuring him Jeff had confessed to certain things already, for him to lay it out on the table.

As Warren explained, when the two were working together during Warren's orientation, Sanchuk had more than once insisted on handling things by himself during certain traffic stops. He'd even seen money exchanged on a couple of occasions, which he chose to file away as potential personal transactions.

I got the gist Warren didn't want to be a whistleblower, but as I explained to him, under my leadership there is no place for brotherhood nonsense. No covering for, or even turning a blind eye to, a colleague's bad behavior, because one bad apple reflects on us all. This kind of misguided loyalty undermines the integrity of the department and I made it clear, I would not stand for it.

I gave the same speech to KC, which led him to confess he'd seen some of that same behavior from Jeff. He even admitted he'd had lunch with him at the Bread & Butter diner a few times. A lunch they didn't pay for because apparently Sanchuk caught the chef's son with an amount of weed in his possession that exceeded the personal use limit. The kid could stand to lose a much sought after football scholarship with Ohio State he'd just been offered, so Sanchuk cut him a break, but used the incident to pressure the boy's father into feeding him free of charge.

That confession left me in a bit of a pickle. I should be disciplining KC since he participated in something he clearly knew was wrong, at the very least he enjoyed the spoils of what amounts to extortion. Yet, at the same time, I recognize as a rookie officer, he felt pressured into a difficult situation. He'd felt guilty and claims he never joined Sanchuk for a meal again. Instead of some kind of sanction, I'm giving him the benefit of the doubt, since he came clean about the diner. I told him I'd make a notation in his file but would remove it if he kept his nose clean for the next two years.

When I confronted Hugo with what had been going on, he shook his head. He admitted he'd been overwhelmed with what had been going on in his personal life, he'd barely been able to focus on his own job, and opted to ignore anything else.

I've got three more guys I need to sit down with—I can hopefully catch Lloyd this afternoon when he comes in— but I get the sense I'll probably hear similar stories from all three of them. They saw or knew about it, but chose to ignore it, and that would be the best-case scenario.

To be honest, I've been thinking back to my own time as a deputy, working alongside Jeff Sanchuk, and there were times I was guilty of turning a blind eye to things I suspected weren't on the up and up myself. Heck, even as sheriff, I've known for a while Sanchuk couldn't really be trusted, but it's taken me until now to do something about it.

I'm as complicit as everyone else.

The yoke of this office has never felt heavier on my shoulders than it does now.

Getting this department back on track is going to take some doing, but there is no shortcut. For us to be a reliable, cohesive unit, I have to first upset the apple cart.

"Are you okay?" Hugo asks, interrupting my thoughts.

I realize I've been standing here, staring at the whiteboard we've got this weekend's schedule marked up on.

"Yeah. I'm sorry, too much going on, my head is spinning," I confess.

"Why don't you leave the Harvest Fest schedule with me? I'll get Brenda to help me make some calls, so you can focus on Ben Rogers's case."

He's right. The problem trying to tackle too many things at the same time is that none of them will get the attention they deserve. I need to start scratching things off my list, not adding more, just because I want to prove I can do it all by myself. That's ultimately not how I best serve and protect the public, which is my job.

Delegation it is.

"Okay. That would be great. And I've asked my father to use his connections with the county commission to see if we can get some more funding for additional deputies."

"Doesn't help if we can't even fill the current positions," Hugo points out.

Admittedly, that's an issue.

"Get Brenda to list the two positions to start on local, state, and federal government websites, law enforcement job boards, any applicable professional organizations, and wherever else she thinks is appropriate. And I'd like you to scan any incoming applications," I add.

"Okay. And, if you don't mind a suggestion, why not make one of those extra deputies you're trying to get money for a detective's position. Someone with investigative experience, so it won't always fall on you to head investigations. You already have an important job running this department."

I'm trying not to hear the criticism in that suggestion, but I do. It's a gentle reminder where my focus should be.

Be that as it may, in our current situation, I don't have much of an option, which is why I get to my feet and fit my ball cap on my head. Then I snatch my jacket with the Sheriff's Office blazoned across the back, and head for the door.

"I hear you, but for right now I have to get out to Quarry Road. I'm already late for my meeting with Wanda."

Wanda is not the one opening the door at her place, it's Dozer. There is no mistaking the reason he is here when he leads me into the living room and takes a seat beside the new widow and drapes his arm around her shoulders, tugging her close. He does it with purpose and intent, clearly keen to bring the suspected affair out in the open right off the bat.

As much as I can appreciate the blunt honesty of the gesture, I'm afraid neither Dozer nor Wanda are doing themselves any favors. Not with Ben lying on a cold slab in the county morgue, his face unrecognizable from the lethal beating he took.

"Wanda...Dozer...I don't need to tell you, your timing is not good."

"We beg to differ," Wanda speaks up. "There were already a few tongues wagging, and we figure trying to hide would do more damage than good."

I pinch the bridge of my nose. She's not wrong, but now the whole town is going to wonder whether the two of them didn't collectively decide to get rid of Ben. I'm sure some of them were wondering as much already.

The kicker is, I don't think many would blame them, at least not Wanda. His abuse of her was well documented and he wasn't a particularly loved resident of Silence. He would get drunk, belligerent, and got into altercations with people all the time.

The truth is, there likely are plenty of people who might have wished Ben dead at one time or another. However, there is only one person who followed through on it.

It's up to me to find out who.

Nate

"We missed you last night."

I turn around to find Tim, Roy Battaglia's dart buddy, standing next to an SUV in the next driveway over from Savvy's place.

"Hey," I greet him, cocking my thumb at the well-tended bungalow next door in contrast to Savvy's somewhat rundown place. "Didn't realize you lived here."

"My mom does. I'm just checking in on her. She hasn't been feeling well."

"I'm sorry to hear that."

"She's that age, you know, where the body starts giving out. We've been talking about maybe moving her to Snowcrest Manor. She already has friends living there, but she hates giving up this house."

I catch him studying the place.

"It's tough," I commiserate, even though I know nothing about the kind of situation he finds himself in.

My mother died relatively young—not much older than I am now—and I have no clue who my father is or whether he's alive or not.

"Anyway, I thought for sure you'd be back so we could kick your ass in darts this time," Tim pivots the subject back to Monday night.

"Maybe next week."

"Sounds good."

He looks like he's ready to get into the vehicle when he turns back.

"Hey, what are you doing over there at the sheriff's place anyway?"

"I'm...um...a contractor. She's asked me to look at some work she wants done to the house."

He nods and checks out the bungalow behind me. "Sure could use it." He reaches for the handle and opens the door. "Anyway, I'd best get going. I'll see you around, yeah?"

"For sure."

First thing I did when I got here was walk around the outside of the house to look for any obvious issues. Lucky for Savvy, the roof appeared to be in good condition and the windows look like they were replaced within the last couple of years. I couldn't see any cracks in the foundation on the outside, but we'll see once I get into the basement.

I hear a whizz and the sharp click of the lock opening when I punch in the code on the keypad. That and the front door are obviously upgrades as well.

It's a promising start, the house looks to have good bones —although I'll have to confirm that once I've had a look at the basement—and it's sitting on a nice, large and mature, pie-shaped lot.

It's a little weird, walking through Savvy's house without her here, it feels a bit stalkerish. Still, I whip out my tape measure and start jotting down measurements and rough sketches of the layout. I have software on my computer at home that will translate the measurements and markings I enter into an easy to navigate 3D image of the house and each individual space, with walls, windows, and doors all marked. I'll be able to move or adjust all the individual components to show what is possible for the overall space.

The place has three bedrooms. One is used as extra storage, and the second one is set up as a home office. When I put my hand on the door to the third room, I know I'm about to go into Savvy's bedroom and hesitate for a moment.

I'm surprised at its starkness. The entire house is lacking in personality, but I figure that was because she wanted changes made before investing time or money into decorating. Her bedroom, however, I would've expected to show a little more of Savvy.

The bed was straightened in a hurry, and one drawer of the white dresser against the wall across from the bed was left open with some of the contents hanging out. A laundry basket sitting next to it is overflowing, yesterday's uniform on top.

It smells like Savvy though. Nothing heavy, just a hint of the shampoo or body wash she must've used in the shower this morning lingering in the air. It's good, fresh, wholesome, and yet my body responds like it's the most mysteriously seductive scent.

The only other thing standing out to me is the picture frame on the single nightstand. Curiosity has me approach and pick it up. Even though I had a reasonable expectation of what the image might depict, it's still a bit of a shock to the system. Savvy, happy in the arms of another man, with Auden in the background, photobombing the couple as he smiles at the camera.

So this is Matt.

As much as I want to, I can't envy a man who died way too young. I can, however, regret missing any opportunity to make Savvy happy going forward.

CHAPTER 21

Savvy

"I CAN DO THAT, YOU KNOW," Brenda offers, poking her head into the roll-call room.

I've set up shop in here because of the two large whiteboards. I needed a way to outline what I have on Ben's murder, so I could see it all laid out at once instead of flipping through the pages of my notepad to put all the details together.

The conference table is bigger than my desk too, so I can spread out my notes and reports without getting anything lost in stacks of other paperwork waiting for me.

This is now my war room.

"It's okay," I tell Brenda as I'm transcribing some of my notes from the pad to the whiteboard. "It helps me to go through this process."

"Okay, if you say so. Your father just got here, by the way. He's talking to KC in the lobby."

"Good, can you tell him I'm in here?"

I went looking for him last night, but no one was home, and my call went straight to voicemail. I left him a message I needed to speak with him as soon as possible. I'm conflicted, I'm still angry at him, but I also need him to make a push on the extra funding with the county commission.

In addition, I need to talk to him about the things that came out of the last interview with Sanchuk, and that's the part I dread the most. I have a hard time believing my father would've condoned any of the things Sanchuk copped to, but I need to hear it from him.

"Will do. I'm popping out to pick up some lunch at the diner, can I get you something?"

I called Nate last night when I got home around ten. I'd thought about going back to his place to sleep, but I really need to do a few loads of laundry and collect some things that need to be dropped off at the dry cleaners. Maybe I'll have a chance tomorrow.

Anyway, Nate mentioned he'd been at my place and had a look around. He talked about going into Spokane this morning to hammer down some prices for building supplies he would need. Something about setting up a contractor account so he could get better rates.

He was very sweet and apologized he wouldn't be around to bring me lunch today.

"Yes, if you wouldn't mind picking me up a club sandwich on rye and a large ice tea, half-sweet, please."

The ice tea at the diner is the real deal, made with steeped tea and lemon, and is delicious, except for the fact they usually put in too much of that syrup to sweeten it. Hence my half-order.

"Sure. Piece of pie for dessert?"

It's on my lips to say no. Then I remember my pathetic dinner last night, that consisted of an expired packet of ramen noodles I found in the back of the cupboard in our little kitchen, when I went digging for food at eight thirty.

I can have the pie for dinner.

"Yes, to the pie. Whatever is on offer today."

Brenda mock salutes me before she backs out of the room.

I take a couple of steps back from the whiteboards to check out what I've put up there so far. A mugshot of Ben from a drunk and disorderly we brought him in for several months ago is in the center of the board on the left. Underneath it I stuck a few pictures the State Patrol crime scene team took at the site.

One image is of the blood-covered rock that was found in the underbrush several feet from where Ben's body was discovered, where it was likely tossed after the attack. Another is of half a boot print, found in the damp soil partially underneath a fern. The only boot print recovered, which leads me to believe some effort was made to erase any possible incriminating evidence. Unfortunately, the imprint appears to have come from a tactical boot. The type is widely worn, including by most first responders. It wouldn't be the first time someone inadvertently left evidence behind at a crime scene. It happens.

We're in the process of taking prints from all personnel on scene for comparison, but it's tedious and until we can confirm either way if the print belongs to one of us, I'm keeping the picture up on the board.

The one other item found at the scene that could become important evidence, once we have something to compare it to, is a small tuft of fabric stuck to a bramble bush less than three feet from the victim. We've already ruled out it came from anything the victim was wearing.

I've drawn lines out from the victim's image, connecting him to locations and any related social connections. For instance, home would connect him to Wanda and Dozer, as well as a handful of other neighbors on the street. The Kerrigan Pub is another frequent location, but the list of names there is much longer. The diner is on there, although reportedly he only really talked to the waitstaff. I've also added the trucking company he worked for prior to being let go and the few people on staff he would have had contact with. Long-haul trucking is a solitary job.

My objective is to throw everything I know on the board and start eliminating possibilities. It's frustrating because the ones with the best motive did not have opportunity. Both Wanda and Dozer had pretty solid alibis for the window of time the ME concluded he was killed in. Wanda's sister and husband vouched for Wanda, and Dozer's cell phone pinged off the same tower from the Wednesday he said he left until the morning we were called to the Rogers's house. Besides, he'd had a buddy there to help him fix the roof. He was accounted for.

"Putting it on the big board? Is it helping?" my father asks as he walks in.

"Not yet, but I hope it will."

Dad is actually the one who taught me laying out a case on the whiteboard sometimes helps you see the forest through the trees when you get stuck.

I turn to face him.

"You wanted to see me," he reminds me.

He's standing on the opposite side of the conference table, illustrating the divide I feel between us.

"Yeah. Would you mind closing the door? And take a seat."

Five minutes later he jumps to his feet, his face a worrisome shade of purple as a vein pops on his forehead.

"What?" he barks.

"Dad, you need to take it easy."

"You're gonna have to spell it out for me, Savannah," he indicates with barely contained anger as he braces his knuckles on the table.

"Jeff Sanchuk has been making false traffic stops to pilfer money off tourists. He's been extorting people and businesses in town for free meals, free goods, or whatever. Some of the behavior has been corroborated by other deputies working with him."

"Under your nose?"

Damn, that stings, even if he's right.

"And under yours," I return, not feeling good about it.

If I wasn't a hundred-percent sure to begin with, I'm absolutely positive now my father had no idea. His only culpability is the same as mine; complacency.

"Tell me that bastard is still here in the holding cell so I can have a word with him."

"He was moved to the jail at the county courthouse, Dad. And you're not going to throw your weight around to try to get in to see him either. You're going to leave it to me," I state firmly.

From the mutinous look on his face, I can tell he's not on board with that idea. Too bad for him, that's the way it's going to be.

"You know what you can do for me? Get going on the extra funding for the department, so I can plug some holes and start building a cohesive unit. In addition to the two deputies, I need a properly trained detective, preferably with plenty of experience, because I need to focus on getting this department running like a well-oiled machine. Can you do that?"

He nods, a serious expression on his face.

"I'll call in some favors; consider it done."

"Good, because I've got Brenda and Hugo already actively recruiting," I confess, which makes my dad chuckle.

"You never did have patience," he points out.

"I didn't get that from a stranger," I return.

A brief silence falls over the room before Dad speaks again, in a different tone this time.

"Are we okay?"

I don't like the vulnerability I hear in his voice, but I'm not ready to just brush my feelings aside.

"Give me time. I'm sure we'll get there."

He seems to mull that over before he asks, "Will you be there Friday?"

"That's the plan."

He nods and turns his back, reaching for the door.

"Love you, Toots."

"Yeah, me too."

∼

NATE

"FANCY MEETING YOU HERE."

I drop the pineapple I'd been testing for ripeness and turn to find Savvy behind me holding a basket with a couple of bananas and a few containers of plain Greek yogurt.

"Dinner?" I ask, pointing at her haul.

"Don't judge. I need a few quick and easy things to grab for lunch and dinner that aren't fast food or swimming with preservatives." She sighs, patting her stomach. "My body is revolting."

"There should be good food at the cookout tonight," I point out.

That's why I stopped at the grocery store after dropping Tate at school. I needed ingredients for the Bombay salad I offered to make, and I was out of the dates I need for my brownies.

"About that..." She grimaces. "I don't think I'll be able to make it. I've got a full day with meetings scheduled well into the afternoon. I'm just swamped."

I'm disappointed, but not really surprised. The last time I saw her was when I brought her lunch on Tuesday. We've texted once or twice, mostly me checking in on her, and her letting me know she'd be working late or was out of the office.

Well, if she's not going to come tonight, I may as well capitalize on this chance meeting in the produce department.

Walking up to her, I bend down to drop a kiss on her lips. She acts embarrassed when one of the baristas from Strange Brew walks by and gives her an enthusiastic thumbs-up.

"Oh great. It's gonna be all over town now," she mutters.

A little offended, I take a step back. "And that's a problem? Because if there are bounds I'm overstepping, I'd like to know."

"What? No, I don't mean it that way," she hurries to clarify, grabbing my arm to pull me to a quiet corner. "It's just...

there are already rumblings in town I'm falling down on the job. There's a lot of pressure to get both murders solved, one of my own deputies is in jail, my department is falling apart, and the mayor is not happy he had to wait for thirty minutes for one of my deputies to show up at the scene of a fender bender that took out the rear bumper of his Mercedes GLS," she rattles. "So now he's on my case."

"And…you're worried being seen with me might be considered a distraction from where your focus should be?" I make a wild guess.

"Sort of." She winces as she says it, offering me a guilty smile.

I stroke the pad of my thumb under her eye where dark rings betray a lack of sleep.

"Am I?" I ask her softly.

"Are you what?"

"A distraction."

"Only of the very best kind," she returns with a warm look in her eyes.

"Good, because I've left you alone these past few days, figuring you were juggling a ton, but I'm starting to wonder if that was a mistake. It doesn't look like you slept much, and you're obviously not eating right." I rest my hands on her shoulders and give her a gentle shake. "So, here's the thing; you're not going to do anyone any favors by running yourself in the ground. I realize you have an important job, but you're allowed to have a life too. You need balance, and you don't have any."

"I have balance," she sputters.

"Savvy…your house has the personality of a hotel room. You have a massive backyard but I bet you haven't spent any time out there. You don't even have a chair out there. You don't own a single throw pillow or candle, your closet is full of uniforms, and there is dust on your remote control."

She barks out an incredulous laugh. "Boy, you really snooped around my house, didn't you?"

"Snooped? I opened doors so I could take measurements, it's not like I went through your drawers. Besides, there was nothing to see."

Her eyes drift over my shoulder and I can tell she's upset. I guess I wouldn't appreciate someone coming in and analyzing my life either. But I care about her, and from what I've seen, she's barely lived and buried herself in work since her fiancé died, which is such a waste.

"Look, Savannah...all I'm saying is, you're not a robot, and even those need to recharge their batteries every so often. No one can fault you for that. We all need rest, we all need nourishment, we all need moments of downtime, so we can function better when we're called on."

She comes willingly when I pull her against me and wrap her in my arms. Her head falls heavily against my chest. I duck my head and brush the shell of her ear with my lips before whispering, "Just come tonight. Eat some good food, have a drink or two, and then come home with me. I'll help you sleep. I'm willing to bet you'll be far more productive tomorrow."

She moans into my shirt. "You make it sound so reasonable."

I chuckle. "That's because I'm right and you know it."

She tilts her head back and studies me.

"I can't make any promises what time I'll be there."

"I'll wait for you," I promise with a shrug.

"All ri—"

My lips are on hers before she has a chance to finish what

she was saying. I groan into her mouth when she presses her body against me. There is something deliciously illicit about making out with a woman in uniform against the organic root vegetable bin. My hand is just sliding down over the curve of her ass when we're rudely interrupted by a fellow shopper.

"Get a room, already!"

CHAPTER 22

Savvy

I SIT BACK IN SHOCK.

"Are you serious?"

The way my days are going, I no longer flinch at the unexpected, but this one hit me from left field.

"As a heart attack," is his curt response.

I tried to get Brenda to refer CdAP Detective Rick Althof's call to the CID, assuming he had information on the Franklin Wyatt case, but she thought I should be the one to take his call. She was right.

"You realize there's no way we could match whatever it is you're making in Coeur d'Alene, right?" I point out.

"Trust me, I wasn't on the Idaho list of top earners anyway. Not to mention, for what I paid for my condo here, I can buy a whole house in your neck of the woods."

"Look," he continues, I realize I'm trying to bypass whatever protocol you have in place, but you've gotta admit; me catching your ad on the police union's career center page was some kind of karma. You're looking and I'm in the market for a change."

"But why?" I blurt out, trying to make sense of this unforeseen boon. "Why would you leave your job and want to come work for a much, much smaller department in a mountain town off the beaten track, with far less resources, and for less pay?"

"Wow, you're really selling this position, aren't you?" he observes teasingly before continuing in a more serious tone. "I guess you deserve to know. I need a change of scenery in the worst possible way. A healthier way of life, a healthier pace, and some new fucking friends. I just need a reboot. Been doing this work since I got my detective badge as the youngest officer in the department, seventeen years ago. Don't get me wrong, I enjoy the work, but with the volume of cases we handle on a day-to-day basis here, I've kinda lost touch with why I loved this job to begin with. I don't have time to give each case my all, and I don't derive nearly the same satisfaction when I solve one these days."

I wait patiently when he falls quiet, because I have a feeling he's not done yet, but I can't help notice how much I recognize what he is sharing. I get it, the constant daily grind to stay on top of things really starts wearing on you. I've never felt that more than I do now, and I've held this position barely five years. But the difference for me is, I actually have the ability to change my circumstances, which is what I've started doing. Delegating more, fighting for a budget increase so I can afford to hire the likes of Rick Althof.

"And on a personal level..." He scoffs derisively. "Let's just say the job isn't exactly conducive to any kind of relationship or home life. I don't even know what that is, but I'd like to find out."

It's uncanny how accurately those thoughts describe what I'm struggling with.

"When can you start?"

The speed with which the words fly from my mouth unchecked illustrates how pathetically desperate I am.

"I need to give two weeks' notice, and I can get on the horn with a real estate agent right now."

We haven't talked about the details of his employment, and I obviously haven't done any of the prerequisite background checks or reference calls, but that doesn't stop me from smiling big when I say, "In that case, welcome to the Edwards County Sheriff's Office."

One thing off my list, twenty more to go, but we'll take the small victories.

~

My earlier sense of achievement doesn't last long when I answer a call from Tessa Androtti.

"I'm driving in tomorrow morning. Are you going to be in the office?"

"Yeah. That was the plan. Why? Has something happened?" I ask. I like to be prepared for what might be coming my way.

I just talked to Tessa yesterday when I called to let her know the judge had released Sanchuk on bail. He said his decision to grant bail was based on a lifetime of service and past merit. How ironic, given what we now know about Sanchuk's conduct over the years.

Both of us had been quite bummed about letting him walk.

"You could say that. I just came from the lab, and I'm pretty sure our cases are connected."

I sit up straighter.

"Oh?"

"The lab's been processing evidence, giving priority to what was collected from the actual crime scene, but has now also started working on what was found in and around Franklin Wyatt's car and cabin. They recovered several different shoe and foot prints from the porch and from inside the cabin. One men's size eleven boot print found in the bedroom turned out to be a perfect match to the partial at your crime scene."

One print at one crime scene might be explained away as left by accident, but to have that happen at two separate sites by the same person can't be a coincidence. There's no way.

I feel the rush of excitement that usually accompanies the promise of a solid lead. As much as I don't like the arrow possibly pointing to a first responder—even if it turns out to be Sanchuk, which would be the best-case scenario—I want this killer caught.

I have to admit, part of my reaction is also relief this will take the heat off Dozer and Wanda. As ill-timed as it may be to make their relationship public, I wish those two any happiness left for them to grab.

"That's great news."

"It is, and now the size is confirmed it should narrow down our list. But I want to keep the discovery of this print in the Wyatt case under wraps. I don't want that to be public knowledge."

"Absolutely."

"I'm hoping to be there at ten thirty or thereabouts, and I'm bringing a crime tech to take prints. I'm hoping you can gather your men so we can try to make this as quick and painless as we can."

She hangs up before I can respond.

What I was going to say is that it will be impossible to get all the guys together at the same time, because we are supposed to cover the Harvest Fest parade in the morning.

It's not much, a handful of tractors pulling harvest themed floats, the high school drum band, the fire department will have a few trucks in the parade, and the mayor likes to show off his equestrian skills by closing out the parade on horseback. It's a half-hour parade at most, unless one of the tractors breaks down like it did last year, holding everyone up for forty-five minutes until they got it going again.

But we have to close off Main Street and block any intersections for the duration. That takes manpower, which I left in Hugo's hands.

It may not be an issue, since we only need to get prints of those wearing a size eleven boot.

"What size are your boots?" I ask Hugo when I stop by his desk.

"Thirteen, why?"

Relieved to have my right-hand man eliminated right off the bat, I invite him into my office. I close the door before bringing him up to speed on the developments.

"That's a pretty average size, I think," he observes.

"I know. And somehow I need to get everyone with an eleven boot in a room together," I explain. "I'll be pulling the personnel files; everyone would've filled out their sizing information with their paperwork so we could order their uniform. That includes boots."

"Sure, but I remember filling out twelve on my intake form, and I ended up having to go up a size for comfort because my size boots fit too tight. So, make sure you include size tens as well. Unfortunately, I think the only ones who don't fall into that range are me and Warren, who's got barge-sized boots. Which leaves just about everyone else, and I've got more than a few of those guys on this weekend's schedule."

So much for my brilliant idea to tackle them all at once in order to keep the element of surprise.

"Shit. There goes that plan. It's okay, I'll figure something out. In the meantime, can you print me out the schedule you did up for the weekend?"

As soon as he leaves my office, I pull up the department's personnel files. Since I'm still holding out hope Jeff Sanchuk may be our perp and not another one of my employees, his file is the first one I open.

I scan the document until my eyes land on his shoe size —nine.

Damn.

∼

Nate

"She's going to give you gray hair."

I turn to find Brant Colter standing beside me, his eyes on the scene outside the window I was focused on just moments ago. My daughter and Carson look a little too cozy on the front porch swing.

"If I don't pull them out first," I grumble.

It's not like the kids are touching or anything, but I can tell from the way they interact, they're totally into each other. This is going to become an issue. She's fourteen and has two years to go to reach the age of consent, but Carson is already there. Two years is a fuck of a long time for a teenage boy to wait. Especially one who has my daughter looking at him like he hung the moon.

"Fuck me."

"Yeah. Given my own track record, I'm probably not the best person to dole out advice—especially to you," he adds quickly. "But I wouldn't suggest trying to stop them from seeing each other. They'll find other ways that won't be under your watchful eye, and then you'll be in trouble."

I watch as Carson shrugs out of his zippered hoodie and carefully drapes it over Tatum's shoulders.

"*Real* trouble."

"She's just a little girl," I protest limply.

"To you, yes, and probably will be for the rest of her life," he states solemnly, before clapping a hand on my shoulder. "Come on, you need a beer."

Do I ever. I need at least a six-pack of them or maybe a few of something stronger, but that would not be responsible-parent behavior. So, I follow Brant to the kitchen, where I pick a light beer from the collection he has on offer, and head out the back door to join the crowd.

"Five more minutes for the skewers, but the burgers are ready for grabs," Hugo announces when I join him by the large barrel grill.

Next to the grill a table is set up with all the food people brought over. This is quite a gathering, but even for this number of people it's a ton of food.

"Thanks, I was going to wait for Savvy so I could eat with her, but I don't even know if she's going to make it. Besides, I'm hungry; I'll just have a bite to take the edge off."

I feel Hugo looking at me while I make myself a plate.

"What?"

"You and Savvy?"

"Yep," I confirm.

I might as well get ahead of it. Tongues are probably already doing plenty of wagging after our public make-out session this morning.

"I figured as much after I intercepted a complaint call about lewd and lascivious behavior at the Safeway."

I bark out a laugh. "Someone called that in? Jesus Murphy, people have nothing better to do with their time?"

"Some people feel compelled to safeguard the high moral standards of law enforcement in this fair town," he shares with a sharp edge of sarcasm.

"That's funny, given I was just this afternoon getting staples removed from the hole one of Silence's finest left in my head when he attacked me."

"Yeah." He sounds a bit defeated when he follows it up with a mumbled, "And that may not even be the worst of it."

"What do you mean?"

He shakes his head, glancing around. "Look...forget I said anything. All I know is I'm glad I'm not in Savvy's shoes; she's dealing with a lot, which is probably why she's late. But I'm sure she'll be here soon."

I take my plate and find a spot at one of the tables scattered around the large yard, next to Bess, who is in a serious discussion with an older lady who looks vaguely familiar about the merits of pumpkin spice. Not necessarily a topic I have any strong opinions about, but I doubt my input would be welcomed anyway. Plus, this gives me a chance to eat my burger in peace, while quietly observing the people around me.

The peace doesn't last when Bess turns to me.

"Nate, you remember Mrs. Dixon, don't you?"

The penny drops. Now I know why she looks familiar.

Mrs. Dixon used to be the town librarian. I spent a good portion of my childhood in the library until it was no longer considered cool, when I was around Tate's age.

The library had been my sanctuary. The books allowed me to escape to lives lived by other people, to places I didn't think I would ever have an opportunity to see. I still read, not as much as I'd like to, but I'll always have one or another book on the go.

"Of course I do." I smile politely, unsure of the reception I'll get. "Good to see you again, Mrs. D, it's been a minute."

The old woman leans forward as she narrows her eyes on me. "Well now, as I live and breathe—and I'm still breathing, mind you—if it isn't Nathan Gaines. My goodness, you're about the last person I thought I'd see back in Silence. Let alone having dinner at Brant Colter's house. You've got some *cojones*."

I barely register the fact the old librarian is using Spanish profanities. I'm too annoyed by the message she's sending. But then she suddenly turns on a bright smile and reaches out a hand to pat me on the cheek.

"You were always a clever boy, weren't you? Are you still reading, Nathan?"

I grin and shake my head. "Whenever I have a chance."

She scoffs and wags a finger in my face. "Make time every day. It keeps the mind flexible and the heart true. It's the best gift you can give yourself."

"I remember you telling me that."

"Yeah, well...maybe this time you'll listen." She straightens up and puts on a serious expression. "And please, God, tell me you don't partake in this ridiculous trend to put pumpkin spice into anything other than pumpkin pie, where it belongs!"

I'm saved from a response when Savvy walks into the

yard to enthusiastic greetings. I get to my feet to greet her myself when the sight of Auden Maynard walking out right behind her stops me.

From behind me I hear Mrs. D's muffled comment.

"Oh boy."

CHAPTER 23

S*avvy*

THE TEMPERATURE IS DEFINITELY a bit chillier than I anticipated.

Arriving with Auden in tow may have had something to do with that. For the record, that was not my idea.

He happened to pull in right behind me and was asking me about the case as we walked up to the front door. When the CID took over the Watts Lake case, his captain put him back on regular duty, so I guess he'd been out of the loop. I didn't even think twice about the impression we'd make entering the house with his hand at the small of my back.

But apparently it was noticed.

By Nate, for one, but also Mrs. Dixon, who surprisingly is shooting daggers at Auden and sending disappointed looks in my direction. I'm not even sure what the hell is happening here, but it's annoying. Especially Auden, who seems highly amused with the whole situation and is really testing my nerves by constantly touching me and leaning into my space. I've already shifted out of his reach twice, but he doesn't appear to get the message, or is willfully ignoring it. I think he's purposely goading Nate.

The last thing I want or need is to say something and possibly create a situation that draws even more unwanted attention, but I'm afraid if I don't step in, Nate may lose his shit and then we'll have a real public spectacle.

Rather than trying to control Auden, I opt to grab Nate's hand and pull him up with me.

"Would you excuse us please?"

I smile at Bess and Mrs. Dixon, and pointedly ignore Auden, as I drag Nate around the side of the house and toward the barn.

I welcome the familiar smell of warm hay and greased leather the moment we step inside; it settles me. The only thing missing is the occasional whinny or a dull clomp of a hoof from one of the horses, but they're still out in the field. When I was young, this place was my refuge, a place to hide out.

"What's going on?" Nate asks when I turn to face him.

"This."

Placing my hands on his face, I lift on my toes to kiss him. His hands instantly find the curve of my hips to pull me closer.

"Mmm, you can drag me away from my dinner for this any time," he mumbles against my lips.

"I'm so sorry," I rush to apologize. "That was rude of me."

But he grins and shakes his head at me. "I'm just teasing, and not complaining at all. I wasn't sure you were going to make it."

"Neither was I," I confess.

I don't want to admit it was a phone call from Phil half an hour ago to ask me where the hell I was that got me out of the office.

"We had a bit of a break in the case and I lost track of time."

Close enough.

"Well, I'm glad you're here now."

A soft rustle from the direction of the goat's stall in the corner draws my attention. I could've sworn I just saw Angus in his outdoor enclosure. Disentangling myself from Nate, I move closer to have a look.

The stall is empty, but a little trickle of dust falls down from between the boards of the overhead hayloft. Then I hear a soft shushing.

Someone is up there.

"What are you—"

I turn around to Nate, my finger pressed against my lips. Then I point up and motion for him to wait. I should've known Nate doesn't follow instructions very well, he follows close behind me as I make my way to the ladder by the tack room.

My head barely clears the opening in the floorboards when I hear, "We were just looking at the view."

Nate's growl behind me indicates he recognizes Carson's voice as well.

The kid is so flustered, he knocks his head on a low beam when he scrambles to his feet. Tatum is still sitting in the open hay door, which really has a great view of the creek and the mountains at the back of my dad's property. I spent enough time up here myself enjoying it.

A quick scan tells me nothing too dramatic has gone on here. Their faces are a bit flushed, which could be from making out a little, or just from getting caught, but their clothes seem to be in place. Thank God for that.

"Tell me my daughter isn't up there," Nate grinds out, trying to push me farther up the ladder.

"I'm fine, Dad."

"She is," I quickly confirm over my shoulder. Then I turn back to the kids. "Why don't you guys come down so we can talk?"

Then I turn around and motion for Nate to get down first.

"Listen first," I hiss at him when I see him waiting at the bottom, glaring past me at what I think is Carson following me down.

"Mr. Gaines, I was just showing Tatum the mountains. The view from up here is the best in the valley."

The kid is not wrong, but I'm not sure Nate is buying what he's selling.

"And I guess your hands were in your pockets the entire time, right?" he sneers, but the anger melts from his eyes when he catches sight of his daughter coming down the ladder, unharmed. However, Tate herself looks pretty riled up.

"Yes, they were, Dad. He didn't touch me, and you're embarrassing me. Besides, you're one to talk; you're the one hiding in the barn, making out," she spits out, stepping in front of her father with her fists on her hips.

The soft-spoken girl isn't as meek as she might appear. She's got the kind of spunk I can't help admire. Still, I'm pretty sure her father wouldn't appreciate the applause I'm tempted to give her, so I curb my enthusiasm and keep my own hands in my pockets.

"Tate, honey..."

"No, Dad. That was not cool."

"Neither was not telling me you were coming out here," Nate returns, also making a good point.

"I didn't think it would be a big deal," the girl mutters.

"Really, Tate?" he probes.

She shrugs in response, suggesting she did know better but chose to ignore it.

It's almost funny how much this exchange reminds me of my childhood squabbles with my dad.

"I'm sorry, Mr. Gaines, we'll be sure to ask your permission next time," Carson wades in courageously, earning a hint of appreciation from Nate, but an annoyed look from the girl.

"Guys, have you eaten anything?" I change the subject, hopefully deflecting a different storm brewing between the two kids. "You should grab some grub while you can. Dessert is pie from Strange Brew, courtesy of Bess, and I can guarantee you that won't last but a minute before you'll find nothing but crumbs."

The pie is a calculated guess, since that's what Bess usually brings to potlucks by popular demand.

Carson flashes me a thankful grin, grabs Tatum's hand, and pulls her along as he beelines it out of the barn.

"Nothing happened," I reassure Nate, who stares after them from the doorway.

"How can you be so sure?"

"I'm a trained investigator, remember? The clothes were all on straight, other than Carson knocking his head into the beam there were no nervous movements, neither of them had hay stuck in their hair, and the dust is so thick up there it would've been obvious if they'd been messing around."

He turns around when I touch his back, and takes me into his arms.

"She saw us."

"I know."

"I should probably have addressed that," he grumbles.

"Better to let things cool off before you do," I suggest with a smile. "To be honest, she seemed more upset with the double standard than she was with the fact you were kissing me."

I catch a flash of humor in his eyes.

"Don't you mean when you kissed me?" he teases with a smirk.

"Is that what that was?" I play along.

Smiling, he takes my mouth for a repeat, leaving me almost gasping before he lets me come up for air.

"That...was me kissing you."

∾

NATE

IT'S AN UNSEASONABLY WARM MORNING.

Perhaps the last one before the temperatures drop. The forecast indicated we might get some snow up in the mountains toward the middle of next week.

Unfortunately, I'm enjoying the morning by myself on my back deck. I just heard the shower turn on in the bathroom upstairs, which means Tate is finally up, and Savvy opted to go home last night, suggesting some one-on-one time might be warranted, given the earlier confrontation in the barn.

Probably a wise suggestion, but as it turned out, Tate—who apparently can hang on to a snit longer than her old man can—froze me out on the way home and shot upstairs the moment we walked in the door.

So, I'm sitting out here on my own, sipping my second cup of java and absorbing as much vitamin D as I can before the sun disappears for the winter. But I am determined to have that one-on-one with Tate before she heads off to meet up with Naomi to check out the parade.

I keep half an eye on the sliding door, not putting it past my daughter to take off before I have a chance to talk to her. To my surprise, she voluntarily comes outside, carrying a banana and a glass of milk, and sits down across from me at the table.

"Nice out," she comments, peeling her banana and taking a big bite.

"It is. Great weather for the Harvest Fest. I remember this one year we had an early overnight frost and there was a layer of ice on the water in the dunk tank. Mr. Gibbs was my math teacher at the time and he had first shift in the chair. Naomi's dad, Roy, and I spent all our money for the day trying to dunk Mr. Gibbs in that freezing water before the ice melted."

I smile at the memory. In a generally miserable childhood, that's one of the good moments that stands out in sharp contrast.

"Did you?" Tate wants to know.

"Last ball."

I snicker and shake my head. I can still see the arrogant smirk on that guy's face and the way his expression changed in an instant when the chair dropped out from under him. The best part was the applause of the crowd that had gathered around the attraction. Apparently, Roy and I weren't the only ones with a healthy dislike for the man.

It's good to see Tate hide a little smile behind the next bite of her banana. A good moment I don't necessarily want to spoil by addressing something that might upset her.

Turns out, I don't need to. It's Tate who brings up the subject.

"She's nice...the sheriff."

"I'm pretty sure she's okay with you calling her Savvy," I suggest, following it up with, "and yes, she *is* nice."

"You knew her from before, right?"

"Correct."

"Was she more than just a friend?"

She studies me, her head tilted slightly to the side.

"She was much more than just a friend," I admit.

It's silent for a moment before she asks the question I knew would be inevitable.

"What happened?"

I'm not sure I want to get into the whole sordid story, so instead opt to keep things simple.

"I messed it up, and I'm incredibly lucky to get a second chance at doing it right this time around."

She nods, her eyes fixed on her hands, picking at the banana peel.

"I like her," she finally says. "I like her for you. Much better than some of those other women you used to hang out with."

I wince at the reminder my judgment wasn't always the best...obviously.

"I'm glad, because if I have my way, you'll be seeing a lot more of her. Now, about you and Carson," I change direction, venturing into another potential danger zone. "I know you like him, and I believe he's a decent kid but, Tate, I need you to be smart. Don't put yourself in situations that could turn into something you're not ready for."

"I know, Dad. Which is why I was going to ask you if it's okay that Carson drives Naomi and me to the church hall this afternoon to practice the dance before the youth group meets tomorrow morning? There's a whole group of us going, including the youth leader," she quickly answers.

I chuckle. Clever girl, twisting the conversation to suit her own needs. I take a moment to think about it, but there really is nothing to object to. It's not like she'll be alone with him, and although I'm not a fan of church, I do like the fact Tate seems to have found a group of kids to connect with.

"Yeah, sure thing. But I expect you back by six at the latest, because you and I are going to have corndogs and funnel cake at the park for dinner."

"Sweet. Thanks, Dad."

She gets up and comes over to kiss my cheek, and then I watch as she skips off inside.

CHAPTER 24

Savvy

"And what is this for?"

Lloyd McCormick, who's been with the sheriff's department since long before I came on board, is annoyed when I ask him to take his boots off. Chris, the crime tech Tessa showed up with earlier, prefers to take prints that way.

"It's just for elimination. There were boot prints found in both these recent cases and we want to know which ones belong to law enforcement so we don't waste time on those. We're collecting prints, even from those who weren't at either of the sites. They'll be handy to have on record for everyone, like we do with fingerprints. Makes life a lot easier for forensics," I spin him the spiel I've used on everyone else.

So far the story seems to do the trick, although Lloyd still looks a bit put out.

After his boots are printed and handed back to him, he walks out on his socks, boots in hand, mumbling something about needing a shoehorn.

"Is that all of them?" Tessa inquires.

Thanks to Hugo, we have the prints of most of my deputies. He made sure the parade was covered by rotating through all the guys he had on his schedule—including the volunteer deputies—sending them back to the office to get printed. I got a hold of one of the guys who is off this weekend, and he showed up twenty minutes ago to get his done, which in itself makes me think he can be scratched off the list.

"Almost," I inform her. "I haven't been able to get a hold of KC Kingma yet, but he may be out of reach. He likes his outdoor activities, so he could be out of cell phone range. I could swing by his place to see if he's home, otherwise, we'll be able to find him tomorrow morning at the New Horizons Church. He's a youth group leader there."

"Sounds like a wholesome guy," she observes, but she says it with a detectable edge. "Tell me about him. Young? Older? Married? Single? Straight? Gay?"

It's clear what directions her thoughts are going in, but I'm having a hard time seeing KC in that light. He's like a little brother to me.

And yet...

"Young. Our youngest deputy. Single, and I'm pretty sure he's straight. He's a good kid. Like I said, he runs the youth group at the church, I mean..."

"Surely you recognize religion isn't necessarily a deterrent for depraved behavior," she challenges. "Not when we have men of the cloth who turn out to be pedophiles and predators."

I get her point, but I still find it difficult to consider KC as a violent killer. Although, he was with me that last encounter with Ben Rogers.

"Look," she mitigates, recognizing the doubt on my face. "He's probably a really nice kid and exactly the Dudley-Do-Right he appears to be, but so was Ted Bundy. Remember that evil can hide right under your nose."

I scoff. "Boy, aren't you a barrel of laughs today."

She bends her head and presses her thumb and index finger against her eyes.

"I'm sorry. I'm tired and eager to get this case off my desk. It's been so slow going, and now we finally have something to put our teeth into."

"I hear you, but let's not do that at the expense of my deputy," I propose. "At least not without some evidence."

"Fair enough. Do you have a space where I can set Chris up to upload what he has so far? And, if you don't mind, I'd like to have a look at the schedules and dispatch logs for the last few weeks, leading up to each of the murders, at some point. But first I think you and I should pay Mr. Kingma a visit, see if we can convince him to come in so we can get a print off his work boots."

I grab my ball cap, my keys, and my cell phone, leave the crime tech in Brenda's capable hands, and lead Tessa to my cruiser. I'm hoping like hell I'm not wrong about my young deputy, because judging from the determination on the agent's face, she likes him for this.

"What motive?" I ask her when I get behind the wheel. "I can tell KC raised some flags for you, so let's play this out. What could possibly have caused him to turn like that?"

She shrugs. "In my experience, it doesn't have to be much. Both sociopaths and psychopaths are sometimes able to fly under the radar for the longest time because they can be charming, and use it to manipulate. Yet, something as simple as a careless remark, or a perceived offense can suddenly set them off. Psychopaths tend to be a bit more detached and impulsive, but either can quickly turn to violence. For sociopaths there is usually a reason they resort to extreme violence. Psychopaths, however, might find satisfaction in the act of violence itself, and are therefore more likely to repeat behavior to elicit the same sense of gratification without any provocation."

She sounds like my psychology professor. One of my elective college courses was called *The Mind of a Serial Killer*. It was one of the most popular courses at the time, because of the TV show *Criminal Minds*. Everybody wanted to become a profiler.

She catches me looking over and immediately winces.

"I'm sorry, I was lecturing, wasn't I? My kids always accuse me of doing that." She shakes her head and returns her focus out the windshield. "I've always been fascinated by the human mind, and I have a tendency to talk too much when I'm into something."

I flash a grin at her.

"No worries. Profiling always fascinated me too, but I have to admit, I don't think I'd be cut out to chase killers day in, and day out. It invades every aspect of your life."

She chuckles.

"Tell me about it."

I pull up to KC's apartment building behind the grocery store plaza, scanning the parking lot for his black Chevy Blazer, but I don't see it.

"I don't see his car, but I'm just going to knock on his door to make sure," I announce as I turn into an empty parking space.

Tessa gets out of the cruiser with me and falls into step

as I walk up to KC's main floor apartment door. I ring the bell and knock a few times, but there's no answer.

It's Saturday, you'd expect a young guy to be out and about, enjoying his day off.

So why does the silence on the other side of the door feel foreboding?

~

NATE

My body is stiff from sitting hunched in front of the computer screen for most of the day.

At least the three-dimensional renditions of Savvy's house are finished, both present and future versions. I haven't used the software in a while, so it took some time to relearn how to work certain things, but I was able to come up with two possibilities to maximize her living space and improve the flow of the house. I've even priced them both, one option more expensive than the other. Both would give her an open concept living space with a very similar kitchen layout. In the more expensive version, I've included a large window wall at the back of the house to continue to flow onto the new back deck. The most substantial difference is the addition of a vaulted ceiling, exposing the beams and trusses, creating the illusion of more space with the same footprint.

In both versions the bathrooms get a facelift, but the finishes are more elaborate and expensive in the second one.

And finally, I didn't change the exterior much in the first one, just a nice door, a lick of paint, and a bit of landscaping.

But on option two I've added an enlarged, modern beam portico over the front door that leaves space for a bench or a small seating area and adds a ton of architectural interest to the property.

I'm actually pretty pleased with the way both options turned out. These plans don't really change the footprint of the house, leaving it possible to add a larger main suite at some point in time, if that's something she's interested in doing.

A quick glance at my phone screen tells me it's after five already, and I haven't even changed out of the sweats I put on this morning. I should have a bit of time to hop in the shower and let the hot water work on the knots I put in my neck and shoulders before Tate gets back.

Twenty minutes later I head downstairs, properly dressed and feeling a lot better after a nice, pulsing water massage. Tate's not here yet, so I check my phone to see if there are any messages, but there's nothing new. Nothing from Savvy either, so I send her a quick message.

> Just checking in. I'm taking Tate to the fest for a deep-fried dinner. ;)
> Feel free to join us if you have time.

I DON'T HAVE to wait long for a response.

> Sounds wholesome. I'm just heading back to the office to finish up something, but I can try to meet you guys a little later. Where are you going to be?

Inside Silence 273

. . .

From what I remember, they usually have some kind of entertainment. If they're any good, maybe we can listen for a while.

We'll be hanging out around the bandstand.

She sends me a thumbs-up emoticon in response, and I tuck my phone in my pocket.

My laptop is still sitting open on the dining room table and I take one last look at my designs, making sure I have them saved before I shut down the computer and tuck it out of sight in the drawer of the TV stand. I'm excited to show Savannah, but when she has time to sit down with me so I can explain what I envision.

Shit, ten to six and still no Tate. She's cutting it close to the deadline I gave her this morning. I shoot her a text.

Ten-minute warning, kiddo. You'd better be on your way home.

To kill time, I turn the TV on and find my favorite news channel to get the latest updates on the state of the world. As per usual, it's pretty depressing, but I get caught up in a lively discussion around climate change. It's a subject that interests me. In my recent years building in the Nevada heat,

I started introducing more and more alternative energy sources and maximizing the use of environmentally friendly materials where possible. Hell, I even looked at an electric vehicle but, aside from the ridiculous price tag and the limited availability in heavy duty pickups, there simply isn't enough infrastructure yet to support those vehicles. I've only seen a few charging stations here in Silence, and once you get out of town...good luck finding any.

At the next commercial break, I try calling my daughter's cell, but I'm bumped straight to her voicemail. I send another message.

> You're officially ten minutes late. Call me, now.

AT SIX THIRTY I'm too restless to watch any more TV, so I turn it off. Then I dial the Battaglias. Maggie answers right away.

"Hey, Maggie. Is my daughter there by chance?"

"No. She was hanging out with Naomi this morning, and they were supposed to have a dance practice this afternoon. Naomi wasn't feeling well, so she was dropped off at home, but as far as I know, the other kids were heading to the church hall. Was she supposed to be home?"

"Yeah. Six at the latest. I think I'm gonna head out and have a look at the church, see if maybe they're running late."

"Yeah, that's always possible. Let me quickly check with Naomi to see if she's been in touch with her this afternoon at all."

A couple of minutes later she's back. "No, she hasn't. She just tried calling her but it goes straight to voicemail."

"For me too. Okay, I'm heading out. Let me know if she happens to show up there or gets in touch with Naomi."

"Will do. Let us know when you find her."

I'm already halfway out the door to my truck when I hang up. The moment my phone links to the audio in my truck, I dial Carson's father.

"Hey, coincidence. I was just about to call you," he opens with.

That doesn't feel particularly encouraging.

"Don't tell me you're looking for Carson?"

"I am, actually."

"*Fuck.*" The profanity slips out before I can stop it. "I can't get a hold of Tate; she was supposed to be home by six."

Outside the truck, dusk is setting in and I don't like it.

"Shit. Same for Carson. Where are you?"

"On my way to the church to see if—"

"Don't bother," he interrupts me. "I just came from there; the place is dark and locked up. I got hold of one of Carson's buddies in the group and he said practice ended around four."

Fucking four o'clock? Where the hell have they been for the past three hours?

Only one place comes to mind, and I pull an illegal U-turn in front of the diner.

"I'm heading to the park to look, where are you?"

"A step ahead of you. I'm already there."

CHAPTER 25

S*avvy*

WELL, KC wasn't at home, and he apparently never showed up at the church hall for a youth group practice, so I'm really starting to get concerned.

It's still possible he went up in the mountains for some R&R and simply forgot about the practice, but something tells me it's not going to be that simple. I've had a funny feeling in my gut this past hour or so.

Restless.

When Tessa and I got back to the office, I tried focusing on work but after a while I realized I'd been doing little more than staring off into space. I ended up leaving Tessa and Chris working in the large meeting room, and decided to go join Nate and his daughter in the park.

Who knows, maybe KC is checking out the fair and I'll bump into him there.

I'm surprised at how busy it is. The town center is bustling with people checking out the sidewalk sales, and from what I can see of the park, it is equally crowded.

Randal Donahue, a retired deputy who now volunteers for special events, is directing traffic. He walks over when he spots my cruiser and directs me to a small portion of the parking lot behind the park's public washrooms they've sectioned off for emergency vehicle access. I'm grateful to see there is room. Even though I'm not here for an emergency, I could get called out for one any time and I don't want the cruiser too far.

Pulling in, I find a spot well out of the way of the ambulance already parked there as a precaution so they can get out in a hurry if need be.

Of course, I bump into plenty of people I know, getting held up saying hello a few times as I make my way to the bandstand. The music is pretty good, a Fleetwood Mac cover band by the sound of it, and it's drawing a good crowd.

The smell of fried food has my empty stomach rumbling and I briefly consider grabbing something before joining Nate—they've probably long eaten—when I hear someone call my name.

"Savvy! Over here!"

I turn to find Nate and Hugo stalking over to me, and all it takes is one look to recognize something is wrong.

"What is it?"

"You haven't seen Tate anywhere, have you?" Nate asks.

Hugo, who looks equally worried, adds, "Or Carson?"

"They're missing?"

I do my best to stay calm, but inside I'm wondering what the hell is going on in my town.

"Last seen leaving the church hall at around four," my right-hand man explains. "Nothing after that. Neither is answering their phone and both go straight to voicemail. They're turned off. We've checked friends, searched around the park thinking they may have come here. I even checked with dispatch to see if maybe an accident was called in involving Carson's car, and I called Dana at the clinic as well. I know it technically hasn't been that long, but this doesn't feel right."

By this time, it's been almost four hours since they last were in contact with someone. They're teenagers, they live on their phone and for both of those to be turned off is disturbing to say the least. I'm also not discounting Hugo's gut feeling, because combined with my own sense of doom, I'm convinced something is very, very wrong here.

There is still a killer out there somewhere.

"Any chance they could've run off together?" I hold up my hand to stop Nate from reacting. "We have to consider the possibility, and I'm sure you remember how upset Tatum was last night."

"Carson told me what happened in the barn," Hugo contributes. "And I know I'm trained not to rule out any possibilities, but I'm willing to stake my badge on it; they did not just take off together. Not over that. I don't believe Carson would do anything to put Tatum in danger."

"I don't see it either," Nate agrees. "Tate and I talked this morning and she was fine, not upset. They didn't run off, but something happened."

I nod. "Okay, Hugo, you call in to dispatch to put out a BOLO for the kids and the vehicle. I'm heading back to the office to write up a warrant for Judge Crombie to sign. We need to get on the horn with the cell phone company to find out where those cell phones last pinged. Or maybe the CID team back at the station can help us fast track that."

I glance over toward the bandstand.

"But first I want to make a public announcement. Are you guys okay with that?" I look each of them in the eye. "If it turns out the kids took off somewhere on their own, this could be embarrassing for them."

"Do it," Nate immediately replies.

Hugo just nods.

The fact neither of them even hesitates shows the level of their concern, and mine is mounting with every second.

Time is of the essence, which is why I don't stop to wait for a break in the program, but instead march right up on the stage mid-song.

"I'm sorry, it's an emergency," I tell the startled singer, who immediately offers up her microphone and moves aside.

Both Hugo and Nate step up next to me.

"Good evening, folks," I start, moving back a little when the mic starts to squeal. "I apologize for the interruption, but we are urgently trying to locate Tatum Gaines and Carson Alexander and are calling on the public for help. Anyone who has seen either Tatum or Carson, or Carson's vehicle." I step aside to let Hugo share the car's details, before I continue. "Or has spoken to either of them, or knows anything about their possible whereabouts, please contact the Sheriff's Office directly."

I rattle off the number for the office before apologizing again to the band. When I start down the steps, my father is already walking toward me, Phil, looking very concerned, by his side.

"What can I do?" Dad asks.

"I may need help with the phones at the station, and I need someone to prioritize tips as they come in."

"Done." Then Dad looks at the men to my side. "We'll find the kids. You'll see."

He immediately turns, grabs Phil's hand, and starts walking, Hugo right on their heels.

"What should I do?" Nate asks, looking so lost my heart constricts in my chest.

I'm about to tell him to tag along with me, when I catch sight of Roy Battaglia with a couple of other guys approaching.

"We're gonna drive around. Any idea where they were last seen?"

"New Horizons Church, but that was around four o'clock," I inform them.

"Okay. We'll head over and spread out from there."

Good. We could use all the help we can get.

"I'm coming with you," Nate announces.

Shit. I would've preferred him to stick close to me instead of going off on his own. God only knows what he might run into. I already have two kids and a deputy missing. Luckily, Roy Battaglia is a veteran, a trained security specialist, and has a good head on his shoulders. I'm sure he'll keep an eye on Nate.

I shoot him a pointed look and he nods his understanding, before clapping a hand on Nate's shoulder.

"Come on, man, let's go find your kid."

"Call my cell if you find anything," I call after them.

"You too," Nate returns over his shoulder.

For a brief moment I watch them, their combined long strides eating up the distance to the parking lot, before I turn to where I left the cruiser.

My phone is already to my ear.

∼

Nate

. . .

NOTHING.

Myself, Roy, Omar, and Larry have been driving around in circles expanding out from the church for what feels like a long time. Then again, I'm discovering every minute feels like an eternity not knowing where my little girl is.

Flashes of dark thoughts pop in my head, and I shove them down and out of sight as soon as they appear. I don't want to allow my mind to go there, but as much as I ban the horrible possibilities from my mind, my body still responds to the visceral fear associated with them.

Roy is already getting out of his vehicle in the church parking lot when I drive up. The other two guys roll up right behind me. Another loop finished without a sign of the kids.

"Those kids had two hours to kill before they had to be home after they left here," Omar points out. "Where would they go?"

I've only asked myself that question a hundred times while driving around.

"The fair makes the most sense. You'd think kids would be drawn there," Larry suggests.

You would, except that these are kids who chose to sit up in a hayloft so they could watch the sun go down behind the mountains instead of joining the crowd at a party just yesterday.

I voice my doubts out loud.

"I'm not so sure," I drawl, my thoughts spinning as I turn to Roy. "Remember that old logging trail to the Lizard Peak summit?"

He and I would steal whatever alcohol we could get our hands on and drive his grandpa's old pickup, bouncing up the trail to catch the sunset from the ridge over the quarry. It was a popular hangout for kids but I didn't think any adults knew it was there, until one night we found that bastard Sanchuk waiting for us at the entrance of the trail by the road.

"I don't think that trail exists anymore. Last time I was out that way..." He appears to be thinking before he adds, "Fuck, that was probably with you."

Except that wasn't my last time up there, that would've been with Savvy, about seven years after, when I took her up there on our second date. The trail had been in much worse shape so we ended up ditching my pickup and hiking the rest of the way.

"Are you talking about the one off Quarry Road, leading to the lookout point?" Larry wants to know.

"Yeah. Do kids still go up there?"

"Nah. They blocked access to that trail many years ago. You wouldn't be able to find it now, it's all overgrown."

Okay, so maybe not that spot, but that doesn't mean there isn't another pretty spot somewhere that kids these days go to hang out.

My phone is in my hand and I dial Hugo's number.

"Got something?"

It sounds like he's driving.

"Not yet. I have a question though; do you remember the ridge on Lizard Peak?"

"That's going back more than a few years, but yeah. Why?"

"Do kids nowadays have a hangout like that? Somewhere you can see the sunset? Does Carson?"

It's quiet for a moment before Hugo comes back.

"Not sure about other kids, but when he was young Carson used to ask me to stop on the bridge across Watts Lake. The setting sun would reflect off the water creating a mirror effect, and he used to say you got a two-for-one sunset there. We haven't done that in years though."

I'm already climbing behind the wheel of my vehicle when I mumble a thanks and hang up. When I start the truck, Roy jumps into the passenger side.

"Where are we going?" he asks as I tear out of the parking lot.

"Watts Lake," I inform him.

The blood is going cold in my veins at the thought of my daughter being anywhere near the place where a man was murdered less than a month ago.

I focus on the dark road heading out of town and don't pay much attention to Roy, who is talking to someone on his phone. It's less than a ten-minute drive from the church but already my hopes climbed so high, it feels like a punch in the stomach when I reach the bridge and it is empty.

No sign of the vehicle or the kids.

I pull off to the side in the middle of the bridge and get out. Roy exits at the same time, and we walk up to the railing.

It's dark out here now, only a watery light coming from the lampposts at either end of the bridge, but it doesn't quite reach the middle. The moon is mostly hidden behind the clouds, so you can't see more than the occasional silver ripple in the water where it catches the light.

When I lean over, looking straight down, I see a glimmer of something reflective just under the surface of the water. At that moment the moon briefly breaks through the cloud deck, revealing the outline of two rear lights and a bumper in the water.

My heart stops as my feet start running.

CHAPTER 26

S *avvy*

I WAS ALREADY on my way to Watts Lake when Hugo called me.

Tessa had been able to pull a few strings and managed to get us an approximate radius where the kids' phones pinged for the last time. Unfortunately, the radius is approximately a square mile, but what is interesting was the coverage included part of the lake.

I'd barely hung up with Hugo when Roy's call came in and had me in an even greater hurry to get there.

So, when a call comes in over dispatch of a vehicle in the water, I already have eyes on Nate's truck parked on the bridge ahead. But no sign of Nate or Roy.

I pull off as close as I can along the guardrail at the base of the bridge, grab my Mag light, and climb over onto the steep embankment. I try to keep my footing as I make my way down, shining my flashlight until I spot one man standing up to his hips in the water.

"Nate!" I yell, but when he turns and I shine my light on his face, I see it's Roy.

Ten feet from him a head and shoulders surface, spraying water, and I take a deep breath when I hear Nate's voice.

"I need that light!"

He comes wading to the side just as I get to the water's edge.

"Emergency crews are right behind me," I tell him when he reaches for the light.

"No time," he pants, clearly out of breath as he reaches again. "They might still be in there."

"Catch your breath before you kill yourself, buddy," Roy cautions him as he joins us. "Let me have a look."

I quickly hand the flashlight off to Roy, who wastes no time diving into the dark waters. I pull Nate to my side as he gulps in air and watch the eerie play of light of my Mag torch under the surface of the water.

"I'm going back in," Nate mutters, trying to pull his arm free, but I'm holding on.

"Give him a chance," I plead, digging my heels in before he drags me in the water with him.

Just as he rips free from my hold, the light surfaces and Roy's head pops out of the water.

"It's empty," he gasps. "No one's in there."

"Are you sure? Did you see any of the windows open or broken? Any external damage to the car?"

I rattle off questions as fast as the thoughts hit my head.

"No broken windows, but I managed to open a door to get a better look inside," Roy informs me.

In the background I can hear the whine of approaching sirens.

Hugo is the first to come barreling down the embankment, losing his footing several times, but that doesn't seem to slow him down.

"Are they—"

"It's the car but they're not in there," Nate quickly shares.

The big man bends over, bracing his hands on his knees as he takes in big gulps of air.

"Windows look to be intact," I explain. "I don't think they were in the car when it went in the water."

But then where the hell are they? It looks more and more like we're dealing with foul play here. If these two were runaways, they wouldn't be ditching their only mode of transportation in the lake. The only reason to do that willfully would be to hide a crime.

Worry about the kids' fate just ramped up to the highest gear.

If their car is here, you would think the kids were here at some point as well. Maybe we can find evidence of that, if we haven't already trampled all over it.

"Guys, let's get up to the road before we destroy whatever evidence there is. We need this road closed off and get some lights set up so we can see what we're doing."

Hugo leads the way and is already off talking to the fire chief, by the time I swing my leg over the guardrail. Tessa and Chris's SUV is just pulling up behind the fire truck, and I head in their direction with Nate sticking close to my side. Roy joins a small group of men on the bridge.

I quickly fill Tessa in on what we discovered.

"Not a coincidence it was dumped in the same lake we found the first victim," she observes.

A fair conclusion, although I do wince at the mention of

the dead man in the lake, and quickly glance at Nate. A muscle ticks rhythmically in his jaw as I'm sure his mind is working its way to the same conclusion we're fearing.

"I put a call into the rest of the crime scene unit, but it'll be at least a couple of hours before they can mobilize and get here," Tessa continues. "In the meantime, we'll do what we can."

Just then Auden's State Patrol cruiser pulls up as well and he rushes over to us.

"I picked up the call on the radio. Tell me what I can do."

I can feel the air go heavy around us and move a little closer to Nate. I know he's not a fan of Auden and the encounter last night didn't really help. I hope whatever is simmering between these two guys gets resolved at some point, because both are important parts of my life, but that will have to wait.

We have much, much bigger priorities now.

NATE

I TRY to stay out of the way, but still stick close enough I don't miss anything being said.

It takes a lot of self-restraint not to go off in my truck and actively look for my girl, but I wouldn't even know which way to turn. So instead, I'm waiting for anything that might give me some direction so I have a place to start.

I gather it's still going to be a while before the forensics people get here, but in the meantime, Savvy had one of her deputies set up floodlights that bathe the embankment in bright light. What we hadn't been able to see in the dark were the tracks leading down the embankment. The car had traveled the steep slope from the shoulder of the road right at the start of the guardrail, to the lake below.

One of the firefighters, who'd gone into the waters in scuba gear to check out the submerged vehicle, surfaces and removes his mask to report a paver had been used to weigh down the gas pedal, and he observed two cell phones in the footwell on the passenger side of the car.

I listen in while the crime tech gives the diver instructions on how to collect those cell phones to preserve any evidence.

"Will they be able to pull off fingerprints on the spot?" I ask Savvy, who doesn't seem to veer too far from me.

Neither does Roy, as a matter of fact. His buddies left, but he's hovering a few feet away. Maybe they're afraid I'm going to lose it, which I feel on the verge of doing, to be honest.

So I try to focus on details and am guessing whoever took the kids would have had to handle the phones to turn them off. Hopefully they left fingerprints that will give us a lead.

I refuse to consider the possibility it might already be too late.

"Look, those phones have been in the water for a while; chances they'll be able to pull usable prints of those are pretty slim," Savvy explains. "And I'm not sure if Chris can do it right here or if he has to try back at the lab, but my guess is he won't find any."

"Why do you say that?"

She blows out a shaky breath before answering, "Because I'm pretty sure whoever is responsible is toying with us. I think this was all set up as a distraction."

"A distraction from what?"

She shakes her head. "I'm not sure, but I think I should head back to the station." She puts a hand on my forearm and looks me in the eye. "And I think you should come with me."

"I wanna stay. What if they find something here?"

"If they do, we'll know as soon as anyone else does, and in the meantime you can help me go over some of the tips Dad messaged me are starting to come in."

Either twiddle my thumbs here or get busy at the sheriff's office. It's not a difficult choice.

"Fine, I'll follow you."

I catch a look shared between her and Roy, who is flanking me on the other side.

"Go with Savvy, and leave your keys with me," he suggests. "I'll get your truck back to town."

I'm not sure I like being without wheels which, I sense, is their objective. However, Roy did drive up here with me and will need a way back to town.

"Sure," I concede, tossing him my keys.

~

I'M STRUCK speechless to find how busy it is when we walk into the sheriff's station. Brenda is manning the phones at the front desk and looks busy when we walk by. Inside the large open office space, I'm surprised to see Bess and Ginny sitting at desks alongside a deputy, whose name escapes me, and Brant Colter. All appear to be on the phone.

"Well, holy fuck, honey. Come here."

Brant's wife Phil slams the coffeepot she was carrying on a desk and pulls me into such a tight hug, I'm finding it hard to breathe. Except when she lets go of me a moment later, I still can't seem to get a full breath of air in my lungs.

"You need something to eat," she announces, patting my cheek as she appears to wipe a tear from her own. "Keep up your strength."

She swings around at Savvy, wagging an admonishing finger at her. "And you too, missy. I'm willing to bet my 1962 Fender Esquire you probably didn't have anything since breakfast, if you even had that."

"I need to talk to Dad," Savvy protests.

"Nothing says you can't eat and talk at the same time," Phil stubbornly observes. "So go talk, I'll bring you guys some coffee and a sandwich. Carlos at the Bread & Butter dropped off a couple of trays after the diner closed."

It's got to be getting damn near ten thirty, and the only reason these people aren't home getting ready for bed is because they're all helping to find my daughter and Carson.

It's overwhelming, and I abruptly turn on my heel and head for the restroom when I feel the burn of tears in my eyes. Safely locked in a stall, I can't hold back the raw sob that rips painfully from my chest. Allowing myself a moment, I let go of the emotions I've been trying so hard to keep in check these past hours.

At some point, I hear a throat being cleared on the other side of the door, and I grab for the toilet paper, mopping up my face. Then I quickly relieve myself, flush, and step out of the stall, hoping my face doesn't look too ravaged.

"Hope you don't mind; I just came to check on you."

Of course it would be Brant Colter waiting by the sink. He turns on the faucet to run the water.

"You may wanna splash some cold water, son."

"Not a good time to fucking be nice to me, old man," I grumble, sticking my whole head under the cold spray when the waterworks threaten to start up again.

The bastard chuckles as he claps me on the back.

"I'll leave you to it. Savvy's doing up a war board in the large meeting room, and Phil is putting out some food in there. Join us when you're done here."

"I'm done."

I take the wad of paper towels he holds out to me and wipe my dripping head. I'm about to follow him into the hallway when my phone rings in my pocket.

"It's Roy," I announce when I see who's calling. I answer with, "Yeah?"

"I tried the sheriff's office and dispatch but the fucking lines are busy. I drove by the church to lock my vehicle, which I hadn't done when I jumped into your truck, and there is something wrong here."

"What do you mean, something's wrong?"

My question alerts Brant, who shoots me a look of concern. I immediately put the call on speakerphone so he can hear.

"I hear yelling, and I think it's coming from the church basement."

CHAPTER 27

T *atum*

EARLIER IN THE DAY.

"So weird KC didn't show."

I turn to Carson, who is focusing on the road.

"I know. I could've sworn that was his SUV pulling in behind the church."

"When did you see that?"

"When I went to the bathroom, I was just passing the hallway window when I noticed this black vehicle pulling in. It looked like it was him driving. I even waved."

Carson shrugs. "Guess it wasn't him."

Guess so. No wonder he didn't wave back, I know it made me feel pretty stupid.

"So what's this place you're taking me to?"

"Watts Lake," he says, shooting a smile my way.

I love it when he smiles. He has really white teeth, and a dimple on one side of his mouth that only shows when he's smiling.

Carson is so good-looking, easily the hottest guy in school, and sometimes I catch some of the other girls looking and talking about us when he sits with me for lunch. The best part about that is he doesn't even seem to notice all the attention. Or maybe he does and is used to it.

I'm not used to it though, and I normally don't really like people checking me out, but it's different when I'm around Carson. He only talks to me and ignores everything else, and that makes me feel pretty special. Like it's just the two of us.

"What's special about Watts Lake?"

"It's pretty. Not as pretty as the view from Sheriff Colter's barn, but still pretty. We won't be able to stay for the actual sunset if we wanna be back before six, but since practice ended early anyway, I thought I'd quickly show you. When the lake is calm, the water is like a mirror and it reflects the mountains. When Mom was sick and after she died, I used to go there quite—"

He abruptly goes silent as he glances in the rearview mirror, but when I start to turn around to see what he's looking at, he grabs my arm.

"Don't. It's just gonna make us look suspicious."

I'm about to ask him what he's talking about when I catch lights flashing behind us in my side mirror and hear a few short bursts of a siren.

"*Shit*," Carson curses softly before pulling over to the side of the road. "Just stay quiet, let me do the talking.

My heart beats in my throat. I've never been pulled over by the cops before. Are we going to be in trouble?

Carson rolls down the window and turns his upper body so I can't really see who's outside, and it would be hard to see me from the outside. I'm pretty sure he's protecting me again.

"Did I do something wrong, sir?"

Instead of an answer I hear a loud crackle and suddenly Carson jerks and slumps over, knocking me sideways. I struggle to push him off me and try to find the handle to open the door to get out, when suddenly the door is ripped open. Next thing I know, I'm being dragged from the car, an arm wrapped around my neck making it hard to breathe.

The last thing I remember is something sharp jabbing my shoulder.

∽

My head is throbbing.

I try to open my eyes, but it's hard. My eyelids feel like they weigh a ton and I can barely lift them a hair.

I don't know where I am. It smells a little musty, like the time I forgot to move the sheets from the washer to the dryer like Mom asked. We had to wash them again to get the smell out. I'm lying with my face on concrete, I think. Or some kind of stone. It's cold and rough, biting into my skin.

Why can't I move anything? Where is Carson?

Who was that?

I manage to open one eye to a crack but it takes a few moments before I can actually make anything out. The light is faint, coming from a small window high on the wall. It looks like I'm in a basement. When I try to lift my head to see better, I hear a rustle and find the source in the far corner of the space. There's a man crouched down over someone lying on the ground.

I immediately freeze, too scared to even breathe. Memories of the flashing lights, Carson slumping over, being pulled from the car, and the arm around my neck come flooding back.

Was I drugged? Is that why I can't move?

I watch as the crouching man seems to be tugging on the feet of the person lying down. Is he hurting him? Then I see him remove the other man's boots.

Suddenly the guy turns his upper body around, and I snap my eye closed, holding my breath, hoping he didn't see me.

I only got a glimpse of his face but enough to recognize him, and I know I'm in deep trouble.

It's eerily quiet. I listen for any movement, almost waiting for him to come over. If he does, I won't even be able to run.

My eyes burn with tears I hope won't escape or he might see.

I want my dad. I didn't even have a chance to text him where we were going.

I wonder, would it hurt when you die?

When the sounds resume in the corner, I'm almost surprised. I was so sure he'd seen me looking. But I resist looking now, keeping my eyes firmly closed.

Even when moments later I can hear him moving, footsteps on the concrete floor coming toward me. I start chanting in my head.

If I move...I'm dead. If I move...I'm dead

It's so hard not to react when he lightly kicks my foot. Then he kicks it harder, but I don't cry out and I don't move, even though it hurts and I want to puke.

His boots crunch on the rough floor as I can feel him crouch down beside me, his hand brushing over my hair.

"Didn't exactly plan it this way, but this may just work out perfectly," I hear him mumble, as he removes the hair clip holding back my ponytail.

That was the last thing Mom gave me.

She'd come home drunk the night before, stumbling around the house, knocking into furniture, and throwing up all over the carpet. I had to clean her up, help her in bed, scrub the carpet, and straighten the house. The next day I came home from school and she gave me that clip, telling me I was a good girl for looking after her.

I almost break my silence to plead with him not to take it.

"Almost time..." he whispers.

Then I hear him get up and walk away from me. More rustling in the corner, before the footsteps seem to grow more faint and finally disappear.

∽

I'm not sure how much time has passed; it could be minutes, or hours.

The only thing I know is that it felt like forever.

I've been afraid to try and move, worried he might come back and catch me awake. I don't know what he meant by "*Almost time*," but I have a feeling it can't be good, and that time is fast running out.

This time, opening my eyes is a little easier, and the tingling I've been feeling in my fingers and feet the past little while must've been the drug wearing off. I'm able to lift my head and shift my arms underneath me to push up. They feel like lead, but at least I can move them now.

Sitting up, I brace my back against the brick wall and scan the space around me.

A muted groan startles me, but it doesn't come from the person lying in the corner, it's coming from behind some kind of dresser on the other side of the room.

"*Carson?*" I whisper.

It sounded like it could be him.

I'm able to get myself onto my hands and knees and start crawling toward the sound.

"Carson!"

He's lying on his back, a puddle of blood under his head, but his eyes are open.

"Tate..."

"I'm right here." I move closer and carefully touch his face.

"You've gotta get outta here," he mumbles, his speech so slurred I can barely make out what he's saying.

"I'm not leaving you."

"Gotta get help..."

There's no smile or dimple on his face now. He looks like he can barely keep his eyes open, and I'm really scared he's hurt badly.

I nod. "Okay. I'll try to find a way out."

This time when I try, I can actually stand up. I'm a little wobbly, but with my hand against the wall for support, I manage to go search for an exit.

I try to ignore the still figure in the corner. He hasn't moved at all, and if he's already dead, I don't want to know.

Beyond this room is a hallway with several doors, but I find those are all locked. I don't want to rattle any of them too hard. What if someone is nearby? They might hear me. To get to the window high on the wall—the only one I've seen— I'm going to have to climb up on something, and hope I'll be able to open it.

The dresser catches my eye. If the drawers are sturdy

enough, I could use those as a ladder to get up. I just hope I'm able to move it closer.

I try to push it with all my might, and then I try pulling it, putting my whole weight into it, but it still won't budge. Finally, after taking out all the drawers, so it's a little bit lighter, I'm able to push the dresser under the window.

The legs scrape along the floor, making a lot of noise, but I can't stop. When I looked over at Carson moments ago, his face looked even paler, but his eyes were encouraging me to push on.

With the help of the drawers, I'm able to get myself onto the dresser. My chin comes up to the windowsill, so I can easily reach the latch, which is a little rusty. I can look out, but the glass is so dirty I can barely see anything. The window has to flip out and up, but seems stuck. I have to hit it as hard as I can with the heel of my hand.

By now I've made so much noise, I'm convinced if anyone else was here, they'd have come running.

Finally, the window flies open with a squeak, and I immediately recognize the church parking lot. How did we get back here? At least I know where to run for help as soon as I get out of here.

I grab the sill with my hands and try to jump so I can pull myself up, but that proves to be more difficult than I thought. My hands keep slipping, and my legs are still too weak to give me a good boost.

Frustrated, I'm about ready to cry, when I suddenly hear the crunch of wheels in the parking lot. I immediately pull my hands back and move to the side to stay out of sight. Carefully peeking over the ledge, I almost cry out in relief when my father's truck rolls into sight.

I start yelling.

CHAPTER 28

S *avvy*

"Do not try to go in there until we know what's going on."

I'm flying down the streets toward New Horizons, with at least one more vehicle following behind. I just hope Phil was able to hold back my dad, since he came running out of the bathroom after Nate, who was sprinting for the door.

I was able to stop my father before he could get out, and bolted after Nate myself.

He's now sitting beside me, coiled tighter than a spring, and I just know he's not even going to let me come to a full stop before he's out of the vehicle, hurling himself into an unknown and potentially dangerous situation.

"I mean it, Nate," I emphasize in my most authoritative voice while trying to keep from hitting a cat crossing the road. "I won't hesitate to slap cuffs on you if I have to."

I've been going at full speed through town, but slow

down to turn into the church lot. A State Patrol vehicle pulls in behind me and I recognize Auden behind the wheel, good. I feel a little better going in with backup.

We find Nate's truck parked around the back of the church when we arrive, but there's no sign of Roy. I'd tried getting a hold of him en route after Nate told me about the call, but he didn't answer. I don't even want to think about the possibility something might have happened to him as well.

"Please, sit tight," I plead with Nate, who already has a hand on the door handle. "We don't know if the kids are in there, or under what circumstances, but you barging in could put them at more risk. We don't know until we get a lay of the land. Please..."

I put a hand on his knee. It's on my lips to tell him I love him and can't handle the thought of him getting hurt, or worse, but this isn't the time and I'm not sure it would make much of a difference at the moment anyway.

His eyes stay fixed on the church, a muscle ticking in his jaw, but he finally relents with a quick nod.

"Hurry," he grinds out through clenched teeth.

Auden is already out of his vehicle, eyeing Nate's truck.

"What's going on? I was just on my way home when I heard the call come in about a disturbance at the church. You blew by me with lights flashing a few seconds later, so I followed you."

"Yelling was heard coming from the basement. The kids may be inside."

I notice there is no yelling now. No sound at all, aside from the sudden squeal of brakes announcing the arrival of another cruiser, this one driven by Hugo Alexander, my stubborn father riding shotgun. The driver's side door flies open.

"No," I bark at Hugo, who doesn't even acknowledge us as he starts moving toward the church.

I run to intercept him with Auden at my back. Together we manage to block his way.

"You can't go in there. You're too close and you know that," I enforce, poking a finger in his chest. "Dad, get over here and fucking sit on him if you have to," I snap at my father.

Then I turn to Auden. "Let's go, before this shitshow gets any worse. And be careful, keep your eyes open, because there's no way whoever is in there could've missed our arrival."

As we start moving yet another cruiser pulls into the parking lot. Yeah, a stealth approach, trying to catch any potential perp unaware is no longer an option. We have to go in prepared for anything.

I notice an open basement window when we approach the church hall's side door but I choose to ignore it; I could probably get through, but there's no way Auden would. Door it is. I'm prepared to kick it in, but am surprised to find it unlocked.

I slip my sidearm from its holster and fit it securely in my hand, aiming the barrel at the ground in front of me. The soft snick of a snap being undone behind me suggests Auden has done the same.

We step into a small foyer with the hall to the left and the church straight ahead. A stairway to the right leads up to the choir loft and down to the basement.

Footsteps sound behind us as Lloyd and Warren catch up.

"You guys clear the choir loft and the church; we've got the basement."

I don't wait for their acknowledgement and head toward

the stairwell going down. At the bottom of the stairs, we find the basement door locked from the outside. It's a simple keyed door knob, but we don't have a key.

"*Kick it down?*" I whisper, looking over my shoulder at Auden.

He shakes his head. "Let me try something first."

He reaches into the chest pocket of his uniform shirt and fishes out what looks like a credit card or hotel key or something. Slipping it between the door and the post right above the latch, he jiggles it slightly as he works it down the crack. I can hear the soft click of the latch releasing as he eases the door open.

I flash him a tight smile and a thumbs-up, before I support my gun hand with the other, and slowly move ahead into the dark basement.

∼

NATE

IT GOES against everything I value to stand here and watch Savvy disappear inside that church.

Especially with Auden covering her back. Sure, he's come a long way from the scrawny kid I remember, but I still don't trust him. The guy rubs me the wrong way, and I'm pretty sure he doesn't like me any better. I don't even know the two other deputies following them inside.

"My kid's in there," I hear Hugo protest as Savvy's dad is doing his best to contain him.

The rational part of me knows Savvy is right to sideline both of us, but I'm not feeling very rational right now. Apparently, neither is Hugo.

"I hear you," I mumble, taking a step toward the church.

But when Brant Colter calmly states, "My kid is in there too, but I trust Savvy. I know she can look after herself, and she's the best person to look after your kids as well. Have a little faith," I stop in my tracks.

"I fucking hate it when you're being sensible," Hugo grumbles.

I'm about to agree with him when I hear my name called. I turn my head and find Roy waving me toward him from the edge of the parking lot.

I hurry toward him, hearing the footfalls of someone else behind me. My bet would be on Hugo.

"What the hell happened? We fucking tried calling you."

"Left my phone in the truck. Look, I've got Tate."

My eyes immediately scan the woods beyond him.

"What? Where is she? Is she okay?"

"I was able to pull her out of the basement window. She was scared, rambling, and as soon as you guys pulled in, she took off running. She fucking climbed up a tree like a monkey, man. I can't get her to come down."

"Did you see my boy?"

Roy looks at Hugo. "No, I'm sorry. Tate was mentioning him, but she was shaking so hard, I could barely make out what she was saying. I think he's in there. I think he's in the church."

Hugo immediately turns back to the parking lot where Brant is waiting. His eyes haven't left the door through which Savvy disappeared. My heart is torn but I take guidance from the old man's words: Savvy can take care of herself, but my daughter needs me.

"Show me," I snap at Roy.

I see the bottom of the pink Chucks with daisies she found online and begged me to buy her. Like the sap I am, I spent way too fucking much money on those bitty scraps of fabric and rubber. But Tate had been elated when they arrived a few days ago and has worn them ever since.

Seeing those pink sneakers dangling from a branch a good twenty-five to thirty feet up off the ground makes my heart constrict in my chest.

"*Jesus*," I mumble.

"Yeah," Roy confirms. "Couldn't believe it. She was so fast, I couldn't catch her, and when I tried to get up there after her, she started shaking so hard I was afraid she'd lose her grip."

I can see her shaking from way down here. She's hugging the tree hard, her face pressed into the bark as her wide eyes stare down. But I'm not too sure she even sees us.

"I'm gonna try and get up there, see if I can get her down."

My work keeps me in decent shape, but I'm well past the age where climbing trees is a daily occurrence. Good thing my calluses are thick with the rough bark biting into my palms. I go as fast as I dare without startling her, mumbling soothing nonsense all the way up. Last thing I want is for her to slip or let go completely before I can get to her.

"You're okay, Sweetpea. I'm here. I've got you. I'm not going to let anything happen to you. I promise."

I work my way around the other side of the thick trunk and ease my way closer to where I'm shoulder to shoulder with her.

"Tate, honey, can you look at me? Please, baby, look at me, I'm right here. You've been so brave, but let me take care of you now, okay? Tatum?"

Slowly, she turns her head. The imprint of the bark mars her cheek with angry red slashes, and her eyes are wide and terrified.

"Good girl. Now, I'm going to get you down from here. I need you to put your arms around my neck and your legs around my waist. I won't let you go. I swear."

She shakes her head.

"*He's down there,*" she whispers, her teeth chattering from shock.

I immediately glance down, but Roy is the only one at the bottom of the tree.

"That's just Roy, honey."

"No...not him. It's the man who stole KC's boots. I saw him get out of the car."

I can't make heads or tails of what she is talking about.

"Who, baby? Who are you talking about?" I push, but she's not saying any more. "Come on, Tate, I'm not going to let anyone near you, but we need to get out of this tree before we both fall out. Please, Sweetpea. Let me help you."

The branch under my feet is pretty sturdy, and I keep a firm grip on the trunk with my left as I reach out my right hand to close over her slim wrist.

"Trust me, I'm not going to let anything happen to you," I promise.

Her concession is no more than a slight shift in her eyes before she releases her left hand, allowing me to wrap that arm around my neck. I would prefer to have her at my front, but that would only make climbing down that much more dangerous. It takes a little maneuvering, but we get it done. When she is clinging to my neck, her colt-like legs wrapped around me, I can feel the tremors shaking her small body.

It's not until we're halfway down she says by my ear.

"It's the tall guy wearing the hat. He went inside with Savvy."

A cold fist closes around my heart.

"Roy!" I yell down. "Tell Brant Savvy needs help! It's

Maynard, hurry!"

CHAPTER 29

S*avvy*

THE FIRST THING that strikes me is the silence inside.

A dead silence.

An involuntary shiver runs down my spine, and I shoot off a silent prayer I won't find death inside.

It's also dark down here. I don't bother looking for a light switch, and I don't want to use my flashlight, because that would only make me an easy target. Instead, I blink a few times to help my eyes adjust to the limited light from the parking lot coming in through the small, open window. Did someone come in or go out through that window?

A little spark of hope ignites in my chest. Maybe the kids were here but got out?

I motion for Auden to follow me as I start moving into the basement, keeping my back to the wall. I make out a few random pieces of furniture, clearly the space is used for storage, but right now those are places for someone to hide.

While keeping an eye on the rest of the room, my attention is focused on the large bookcase to my left. One of the sides is maybe a foot and a half or so from the wall, almost creating a room divider. But a foot and a half is enough for me to get through, and if anyone is hiding behind there, they'd have their eyes on the other side, which is wide open to the room. That might give me an element of surprise, because I'm sure whoever is down here is well aware of our presence by now.

I turn and signal Auden with a finger to my lips. Then I point a finger at myself and the route I plan to take, before indicating for him to go toward the other end of the bookcase. That way, if the perp is back there, we'll have him covered from both sides.

God, I really hope there is another explanation for KC's disappearance, because the thought of him having any part in the abduction of the kids makes my stomach turn.

Slowly, I start easing myself through the narrow space, trying not to brush up against anything. Taking in a deep breath, I brace myself for what or who I might be about to face and poke my head around the corner. What I wasn't expecting was the still body of a man, lying on his side facing away from me, but I have no trouble recognizing my own deputy.

I take two cautious steps toward him, making sure this isn't some trap to draw me closer, but when I notice no movement at all, I rush to his side and immediately feel for a pulse.

"Don't worry, he's alive. For now."

My hand immediately reaches for the gun I set down so I could press my fingers to KC's carotid. *Stupid.*

"If you touch that gun, I'll shoot you, him, and then those brats on the other side of that armoire."

My hand is frozen in midair as I stare in disbelief at the man I thought was my friend. The man I trusted to have my back when facing off with a dangerous criminal. Except, he's the dangerous criminal.

Those poor kids. I hope to hell they managed to get out.

I shake my head, trying to make sense of what is going on.

"Auden, what is happening? What the hell are you doing?"

He smiles, and I'm almost surprise to see that familiar boyish smile instead of the evil sneer more suited to this moment.

"Not what I planned, I can tell you that," he responds easily. "But I'm nothing if not adaptable, and I think this way is going to work out even better. The other way was messy, but I might actually walk out of here the hero today."

He laughs, full of himself and, I hope, distracted.

"I know you're smarter than that, Savvy," he suddenly snaps when I inch my hand closer to my gun. "Back away."

When I don't immediately move, he aims his gun at KC's head instead of me. Message received; I crawl backward. That seems to amuse him.

"Imagine that, the great Savannah Colter on her knees for me."

"What are you talking about?" I ask, genuinely confused as he approaches. "What have I ever done to you?"

He's still smiling as he crouches down and picks up my gun with his free hand. When he straightens up, he backs up only a few steps to the bookcase and slides my sidearm on a shelf. Then he turns his own weapon back on me.

"You're funny. You think this is all about you? It isn't," he spits out. "This time it's about me. I'm going to have the upper hand. I'm going to win this one. You want to know how?"

I don't think he's really expecting an answer so I keep quiet, hoping he'll keep talking, so I can figure out my next move.

"See this?" He holds up his gun without ever shifting the barrel away from me. "This belongs to your wonder boy here. He will become the permanent stain on the reputation of this town and your sheriff's department. Sweet justice, if you ask me. One of Silence's favorite sons will go down as the serial killer who terrorized the sweet, innocent town. After all, he's wearing the boots." He chuckles, kicking KC's foot before he continues, "Slaughtering a total of four and setting the church on fire—maybe getting himself killed in the process or on purpose—was the original plan. But this is much better, five victims, and one of them will be Edwards County's beloved sheriff. They'll hear the gunshots, but your father will take charge, and he does everything by the book. They'll come in cautiously, giving me time to take care of the kids."

The pieces of the puzzle start coming together.

Auden? He hadn't even pinged on my radar as a potential suspect. But the boots, the uniform, even the scrap of blue fabric pulled from a bramble bush near where Ben's body was found now makes sense. The state trooper uniform is blue.

He's planning for KC to take the fall for all of it. I can see the scenario playing out now. He'll shoot me with KC's gun, and then he'll kill KC with his own. Justified shooting, and no one would ever doubt him. He'll come out a hero.

But maybe if I can keep him talking. He seems high on his own perceived genius, so perhaps if I keep asking questions, he'll feel compelled to show his superiority, giving others outside a chance to start wondering what the hell is taking so long and come looking.

"But why?" I can't help ask. "Why any of it? What have Franklin Wyatt, or Ben...my God, Auden, and those two kids, KC...what have any of us ever done to you?"

"They threatened me, and I don't like being threatened. Franklin was nobody. A hookup I met online. A quick fuck I could keep out of my daily life, but he wanted more. Said he'd leave his husband for me, and I told him not to bother. He threatened to expose me, called me gutless, so I showed him gutless."

I remember the state of Franklin Wyatt's body and shiver at the callous reference.

Who is this man? Never, in a million years, would I have seen that coming. God, he was almost legendary in town with his endless string of flavors of the day, always women, and never lasting. I've known him for years and would never have suspected he swung both ways.

How the hell did I miss that?

"Ben saw me come up the embankment after I dumped Franklin," he continues, obviously caught up in his own story. "When he heard about the body, he cornered me at The Kerrigan one night, drunk out of his brain, and tried to blackmail me."

He smiles again, but this time I don't see the boyish charm I always thought he was conveying, but a more sinister, dark individual.

"KC is an easy target," he continues his self-aggrandizing confession. "Golden boy wonder of the Evans County Sheriff's department. He can be made to fit any of the evidence collected, which is why he's wearing my boots. And the kids? Well, they will be part of the grand finale. The small details that make this plot entirely plausible. A little divine justice the girl happens to be Nate's spawn. I'm going to enjoy watching him suffer when he loses you both."

The man is insane. Evil personified.

I'm now convinced he wouldn't flinch putting a bullet in me.

Truth be told, at this point, I wouldn't flinch putting one in him either.

I cock my head slightly, positive I just heard movement behind the bookcase, but I quickly cover it by asking, "And killing me? What sins have I committed?"

"You have to ask? Everybody loves Savvy," he says in an exaggerated singsong voice, before he leans forward and stabs a finger at his own chest. "But I loved them first... Nathan."

He almost spits out the name, and I feel like I've been slapped in the face. Nate? He loved Nate? I wasn't even aware at the time they knew each other.

"But of course the princess of Silence, the heir apparent of Edwards County, caught his eye instead," he mocks. "And why wouldn't he? I was just the awkward, bastard son of the world's worst mother and one of the sheriff's underlings whose name she refused to share. But I loved watching you suffer those years after he disappeared."

My God, how could I not have seen how much he hates me? It's clear as day now.

Morbid curiosity has me ask the next question.

"You said you loved *them* first...who else?"

"Don't tell me you don't know you stole Matt from me too."

This is like a one-two punch, and leaves me reeling.

"Matt? But you introduced me to him," I remind him, completely thrown off guard.

"Only because you showed up to my place just as he was leaving after fucking me only minutes before."

I put my hands over my ears and shake my head, unwilling to hear more, but Auden is relentless.

"I had to stand by and watch as you two became the most enviable couple in town. I thought you were the diversion, but it turns out I was. And when I showed up at the quarry to confront Matt—to tell him he belonged with me—he laughed in my face. No one laughs in my face."

He takes three big steps toward me and presses the barrel between my eyes.

"I have lived to see you suffer...you don't deserve another single moment of happiness."

I'm suddenly knocked to the ground, the sound of a gunshot ringing in my ears.

CHAPTER 30

N*ate*

I STAND BY THE WINDOW, watching Savvy get into her cruiser and drive off.

She's barely even acknowledged me since her father led her out of the church, covered in blood and looking like a ghost, but still very much alive.

The blood hadn't been hers, even though, for several very long minutes after I heard the shot go off, I was terrified Brant and Hugo rushed in there too late. Roy had to hold me back from rushing in after them, and he was right, my little girl was traumatized enough and needed me.

"Give her time," Hugo says behind me.

Our kids were placed together in a room. They'd both asked to be and nursing staff readily agreed. The small hospital only has limited rooms and we arrived with three patients at once. Tatum, Carson, and KC Kingma all had drugs in their system, and Carson also had a head laceration and suffered a concussion.

Apparently, the kid had been knocked back by a Taser, which allowed Maynard to subdue Tate. That gave Carson enough time to regain some muscle control and he tried to fight the much bigger man off, but got his head slammed into the road instead. I have a whole new appreciation for the teenager after finding out he's also the one who urged Tate to get out.

All three of them were admitted to the hospital for observation, at least until the lab is able to identify what exactly they've been drugged with.

So I've been stuck in this room for a day and a half now, waiting for a chance to talk to Savvy, but she's been actively avoiding me, even though I've seen her come in and out of the hospital and pass by in the hallway.

"I don't fucking understand, man," I complain, trying to keep my voice down for the kids.

"Listen, she's got a ton to process. She has a severely shorthanded department she has to keep running, she's got several state and federal agencies milling about in her town, and her father is being closely looked at in the shooting of Maynard."

"He was fucking holding a gun to her head," I hiss. "What would they have him do? Ask fucking politely to unhand his daughter? That's bullshit."

"Shh," he shushes me. "I know it's bullshit, I was there, he was completely justified, but that's protocol, and believe me, Brant himself would insist every step is followed. He's retired, a civilian now, there are slightly different standards for a justified shooting."

Hugo gave me the outlines of what went down in that basement, but I'm sure there's a lot he left out. I'm still fuzzy on Maynard's motivations and I'm eager to learn all the details, because the Savvy that walked out of that building is not the same person who went in.

I need to know what changed.

"Look," he continues. "All I'm saying is she's under a lot of pressure, so give her a little time. Believe me, I'm feeling pretty damn useless myself, but our job right now is to look after our kids."

The conversation is over when Doc Wilson walks in with another doctor we briefly saw when we got here.

"You remember Dr. Sharma?" Doc asks.

"Call me Rohan," the man says, holding out his hand for first Hugo and then me to shake. "I don't stand on formalities."

His handshake is firm and his smile seems genuine. I'd guess him to be around my age, maybe by a few years on either side.

"Dr. Sharma is new to town, but I'm sure you'll be seeing a lot more of him," Doc informs us. "He's joined my practice, and will eventually be taking over."

Then he smiles at each of the kids in turn. "So, how are you guys doing? Think you might be ready to go home today?"

"Yes, please," Carson is the first to respond. "I'm bored out of my brain."

"I'm sure you are, kid," the older man says with a grin. "But I have to tell you, you're gonna have to take it easy for at least another week with that hit your noggin took. Rest at home, no strenuous activities, I'd advise against too much gaming so limit the screen time, and come check in with me in a week."

He turns to Tatum. "And you, young lady, should be good to go with another day or two at home. You don't have to come back, unless you have any complaints. And that goes for both of you."

Then he redirects his attention to us. "You'll need to keep an eye out for mood swings, anxiety, any memory loss or impaired cognitive functioning, that kind of thing. Now, I don't think the kids were exposed to the drug long enough, but it pays to be cautious. They were injected with a hefty cocktail of ketamine and propofol. Although, most of the ketamine should be eliminated from the body after ten to twelve hours after administering, on average, some remains and can be detected in the urine up to two weeks after. Propofol dissipates much faster and is already gone from their system."

With a promise a nurse will be in shortly with the kids' discharge papers, the two men are about to walk out when Bess arrives with a bakery box. The older doctor greets her with a nod before disappearing down the hall, but Dr. Sharma pauses, his eyebrow raised as he inspects the box.

"Busted," she grins at him sheepishly. "I hope the kids aren't on any dietary restrictions. I thought they might be allowed a little something sweet."

"They're allowed. I'm partial to sweets myself," the guy smiles back, tapping a finger on the Strange Brew logo on the box. "Yours? I was in there for coffee and breakfast the other day, and I'm pretty sure I saw you pop out of the kitchen a time or two."

I hear a distinct sound of grinding teeth behind me and when I glance over my shoulder at Hugo, he's glaring at the new doctor with a jaw clenched so tight, I'm afraid he'll break it.

Interesting reaction.

"Yup, it's mine," Bess clarifies. "Hope you enjoyed your breakfast."

"I did. I've gotta run, but I was planning to come back, so I'm sure I'll see you around," Sharma returns before he hurries out the door.

I almost laugh at the sharp huff from Hugo. I'm not exactly sure whether he just feels very protective in a friendly way or if he actually has an interest beyond that. I suspect the latter. He most definitely has a strong opinion on that little exchange, and glares at Bess as she approaches the kids' beds.

I shouldn't laugh at his obvious frustration, it's not like I'm doing swimmingly in the romance department myself.

Bess seems oblivious to it all as she ceremoniously whips the lid back off the box.

"Fresh donuts, anyone?"

∾

SAVVY

I'VE BEEN SITTING HERE, staring at the text I received twenty minutes ago, waiting for the knock on my door.

It's been five days since Auden's brains were blown all over me, my father's finger on the trigger.

There are events you know, even as they are happening, will be etched into your brain with excruciating detail. This was definitely one. From the casual, *"Don't worry, he's alive. For now,"* right up to the deafening reverberation of the gunshot that brought a long friendship to a violent and abrupt end, and every moment in between.

I've relived each one of them time and time again as I've

lain awake in my empty bed. The lonely picture on my nightstand found the trash can that very first night, when I finally got home, after spending the night before in the hospital and at the office.

There was no sleep then, and there has been little since. I'm coasting by on coffee, piles of work, and sheer will. Although, I will say the latter is wearing concerningly thin.

And now I get this message from the man I've avoided all week, announcing he'll be here in mere minutes and if I even think about ducking out to avoid him, he vows to hunt me down.

I'm too tired to duck and run, I haven't even had the energy to change into my sleep shirt and go to bed, which I fully intended on doing when I left the station.

The kicker is, I could probably sleep with Nate holding me, but first I owe him an explanation for avoiding him, and don't know that I'm ready. I'm hurt, I'm confused, I feel betrayed, and nothing in my life I thought I knew for a fact was apparently based in reality. As much as Nate does not carry any responsibility whatsoever for any of it, he is entwined in all of it.

Also, if I'm absolutely honest with myself, I have to admit I'm ashamed for being so gullible for so long. I know Nate didn't trust Auden's motivations, but I brushed it off. That could've cost two innocent kids and one of my deputies their lives. As it is, they'll be traumatized for the duration because I couldn't see what was right under my nose.

A sharp rap on my door interrupts the sea of self-doubt and recriminations I'm drowning myself in, and I push myself to my feet with a groan.

I almost sob at the sight of him, so strong and handsome, and I want to throw myself in his arms, despite the angry scowl he's aiming at me.

"You didn't run."

"No."

I step aside to let him in. When I follow him inside, he stops in front of the coffee table, his hands jammed in his pockets.

"Can I get you something?" I ask, almost by rote.

His response is curt. "I'm fine."

I sit down in the same spot on the couch I just vacated, grab a toss pillow to hold in my arms, and curl my legs under me. Even as I'm doing it, I recognize the defensive body language. Nate notices too, and his expression gentles slightly as he perches himself on the edge of the coffee table in front of me.

"Talk to me."

"Where is Tatum?" I ask as a last attempt at diversion.

"Spending the night at Naomi Battaglia's," he answers, before repeating, "Talk to me, Savannah."

I shake my head. "I'm sorry. I'm sorry I avoided you. I could tell you I was busy with work, wrapping up this case, and dealing with the investigation into my father, but as valid as they all may be, they're also just excuses. The truth is, there is so much to unravel and I haven't even really wrapped my head around it myself. As you can see, I'm a bit of a mess, and I was frankly afraid if I talked to you, I would fall apart, and I didn't feel I could afford to. Not until my job was done and I could start processing."

He reaches out his hand and wraps it around my ankle, his thumb softly stroking the strip of bare skin between the cuff of my pants and the edge of my sock. The simple soothing gesture alone is enough to make my eyes well up.

"Look at me, Savvy." He waits until I lift my eyes to his. "I love you. Do you know how hard it's been to see you struggle from a distance and not be able to do anything?"

There's no holding back the tears, not after a declaration like that.

I'm barely coherent when I mutter, "Don't be nice to me, please. Not when I have to tell you things that are going to upset you."

He swiftly moves from the coffee table to the couch beside me and pulls me onto his lap like a child.

"Tell me," he prompts, stroking my messy hair with his large hand.

So I do, starting haltingly, but I don't leave out any detail of my exchange with Auden Maynard. I cling on to his shirt, feeling every reaction to what I'm saying in his body's response.

"Sanchuk," he suddenly interjects inexplicably. At my quizzical look, he clarifies, "The sheriff's underling, it's gotta be him. It would never have occurred to me, but picture those two side by side. The hooked nose, the dimples. There's a definite family resemblance, I can't unsee it now."

He's right, I can't believe I missed it. I wonder if Sanchuk knew, or if my father ever picked up on it. Mental illness runs in families too, and I'm willing to bet both those men could be considered psychopaths.

I slightly shift in his lap so I can look him in the eye.

"Are you okay?"

"Am I okay?" he echoes back. "No, not by a long shot, but that has nothing to do with you and everything to do with that sick bastard."

"I'm so sorry."

I start sobbing again and he immediately gathers me closer and gets to his feet with me in his arms.

"Nothing for you to be sorry about."

"Where are we going?"

"I'm drawing you a bath, and you're gonna relax and let

all of this garbage spinning through your head drain itself, and then I'm taking you to bed so you can sleep."

It's not until much later, after I've cried myself dry and washed myself clean, I nestle in his arms and press my face into the side of his neck.

"I love you so much."

CHAPTER 31

S*avvy*

I WAKE up to the light abrasion of Nate's scruff on the inside of my thighs.

Stretching my arms over my head, I completely give myself up to his ministrations. I'm accustomed to being in control all the time, but with Nate I feel free to let go and have him take the reins.

Something he does fabulously.

We've discovered early mornings are our favorite time of day. With a kid around, quiet times are hard to find, but we know for a fact a cannon couldn't wake Tate in the mornings. She's a teenager.

The muted light, the mellow vibe, no distractions or responsibilities killing the mood. Bodies still warm and lazy from sleep.

It's delicious. Best way to start the day.

"Mmm," he hums against my soft flesh, and I can feel the vibrations disperse through my body.

Unable to resist, I lower one hand to Nate's head, holding him in place as his lips and tongue play my body with great skill and knowledge. Time doesn't exist, just an endless wave of sensation, building and building until one final nudge has it crashing onto shore.

I blink my eyes a few moments later, when he effortlessly slides inside me, his body suspended over mine.

"Morning."

He smiles, softly brushing my lips with his and I catch a hint of myself on him.

I lift a hand to his face as he starts moving inside me.

"Hey."

We fit so well. Not only are our bodies in sync, but our minds are as well.

Now that all the barriers have come down, and every misconception and deception are exposed, there is nothing left but raw, and sometimes brutal, honesty.

Looking up in his eyes, I see the truth of us reflected back at me. The years we were apart have become insignificant against the backdrop of our shared history. Only the means to an end in bringing us right here, in this moment.

"Yesss," I hiss against the skin of his neck, as his strokes become more forceful—demanding.

I brace myself against the headboard with one hand over my head, providing leverage so I can receive each thrust for optimal impact. My eyes roll back in my head as my body flies apart.

"Fuck, baby. Every fucking time," he grunts in my hair as his body goes rigid against mine and bucks through his release.

Then he lifts his head and smiles. "Perfection."

"Do you have time to pick the tile?"

I'm just shrugging into my coat when Nate walks up with a couple of boards with the different tile samples glued to the backing.

"Isn't it a little early to start picking finishes?" I observe.

"Ah, yes, however, the building supply and home center has an end of the line sale going on. I was heading into Spokane today anyway to pick up a new battery charger for my tools, and thought I could put in an order for that flooring you like and tile for the bathrooms and the kitchen backsplash. Some of these are half price, which is gonna make a huge difference to the budget."

We hemmed and hawed a bit over whether to do the work in smaller sections, but after crunching some numbers, we came to the conclusion it would ultimately be cheaper doing it all at once. It would definitely be less disruptive.

Nate started work on my place a week and a half ago, tearing out the kitchen, bathrooms, all flooring, and knocking down a few walls. Dad's even dropped by to lend Nate a hand from time to time. I'd love to be a fly on the wall at some point to see what those two are talking about, but I'm just happy they seem to be getting along.

"Can't you pick?" I suggest, checking my watch since I'm already running a little late on my day.

"It's *your* house," Nate returns, holding up the sample boards.

"It may not always be," I point out.

When he started the work, we briefly talked about what the future might look like, and he mentioned he liked my neighborhood better. I think when he bought his house in the same neighborhood he grew up in, it was a bit of a middle finger to the past, but he seems ready to leave that behind.

"Fine, I'll tell you which ones I think will look good, and you make the final decision," he offers.

It ends up only taking two minutes to make selections we're both happy with. I quickly kiss him, yell a goodbye to Tate—who is probably still trying to drag her butt out of bed—and dart out the door, shivering when the cold air hits me.

At Nate's invitation, I ended up packing a few bags and temporarily moved in with him and Tatum, who didn't seem to mind at all when asked her opinion.

It's been pretty good, and everyone seems to get along. I sure am eating a lot healthier. I never spent a lot of time cooking for myself, but I've started enjoying tackling dinner together when we get home. It's far more fun that way, and even Tate has started chipping in.

Yesterday she asked me if I wanted to do some baking with her in preparation for the holidays, but I'm afraid that might be a little ambitious for me. I didn't have the heart to tell her no though, so I was going to ask Phil for some guidance.

The past few weeks have been ones of transition in a multitude of ways. For one, the weather has decided to skip fall and careened straight from summer to winter. We already clocked our first snowfall two days ago. In town it melted off the roads and sidewalks during the day, but a little higher up in the mountains, it has stuck. It's at least several degrees colder up at Dad and Phil's place and it looks like a winter wonderland.

But the weather isn't the only thing I've had to adjust to. There was also the aftermath of Auden's reign of terror.

Dad's been cleared, of course, but the shooting—justified as it might have been—left its mark on him. There's a shadow in his eyes I hadn't seen there before, one that comes with taking the life of a man you've considered part of your circle for decades. He's had two such cold realities hit him, both with Jeff and with Auden.

It's the kind of betrayal that burrows deep, I know. But Dad and I are both lucky we also have a lot to be grateful for, a lot of love in our lives.

Phil said it best; you can't change the shit behind you but you can damn well make sure you don't let it stain your future.

I hop behind the wheel, and hurry to the station to welcome Rick Althof to the Edwards County Sheriff's Department.

Out with the old and in with the new.

∼

NATE

"Why can't we just buy one at the stand by the gas station?"

I glance over at Savvy, who is hiding a smile, before lifting my eyes to the rearview mirror to look at Tatum, who is whining from the back seat.

"Where's the magic in that?" I ask her.

It earns me a mutinous glare that only makes me grin harder.

My daughter has made me spend close to four hundred dollars in the past few days on Christmas shit. Small-town living has gone to her brain, and she now wants to turn our house into a Norman Rockwell Christmas painting like a lot of others have in town.

She's the one who called me a Grinch—because I've never owned a single Christmas ball or string of flickering lights in my life— and told me we needed a little magic in our lives, so it's fun throwing that back at her.

Not that she was wrong, I haven't celebrated Christmas, or any other major holiday, in a very long time. In fact, the last time I sat down for a Christmas dinner was one Savvy's mother cooked. The entire dinner I felt Sheriff Colter's disapproving eyes on me. Haven't celebrated a single one since leaving Silence.

But things have definitely changed since then. It's a new beginning, and I'm making a lot of clean starts; with Tate, with Savvy, with Brant Colter, and with the town of Silence in general.

The holidays are for family, and although I may never have had much of one, it would appear I have one now. One that, ironically, includes the man I thought I hated more than anyone else, the woman I've never stopped loving, and the daughter I don't deserve.

Phil is out on the porch when we pull in, tying some greenery to the porch railing. She waves when she sees us rolling up.

"Happy Thanksgiving! Are you guys ready to go pick out your Christmas tree? The turkey is in the smoker, I already have the thermos of hot chocolate packed, and Brant is hitching Clovis to the sled."

Clovis is a partially blind Belgian draught horse Phil rescued from the slaughterhouse, much to Brant's dismay, or so the story goes. The animal is to drag the entire family up the mountain to find an elusive perfect Christmas tree for each house.

This whole day was Phil's idea, who has embraced grandparenthood with gusto since she met Tate, and seems to be reveling in the role.

"Do we have to?" Tate complains. "It's cold. Can't we just do the baking?"

That is the plan for this afternoon; the womenfolk bake Christmas goodies, and Brant and I are supposed to build wooden stands for the trees we bring back, peel potatoes, and keep an eye on the turkey.

"Let it go, Tate," I warn her in a low voice. "It's a package deal. You've gotta learn to go with the flow."

"Your dad's right," Phil steps in, draping an arm around my daughter and tugging her close. "You'll be snug as a bug in the sleigh, I've already loaded up the blankets. You never know, you might actually enjoy it if you open your mind."

Still a little in awe of Phil since finding out she is a famous rock star; Tate seems more inclined to listen to her than she ever does to me.

Her soft, "Okay," and conceding shrug are evidence of that.

The sleigh is little more than a platform on runners, stacked with two rows of straw bales behind each other. Brant and Phil sit on the first row, with Brant handling Clovis, and Savvy and I flank Tate on the back row, our knees wrapped in a large quilt.

It's pretty up here. A bit chilly—especially for a Nevada transplant like my girl—but the snow is pristine and the air is clean and fresh. It doesn't take long for Tate to warm up to the experience as well.

I get to do the honors, cutting down the trees we find in a small copse of younger Douglas fir after a short, twenty-minute ride. By now Tate is smiling, accepting the mug of hot chocolate Phil pours for her.

"Can you handle it?" Brant asks, supervising my work.

I suspect it was his wife who suggested he turn over the saw to me.

"I'll finish this tree, but would you mind cutting down the other one? My shoulder is bugging me a bit."

"Sure. I'll take care of it."

It may be my imagination, but it looks like his chest puffed up a little.

"My, my," Savvy mumbles by my side, slipping her arm into mine after I hand off the saw to her father. "You're a fast learner. You handled him like a pro."

"Meh, I've been watching you and Phil, taking notes."

"It shows."

She grins up at me and I can't resist dropping a kiss on those lips.

"Gross. I'm losing my appetite here," Tate objects.

"You didn't seem to think it was gross when I caught you and Carson outside Strange Brew the other day," Savvy returns with a wink.

I'm not quite sure what she is talking about, but I'm convinced I'm not going to like it. "Sorry...what was that?"

Tate bulges her eyes at Savvy, who turns back to me to pat my cheek.

"Not to worry, honey," she informs me in a soothing voice. "I've got it all under control."

My daughter is suddenly very interested in her hot chocolate, while Brant lets out a hearty chuckle.

Phil spreads her arms and inhales deeply.

"Love...isn't it fabulous?"

EPILOGUE

Savvy

"SINGLE MVA on Old Winchester Creek Road, three miles west of the Black Mountain Casino."

The call comes in just as I'm about to head home.

It's been a long week of snowstorms that's had us running from one end of the county to the other with similar calls to this. Poor road conditions and poor judgment can be a dangerous combination, all too often with a life-altering outcome. In addition, I've been plagued with a nasty bug, which I guess is also par for the course this time of year.

The snow started up again an hour ago, so I'm sure the weather had something to do with it, but something tells me this accident—so close to the casino with little else around—may have had alcohol playing a role as well.

Wonderful.

Instead of finally heading home to a warm bed, I'm once again braving the weather to the scene of an accident in the opposite direction. God only knows how long it'll take me to get there.

At least I won't have to bother Nate to let him know I won't be coming home; he wasn't expecting me anyway. I told him if things got too ugly out there, I might just crash at the station. It wouldn't be the first time this winter, which has been pretty brutal so far.

The sparse streetlights barely have an impact on visibility, which is minimal due to the heavy snow coming down. At least they give me some indication where the actual road is. I sure am glad for the chains on my tires and my all-wheel drive, or else I wouldn't have any traction at all.

As much as I want to get to the scene as fast as possible, I'm not about to jeopardize my own safety. I have too damn much to live for these days.

When I'm a few minutes out, dispatch informs me the fire department and EMTs are en route as well, but will be a few minutes behind me.

This part of Old Winchester Creek Road is dark, without street lighting, but it makes the red glow of a set of rear lights poking out of the snow up ahead all the more visible. I'm not sure who called it in, but there aren't any other vehicles around.

I leave my lights running so the location is easy to spot for any emergency vehicles behind me, make sure I have my flashlight, and pull my beanie over my ears before stepping out.

Damn, that wind is cold. The snow hits my face sideways and feels like sharp icicles digging into my skin, while I grab the snow shovel from the back of my cruiser. Grateful for my sturdy fur-lined boots, I make my way to the back of the stranded vehicle, noting the front end disappears into the ditch, which is buried under the deep snow.

To my surprise, the first vehicle that shows up is one of our own, and KC gets out.

"Give me that," he grumbles, grabbing the shovel from my hands.

"What are you doing here?" I inquire. "Your shift doesn't start until the morning."

"I was monitoring the scanner. Why are you out here anyway? Why didn't Warren take this call?"

I stare slack-mouthed at my deputy. I'm not used to him being this assertive, it's borderline rude, and that is not like the KC I know.

"Watch your tone," I caution him.

That seems to startle him.

"I apologize if I was rude, but I worry about you," he clarifies as he keeps shoveling at the snow.

"About me?"

My question gets lost when the fire department rolls up. With their help, enough snow is cleared away for us to be able to open the door. We find the driver slumped over the steering wheel, reeking of booze, with a cell phone clutched in his hand. He must've called 911 himself.

"No pulse," one of the firefighters announces.

I'm shocked when he eases the man back and I recognize Jeff Sanchuk.

"Oh shit," KC mutters.

He pulls me out of the way as the first responders pull Sanchuk from the vehicle and carry him up to the road where they attempt CPR to revive him.

"Wasn't his assault trial coming up soon?"

"Next week, March fifth," I confirm.

Nate had a meeting with the assistant district attorney

just a few days ago to prepare for his testimony. Something I know he wasn't particularly looking forward to.

"I think maybe karma doled out some justice today," my young deputy shares sagely.

I wince, because it's a bit harsh, but he's not lying.

"Maybe."

Half an hour later, the snow has stopped falling, Sanchuk's unresponsive body has been removed by ambulance, the fire department has left, and the tow truck has pulled the stranded vehicle from the ditch. I'm about to tell KC to go back home, but he beats me to it.

"You should get some rest," he suggests. "You shouldn't be out here in your condition."

Once again, I find myself staring at my deputy with my mouth hanging open.

"My condition?"

He blanches at my question and starts sputtering.

"I'm sorry, I saw you throwing up in your trash can when I walked past your office on Tuesday. And yesterday morning I almost bumped into you when you were running for the bathroom. Both times were in the morning, and I thought..."

He doesn't finish his sentence and looks decidedly uncomfortable.

I'm simply too shocked to speak.

"I should get going too. Again, so sorry."

He heads over to his patrol car, wipes the windshield clear of snow with his sleeve, and hops behind the wheel.

I'm still standing in the same spot, as KC drives off in the direction of Silence.

Is it possible?

Nate

"What's wrong with Savvy?"

I glance over at my daughter as I drive her to her youth group rehearsal, which KC ended up moving from the church hall to the high school auditorium. Understandable, given what happened to him, as well as to Carson and my daughter, in the basement of the church.

"She hasn't been feeling too well and she's tired. Work was crazy this past week."

All true, but I was wondering myself when she passed on what has become our weekly tradition of Sunday morning breakfast at the Bread & Butter Diner earlier and opted to stay in bed. I intend to find out when I get home after dropping Tate off.

"Savvy?" I call out, walking in the door.

She's not on the main level, and I don't find her in bed. The door to the bathroom is closed and I softly knock on the door.

"Babe, are you in here?"

"It's not locked."

She's sitting on the floor, her back against the shower door and her bare legs stretched out in front of her and her hands in her lap. She's still wearing the sleep shorts and shirt she had on earlier. Her hair is a tangled mess and her face is blotchy and red.

"Are you still feeling sick?" I sink down on the floor beside her and drape my arm around her, pulling her close to my side.

"Don't," she says, resisting a little. "I reek of vomit."

"I don't care about that. I care about you." I press a kiss

to her head. "I'm worried. Maybe you should see a doctor? Whatever this bug is, it doesn't look like it's letting up."

She scoffs a laugh.

"I'm pretty sure it's not going to let up for a while," she shares.

"What do you mean?"

By way of a response, she hands me a white and blue plastic stick she'd been holding in her lap. It takes me no more than a second to recognize it for what it is, and there is no doubt in my mind what that dark blue plus sign in the small display window means.

She promptly bursts out crying.

"I'm sorry. I swear I haven't missed taking my pills. I don't know what happened."

"I do," I tell her with a chuckle. "I remember exactly what happened. I haven't forgotten a single moment I've spent making love with you."

"But I wasn't supposed to get pregnant. We haven't even talked about—"

"Hush," I cut her off, easing her chin up with my index finger so I can look in her eyes. "We, of all people, should know by now to grab on to those unexpected blessings and treasure them."

I give her a little shake.

"This is a good thing, Savvy. A happy thing. Whatever changes or adjustments need to be made to our lives will be so worth it, and the beauty of it is, we have a lot of months to figure it all out."

She flashes me a watery smile, but her tears are drying.

"Dad's going to flip out," she observes.

"He sure is," I agree. "And Phil is going to go nuts over this baby. And you know who else?"

Now she beams up at me.

"Tatum?"

"Bingo. She'll be in hog heaven."

I lower my head and drop a kiss on her lips.

"Eww..." she mutters, pulling away. "Vomit breath."

I laugh in her face.

"Like I care. You're having my baby, I'm sure there'll be plenty of bodily fluids to contend with in our immediate future."

The expression on her face makes me laugh even harder.

"Oh God, I'm so not prepared for this."

I rest my chin on the top of her head.

"You will be. We'll figure it out."

Bess

I BITE off a curse and immediately cover a second yawn with the back of my hand.

Another early morning after yet another sleepless night.

One of these days one of my employees is going to come in and find me passed out on the kitchen floor. Unless Chance Tanek finds me first. He's the town drunk and I swear he watches this place, waiting to see the light go on in my apartment upstairs.

He is usually already by the backdoor by the time I make my way downstairs in the morning. I normally have a paper bag with the prior day's leftovers ready for him. He's such a lost soul, not a particularly friendly one, but I feel for him nonetheless. I figure there's no harm in giving him some day-old baked goods to soak up all the alcohol he consumed in the previous twenty-four hours. Plus, everyone deserves at least one friendly interaction a day. I'd like to think of it as doing a public service, although a couple of people in my circle of friends may not agree with me.

This morning I was too tired to even spare him a basic greeting, almost tossing the paper bag at him before slamming the door shut and shuffling into the kitchen. This is getting ridiculous; I can count the hours of sleep I've managed to cobble together over the past week on one hand. I'm going to have to ask Dana if there is anything she can prescribe because this is not sustainable.

I have a business to run, bills and employees to pay, and I can't afford to fall down on the job, but that's exactly what I've been doing since that damn phone call last week.

So far this morning, I already over-proofed my Chelsea buns, burned a batch of cookies, and now the apple streusel muffins I just pulled from the oven are collapsing. I can't seem to do anything right, and it's only a little after 6:00 a.m.

Something's got to give.

As I quickly slide the muffins back in the oven—hoping I can salvage the batch—I hear the back door open. Lola, my only full-time employee, pokes her head into the kitchen. She takes one look at the lackluster Chelsea buns, and the discarded tray with my cookies charred remains before turning to me with a sympathetic look on her face.

"Let me put my stuff away and I'll come give you a hand."

I open my mouth to tell her not to bother—she shouldn't have to pick up my slack like she's been doing all week—but she's already disappeared down the hall. Letting my eyes drift around the kitchen, I do some damage assessment. At least the date squares and the bacon and cheese scones came out fine. The Chelsea buns will have to do, and hopefully the muffins will turn out, but I'll have to redo the cookies and should probably whip up a batch of lemon-poppyseed muffins as well, just in case.

Lola grabs an apron off the hook as she walks into the kitchen and ties it on.

"What's next?" she asks, and I swallow against the sudden flood of emotions.

Damn, who'd have thought when I took a chance on the rail-thin girl who answered the help-wanted sign in my window six years ago, she'd become the rock I lean on these days. As it turned out, hiring her was not only the best thing that could've happened to her, but me as well. She has become invaluable to me and Strange Brew.

Lola has shared only bits and pieces of her history with me over the years, but it was enough information for me to realize my own sordid past pales in comparison. The woman has a core of steel though, and has completely reinvented herself. The pretty, well-put-together woman in front of me is a far cry from the skinny kid who first walked in here.

"Lemon-poppyseed muffins and pecan chocolate-chip cookies."

"On it," she states, checking the wall for the recipes.

Every time I add a new item to our weekly rotation, I tack a laminated copy to our recipe wall. I don't have any secrets, at least not with respect to my baked goods.

"Why don't you take a break, go make yourself a coffee," Lola suggests, glancing at me over her shoulder. "You look like you could use it."

Ugh. I purposely avoided looking in the mirror this morning. I figured it wouldn't be an improvement on the pale, haggard reflection staring back at me last night. Guess I was right.

I don't bother arguing; I could use a boost of caffeine if I'm going to make it through today.

"Oh, and I'll take Carson under my wing when he gets here," she adds when I start out the door.

Shoot, Carson. I'd forgotten about him; the kid is supposed to start today.

I overheard him talking to his girlfriend, Tatum, when they dropped in after school last week. He'd been complaining he had a hard time finding an after-school job. It just so happened one of my weekend part-timers gave me two-weeks' notice a few days prior, and I hadn't started looking yet. I ended up offering him the job, provided his father approved. I'm sure working at the local coffee shop wasn't Carson's first choice, but the promise of free baked goods had been enough of an enticement for him to accept.

I'd all but forgotten he's supposed to start today,

"I need him to fill in a few forms for me first, but after that, yes. If he could shadow you for a bit during the rush, that would be great."

The rush is usually between seven—when we open—and nine. After that things slow down a bit until noon, when it picks up again for the lunch crowd. Our menu isn't big, since we're supposed to be a coffee shop and not a restaurant, but especially on the weekends people have a tendency to pop in here for a quick bite while they run their errands. We offer sandwiches and a daily soup or stew during the winter months, but it's all pretty basic.

When I get here at around four in the morning, baking is the first thing I tackle. Usually by the time the doors open, most of the pastries are done, and I start prepping for lunch.

When I started, I was very ambitious and baked all my own breads as well, but that proved to be too labor intensive. I ended up ordering in from Crumbs, a local, artisan bakery with whom I was able to negotiate a great deal. It leaves me more time to spend on salads for the sandwiches and whatever special I am serving that day.

Then after lunch, I normally do my ordering and administration, and when I close the doors at five, I'm dead on my feet.

I haven't had much of a life since I opened Strange Brew eight years ago, working thirteen- or fourteen-hour days, but it has been a labor of love building this place in to what it is now. At least these days, with Lola running things so I can take a day, sometimes two, off every week, I have some downtime.

Tomorrow is Sunday, my standard day off. Normally, I'd be looking forward to the break, but at the moment I'd rather be busy. Less time to think and worry.

I've barely booted up the computer in my office when I

hear the back door fall shut. It sounds like Lola is intercepting whoever walked in, but a few moments later I hear footsteps coming down the hall.

"Hey."

Hugo Alexander, Carson's dad, pokes his head in the door.

"Hi."

I'm annoyed I sound breathless whenever I talk to him. It's ridiculous. Sure, the man looks more like a reincarnated Viking the older he gets, but I've known him forever, and he's not the only handsome man in town. He just appears to be the only one who affects my vocal cords. It's aggravating.

"Are you sure about this?" he asks, obviously referring to his offspring working here.

"Positive. He's a good kid, Hugo, he'll do fine."

He runs a hand through his unruly, straw-colored hair laced with a decent amount of silver.

"I know, it's just...we're friends, and I'd hate to see him fuck up and—"

"And what?" I interrupt sharply, for some reason extra annoyed by the friend label I'm slapped with. "You really think I'd be so petty; I'd take that out on you? Please, you should know me better."

He looks appropriately sheepish and maybe a little surprised at the edge in my voice.

"No, I just meant..." He stalls before continuing with, "I don't want things awkward."

I snort before getting up from my chair so I'm not looking up at him. Well, I guess I'm still looking up at him, since he's a towering six foot three to my modest five two, but standing makes me feel taller.

"Things would only be awkward if you make them so," I return pointedly.

He narrows his eyes on me, scanning my body down and up again.

"Are you okay?"

Instantly self-conscious at his question, I run my hands down my flour-dusted apron.

"I'm fine, why?"

"You don't look fine."

*****

Hugo

Smooth.

Her sharp, "Thanks for sharing that observation. Now if you don't mind, I have work to do," served as an effective dismissal.

Apparently, I'd already put both my feet in my mouth and I figured my safest bet would be to make myself scarce and try again another time.

I don't know why, but I seem to be making an art out of saying the wrong thing to her lately. To my recollection, this was never an issue before, but the past several months I can't seem to say the right thing.

After a quick goodbye for my son with a warning to behave, I walk out to my cruiser, frustrated and brooding. Funny, because I was in the best of moods when I pulled in here five minutes ago. I'd planned to beat the crowd and score a couple of coffees and some pastries to take to the station, but I'm empty-handed when I slide behind the wheel. I highly doubt Bess would be willing to serve me early after I pissed her off.

"Who the hell pissed in your Wheaties this early?" Brenda Silvari, our office manager, asks as I walk into the small office kitchen, looking for a hit of caffeine.

"Don't know what you're talking about," I grumble, reaching for the pot of black tar Brenda manages to brew every morning.

I swear, she adds engine oil to the coffee grinds to create the dark sludge she serves us, but it does the trick when in need of caffeine, and right now, I need that jolt to my system.

"Let's just say, you don't look particularly cheerful this morning," she responds.

"And this conversation is not helping," I point out.

But that doesn't deter Brenda, who is more like a den mother than an office manager some days. She puts a hand on my arm.

"That boy giving you trouble?"

She's referring to Carson, who hit a rough patch there for a while after his mom died and got himself into some trouble. Having two teenage boys herself, I found myself sometimes confiding my struggles with him to Brenda.

"No, it's not Carson. He's fine, he starts his part-time job at Strange Brew today. I just dropped him off."

"Ahhhh." She nods with a smirk. "You didn't run into Bess by chance, did you?"

I have no idea how she manages to zoom in on the sore spot every time. Like I said; den mother.

"Bess?" I feign ignorance, an effort I know is wasted anyway. "Barely. I was in and out of there in minutes."

"Hmmm," she hums, making it clear she's not buying what I'm trying to sell.

I quickly toss a few spoonfuls of sugar in my coffee in hopes of killing the bitter taste, and dart out the door before she has a chance to dig her claws in deeper. The woman is a terrier.

Once at my desk, I can't help but replay my conversation with Bess to try and figure out where I may have messed up. Even under her usual ivory complexion, she'd looked pale, almost gaunt, with dark circles under her eyes. She'd also noticeably lost weight. Even being a small woman, she's always been sturdy. This morning she looked like a stiff wind could blow her over. There's definitely something wrong with her, but in my attempt to get to the bottom of it, maybe I was a bit too blunt.

The radio on my desk crackles with an incoming message, interrupting my trailing thoughts.

"Dispatch to all units, structure fire reported at 217 Main Street. It's Main Street Mechanics, risk for explosion. All units, acknowledge."

Jesus, that's Clem Tanek's auto shop. I just drove past it on my way here and didn't notice a thing.

I snatch up my radio and check for my keys in my pocket as I respond.

"Unit 42 acknowledges. En route."

I rush down the hall and out the doors to my cruiser, as more calls come through from the fire department and two of our sheriff's units.

Engine one of Silence's Fire Department is already on scene when I pull up in front of the building. Smoke is pouring from one of the partially opened bay doors and an orange glow can be seen from within the shop. I don't interfere with the work of the fire department, which is well in the hands of fire chief Randy Nichols, who is already barking out orders at his crew.

"Is anyone inside?" I ask him quickly.

"Not as far as I know; the place doesn't open until eight."

I leave him to it and turn to the crowd forming on the sidewalk and street. Crowd control is my main concern, and I need to get these people back and out of the way. Tons of hazardous and potentially explosive materials inside could go off at any time.

"Hey!" I holler, trying to draw attention as I wave my arms. "I need everyone to back the hell up!"

A few listen and move out of the way, but there are still some folks trying to get closer, getting in the way of firefighters doing their job. But as I try to block their path, I'm knocked to the ground by a massive blast from behind.

My ears ring and I'm disoriented, my vision is obscured by a thick cloud of dust and smoke, as debris rains down around me.

A hand lands on my shoulder and when I look back, I see Deputy KC Kingma standing over me. His mouth is moving, but I can't hear a damn thing. He grabs me under my arms and hauls me to my feet.

"You okay?" he mouths.

Other than that damn ringing in my ears and a slight stinging at the back of my head, I seem to be in one piece.

"I'm fine."

Then I look around me to find chaos. Some of the people I was trying to push back are lying or sitting down, appearing injured by debris from the blast. When I look back at the auto shop, almost the entire front of the building is gone.

Up next are Bess and Hugo in Guilty Silence.
Get your copy here.

ALSO BY FREYA BARKER

SILENCE

FINDING SILENCE

INSIDE SILENCE

HMT 2G:

HIGH FREQUENCY

HIGH INTENSITY

HIGH DENSITY

HIGH VELOCITY (2025)

High Mountain Trackers:

HIGH MEADOW

HIGH STAKES

HIGH GROUND

HIGH IMPACT

Arrow's Edge MC Series:

EDGE OF REASON

EDGE OF DARKNESS

EDGE OF TOMORROW

EDGE OF FEAR

EDGE OF REALITY

EDGE OF TRUST

EDGE OF NOWHERE

GEM Series:

OPAL

PEARL

ONYX

PASS Series:

HIT & RUN

LIFE & LIMB

LOCK & LOAD

LOST & FOUND

On Call Series:

BURNING FOR AUTUMN

COVERING OLLIE

TRACKING TAHLULA

ABSOLVING BLUE

REVEALING ANNIE

DISSECTING MEREDITH

WATCHING TRIN

IGNITING VIC

CAPTIVATING ANIKA

Rock Point Series:

KEEPING 6

CABIN 12

HWY 550

10-CODE

Northern Lights Collection:

A CHANGE OF TIDE

A CHANGE OF VIEW

A CHANGE OF PACE

SnapShot Series:

SHUTTER SPEED

FREEZE FRAME

IDEAL IMAGE

Portland, ME, Series:

FROM DUST

CRUEL WATER

THROUGH FIRE

STILL AIR

LuLLaY (a Christmas novella)

Cedar Tree Series:

SLIM TO NONE

HUNDRED TO ONE

AGAINST ME

CLEAN LINES

UPPER HAND

LIKE ARROWS

HEAD START

Standalones:

WHEN HOPE ENDS
VICTIM OF CIRCUMSTANCE
BONUS KISSES
SECONDS
SNOWBOUND

ABOUT THE AUTHOR

USA Today bestselling author Freya Barker loves writing about ordinary people with extraordinary stories. With 60+ titles to her name, Freya inspires with her stories about 'real' people, perhaps less than perfect, each struggling to find their own slice of happy.

Freya has her hands full with a retired husband, a needy pup, and a growing gaggle of grandbabies, but she continues to spin story after story with an endless supply of bruised and dented characters, vying for attention!

Recipient of the ReadFREE.ly 2019 Best Book We've Read All Year Award for "Covering Ollie, the 2015 RomCon "Reader's Choice" Award for Best First Book, "Slim To None", Finalist for the 2017 Kindle Book Award with "From Dust", and Finalist for the 2020 Kindle Book Award with "When Hope Ends", Freya spins story after story with an endless supply of bruised and dented characters, vying for attention!

www.freyabarker.com